THE CARDINAL LINE

Book Design by Jordan Wannemacher
Author Photograph by Deanna Meadow Photography

ISBN: 979-8-9894270-0-0

THE CARDINAL LINE

a novel

JORDAN FITCH

1

ARIN COPPERTREE WATCHED sleepy students queue up to be shot point-blank in the forehead. She sipped her latte and recovered the delicate foam from her lips.

"Are the Pearly Gates any more objective than this?" Melanie asked as she downed her unadulterated brew from the bench beside her.

"Not given the arbitrary nature of that ticket," Arin answered. "But let me show you this, and you can call me St. Peter. Tall girl with the ponytail, white shirt. She's going down. Kid with the yellow shirt, him too." She surveyed the meandering string of Boston University students awaiting passage through the arched columns of the chapel breezeway.

Melanie surveyed her, turning and scrunching her eyebrows. "What are you talking about? How do you know these undergrads?" She donned that inquisitive journalist-in-training face that Arin wouldn't admit she loved.

"I don't. But I know they're going to fail their temp checks."

Melanie spread her hands wide, maintaining her grip on her cup. "Umm... How?"

"I... I don't know. Look, here's Miss Ponytail at the not-so-pearly gate."

The girl was checked, rechecked, then directed to turn around. She protested for a moment before leaving. A few students later in the queue, Yellow Shirt suffered the same judgment.

"Now you're scaring me," Melanie stated. "How did you know they were getting booted?"

"They looked off—seemed off. Compared to the others, anyway." Arin looked down at her cup. She hadn't mentioned what she'd been seeing. She knew Melanie would pry and she didn't need the distraction. "I don't know. You don't see it at all?"

"That those kids had fevers? From forty feet away? No, Arin, how the hell would I know that? How would anyone without one of those guns? Tell me you have some kind of joke going on here."

Arin hesitated. "I wasn't sure what I was noticing. Thought I was wrong, and each of those kids would walk right through. And maybe others would be sent back."

"But they didn't walk through." Melanie paused, then waved it away. "Whatever, some fluke with the air or something, and you're a lucky guesser. Like everything else about you."

The fall breeze transported wafts of unshowered undergrads and recently fired mid-grade marijuana. Shorebirds passed overhead on the wing to the Charles River. Melanie flicked screens on her phone.

"Did they get your drink right this time?"

"Close enough, but they spelled my name wrong again." Arin spun her cup. "Got a pen?"

Melanie did, of course. Arin couldn't remember the last time she had carried one. She took it and rewrote the name sticker. "It's an odd spelling, my parents being no exception to the trend of unique baby names. Oxymoronic that common names and normal spellings are the exceptions now, but feel fresh."

"That's how fads work," Melanie replied. "Like our capricious support of rotating social causes. The number of dollars and shits given scales with media attention and fades just as fast."

"And you still want to join them? The media?"

"That's why I want to join them." Melanie shrugged. "A girl can at least start with quixotic optimism."

"Cervantes wrote satirically."

"We in media don't recognize that distinction."

Arin blew a strand of blonde hair from her face. "It is a medium lacking distinction, I'll concur."

A trio of young joggers passed their bench, and Arin mentally critiqued their forms. After thousands of hours with her own coaches, she couldn't help it.

"Ooh, someone's been bad," Melanie stated, scrolling with her non-coffee hand. "Journalist chat rumors of an impending arrest warrant for former Congresswoman Carmine."

Arin returned a blank stare, knowing Melanie expected just that. She didn't need to verbalize the question.

"Right, not so tuned into modern politics, are we? Just the ancient stuff. Robin Carmine was a one-term Massachusetts congresswoman years ago. Ran for Senate but flared out. Apparently been working at a K-Street firm, but got on the Fed's radar for doing something she shouldn't have."

"I wasn't even living here then," Arin retorted. "I condemn your condescension of this classics student for not knowing irrelevant trivia."

"Name the current congressional reps from the Commonwealth, then. Or any from your home state of Maryland." Melanie sipped her coffee and donned what Arin called her patronizing bitch face. She knew it well. She had one of her own.

"Name one senator from ancient Rome, my haughty hottie," she replied. Her dubious pursuit of classical studies aided in trivial debates, if nothing else.

"That senate body who kept the ample staff of young, beddable boys?"

Arin glanced sideways. "Have senatorial proclivities changed over the millennia, my budding reporter?"

"They hide it better now, usually." Melanie conceded. "That insatiable desire for control doesn't ebb."

No rebuttals there, Arin thought. She looked back at the queued students.

Melanie followed her gaze. "Hey, choose one more for me. I need to know your little trick is just an aberration, or I won't sleep tonight." She tilted her Sox cap upward and took off her glasses. She squinted, tilting her head as if testing her eyesight.

"Watch the guy in the tie-dye with the scrappy beard," Arin answered. "And a few back, the chick in the too-tiny black shirt and oversized headphones." The line advanced. A short girl with an orange beanie was tagged and sent back. The two students Arin had mentioned both went through, having passed the divine judgment of the temperature guns.

Melanie looked at Arin, who looked straight ahead, silent. "So that's good, right?" she questioned. "Your first guesses were just a freak thing?" She snapped her fingers in her face. "Arin?"

"I said watch those two. They were flittering eyes at each other, and I think they'd make a tasty couple. I didn't say anything about them passing the temp checks." Arin watched the girl with the beanie walk away as she raised her coffee cup.

Melanie looked at it. "You said you were correcting your name."

Arin didn't reply. On the cup, she had written *white girl, orange beanie.*

"YOU DIDN'T ASK FOR HELP in the quad yesterday, but you kind of did," stated Melanie. Arin lifted an eyebrow as Melanie waved toward the café entrance.

"So I reached out to a guy I know. Before you ask, yes, we had a thing a couple years back. Don't be jealous. He's a bit awkward but harmless. Don't refrain from hitting back." A tall guy with glasses and a chipper smile came over. He wore a collared shirt and a yellow tie and was well overdue for a haircut.

"Is that how Ph.D. candidates need to dress, Ross?" Melanie said by way of introduction.

Ross looked down at his tie, back at Melanie, and settled his gaze on Arin.

"Hi," he said, showing big white teeth and extending his hand. "Almost Ph.D. Candidate, indeed wearing a tie. Pleasure to meet you, Miss...?"

"Arin," she replied. "Uh, grad studies in classics. Not dressed up."

"They make us wear stuffy doctor gear, but they don't make you wear togas?"

"Oh, please," Melanie cut in. "So, Ross, I know you're way behind on your thesis."

He snorted in affront as he took the open chair facing Arin.

"As in, you haven't chosen one yet."

"I do indeed have..." He turned to the waitress who had ambled to their table. "I'll take a large black house and three of those pastries on the top," he chirped, then turned back. "I do indeed, as I was saying,

9

have a thesis. In fact, I have three of them, and I just need to pick one. I only have time for a quick cup here, though. What's this about?" "Your thesis ideas? Drop them all," stated Melanie. "You're doing her."

Had Ross gotten his coffee and taken a sip by then, that mouthful would have covered at least their table, if not the next two. "I'm, uh..." He struggled for words as he gaped at the twenty-six-year-old green-eyed track star. "No arguments here." Arin held her mouth firm and threw a sideways glance at Melanie.

"Again, freak, stop it," Melanie continued, "And hear me out. You're focusing on neurological awareness patterns for your studies. Yes, I sometimes actually listen to you as you prattle on. So, whatever you're looking at for your, uh, thesises...?"

"Theses." Arin was happy to supply the corrected plural, if for nothing more than to have a chance to interject.

"Right, whatever topics you've put on your shortlist, if you've actually come up with any, I can promise none are as interesting as her. I don't know what she has, but it's special. She wants to know what it is, I want to know what it is, and you will get published if you figure it out. Published!"

The waitress delivered the coffee and pastries, and Ross distributed them. Taking large gulps of his house brew and larger bites between, he economized his acceptable time looking into Arin's green, almond-shaped eyes before earning another admonition from Melanie.

Arin admonished herself for mentioning the students the day before. She had papers due and didn't have time for extra. Melanie knew that, too. She had no interest in being interviewed by the guy taking liberal eyefuls of her over coffee, but she could play along until she next spoke to her therapist. That's what she does.

2

"SO, ARIN, WHAT do you have?" asked Ross.

Arin took a long sip, letting the oversized mug hide her face. Was she okay with this? She'd grown comfortable showing her abilities on the track and was fine giving academic presentations and the like, but this was new ground. This was something she didn't control or even understand.

But she was with Melanie and a seemingly trustworthy if somewhat obnoxious medical student. In a busy café in the middle of the city. All arranged by Melanie—she'd share her dismay later.

"What do I have? It's more of a show than a tell, I guess."

She turned to look around the room, then settled on the counter. "See those three cups on the counter? They all look the same, right? White paper cups. The nearest one has hot water, probably for tea. The next two are empty."

A barista walked to the counter and dropped a tea bag in the first one, then grabbed the next two to be filled elsewhere.

Ross tilted his head. "So you heard what people just ordered. Or read the little stickers they put on."

"No one can read those," Melanie retorted. "Not even the people who write them. Certainly not her from thirty feet away through the back of her head. And she's been here valiantly taking your endless ogling while the baristas have been churning through that line behind her."

Melanie splayed a hand on the table and leaned forward. "Yesterday, this girl of mine sat beside me and picked out the undergrads who were going to pop on their temp screens. While they were standing in line a dozen yards away. How is that possible?"

"I have no idea. Anything else? What other things can you see?"

"I can't see those things," Arin replied. "I just know it somehow—it's a perception."

"Perception. Right, we have senses that we can't sense in the traditional... sense. Damn, you have me sounding insipid." He gathered his thoughts. "Our minds receive uncountable stimuli each second, and they filter most of it away as irrelevant. Only a small fraction of that stimuli is converted into signals that reach our conscious awareness. And some of what doesn't reach our awareness can still influence ourbehavior or add to our knowledge, even if we don't understand it. Have I lost you both yet?"

"It's bed o'clock in the morning, you'll need to slow down." Arin rubbed her forehead. "Do you mean how we have a sense of balance?"

"Right, great example!" He shouted and stood up, then sat back down as he gathered looks from around the café. "That's one of the senses beyond the normal five you were taught in grade school. We know when we're off-kilter, and we make moves to correct it, but may not really understand what's happening at the moment or even process it at a conscious level. Our sense of space is another hidden tool we use. But back to whatever is happening with you. Can you think of

12

other times when this... perception or whatever comes up? When it may elicit a response that you're not aware of?"

"That I'm not aware of? No, I can't imagine why I wouldn't notice something I'm not aware of."

"Fair enough, let me think," Ross replied.

As they sipped their drinks and picked at their pastries, a woman with three young kids entered and joined the queue, struggling to corral her brood. One of the younger kids ducked behind a merchandise stand, and the woman performed a frantic pirouette when she realized she was short a kid.

"Hide and seek," stated Arin.

"I'm sorry?" said both Melanie and Ross in unison.

"Hide and seek—I was ruthless. A wicked little warrior as a kid. I'd always win. Does that help?"

"Yeah, that may help." Ross's voice trailed off as he lost himself in thought.

Arin looked on with apprehension, feeling like a lab rat. Ross's gazes had turned from the usual flirty type, to which she was accustomed, to an analytical and much less comfortable stare.

"Hide and seek. Where you do well if you can see a player behind a curtain or know where someone had walked or placed their hand a moment before."

"I assume you played it as a kid when you weren't playing doctor with yourself," Melanie chimed in.

"Easy now. Recall that you texted me to come here," Ross sneered. "Want my brilliant insights or not?"

"Children!" Arin cut in. "Whatever history you have, I don't care. Ross, I'm glad Melanie contacted you. I'm eager to hear what you think." She wasn't sure if that was true.

"What I think is that I need to study you further." He snapped towards Melanie. "No comments."

He brought up his phone and scrolled for a moment. "Let me make a call." He put in an earbud as Arin finished her drink, listening to the local half of the conversation.

"Hey, you have an fMRI slot this Saturday, right? And you wanted some more time to prep? Surely you could stand another few weeks? Yes, a swap for mine later in the month. Well, a perfect opportunity just presented herself, and I can't wait that long." He smiled at Arin. Melanie clucked her tongue.

"It'll set you back, I know. How many firstborn children do you want? Yes, yes, technically I can only have one." He muted his phone to speak to the table. "We're in. I just don't know what it will cost me yet."

He grimaced as he got his reply. "Three days! How about one? Ouch. Fine, three days, you got it." He set his phone down and glared at them both.

"This better be worth it. I just gave up half of my slopeside rental on New Year's week. Ah, the perils of helping friends, right? So, I've got some ideas, but need time to prep. Meet me at the medical campus Saturday morning, 8 am sharp. Mel, I suppose you can come too, but one snide remark and I'm kicking you out."

He stood, looking at the table. "Arin, fantastic to meet you, and I am deeply interested! Mel, you can get the check."

THEY MET IN THE LOBBY of Boston University's Medical Campus on Saturday morning, and Ross led them through the hallways to the MRI waiting room. He gave Arin a gown and some imaging goggles, and after she was changed, he explained the test.

"I set up as much as I could on short notice, but I think we'll get some answers, one way or another. These glasses are small enough not to interfere with the scans, but you'll be able to see fine if you look straight up. Once inside, I'll show you a series of images. Some are photos, and some will just be colors or patterns. All you have to do is thumb this," he held up what looked like a fat marker with a button on top, "when you see the image. Any image, you see it, you click the button. The big magnet hole will do the rest. Simple enough?"

"I guess. Don't I need to sign something?"

"Oh, yeah. I think we have a release form we're supposed to use. No real danger here, though. Here, sign on the tablet. Now lie down, and let's see what you're made of! No rings or studs or chains? Anywhere?"

"Mel, keep an eye on him."

"Oh, I will. He's still working through his adolescence, it seems. If he somehow graduates, he'll be facing an ethics board."

"Hey, we're all professionals trying to find an answer. Feel free to kick me if I'm trying too hard. But keep in mind I haven't brought out the straps yet—ow!"

"You're trying too hard," Arin growled, allowing a hint of mirth in her eyes. Melanie cackled through the waiting room glass. Ross grimaced and rubbed his thigh. Even barefoot and lying down, she had nearly toppled him.

"Fantastically strong legs noted—I'll update your chart. But let's focus as I only have this toaster oven for a short block."

He moved behind the glass and pressed a sequence of buttons that drew Arin's head into the cylinder's core, then turned to his laptop. "Are you good in there? Give me a test press. Perfect. Now I'll dim the lights, put on some jazz—I kid, I kid, don't kick me again—and start with the first image."

She saw an image of a rooster. She clicked the button. Next came an image of a wheat field and then a fire. Then a series of colored circles, starting with primary colors, then secondary colors, then more

15

shades in what she recalled were the upper and lower parts of a rainbow. Purples on one end and deep reds on the other. The intervals between each new image were random, so she couldn't anticipate any pattern and wouldn't mistakenly click by habit.

After what felt like an hour but was probably no more than fifteen minutes, Ross's voice carried over speakers.

"Intermission. Everyone good? Going to part two now."

He entered the room and removed her headset, then taped over all of the machine lights and readouts. "Now I'm going to kill the lights and try something else. Just lie there, and click if you see anything."

With all the lights out and LEDs taped over, the room was a tomb. Arin heard him wheel something toward her before he retreated behind the glass. The fMRI started whirring again.

"No clicks?"

"No, should I be?"

"Only if you see something." A few moments passed. "Thank you. I think we're done for now." He turned the lights on and extracted his subject from the machine. She got dressed as he straightened out the room and removed the blackout tape. After gathering their items, they walked toward the hospital exit.

"So..." Arin inquired, "what's wrong with me?"

"With you? I see not a single flaw. Honesty with the subject of one's studies is important. As for your condition, I need some time with the data. But yes—we've got something. And hey, if this is something genetic, what can you tell me about your family?"

3

DANE HARDY LOCKED his bike to an iron pipe in a recess along shadowed brickwork.

Secure enough. Actual alleys are scarce in New York City, despite their abundance in movies, so a fixed pipe behind a haphazard stack of scaffolding would shield all but the most observant eyes. Those, too, were scarce, he'd learned.

It would have to do. He clicked the lock home. He couldn't lose another bike, not this one, regardless of tonight's outcome. The average nut stain trying to ride off with his prized wheels would bail on the first curb, but Dane wouldn't be around to intervene before they figured out how to ride fixed gear or just abandoned it for someone else to snatch.

Crouching down, he hooked the handlebar over a pipe bracket, which freed the front wheel from the ground. He spun the wheel, letting the tuned hub whir as his colored spokes blended into a dull gray in the shadows.

He had sprayed his front spokes equal wedges of red, white, and blue. Patriotic, sure, but he had always liked those colors, regardless of what flag they were on. There's a balance between those colors, he recalled. Something about light waves, but science class was a jagged memory, and it didn't matter. He'd seen those same colors on plenty of other flags when he rode by the UN building on First. America hadn't done shit for him, anyway.

He let the friction of the hub and the thick city air slow the wheel down from whirring to clicking to a stop. The front fork split the blue colored wedge of his wheel. *First is Early.*

He interlaced his fingers in the spokes, gave the wheel another hard spin, and looked around while waiting. The grate across the street billowed thick steam, which a group of laughing teens jumped to avoid. Incessant subway cars rumbled underneath, drowning out talk and thought alike. The old iron beasts were the same trains he had known since his father had shown him that world as a child. The bike wheel eased from a whir to slow clicks again.

He watched the entrance to a busy bar across the street. *The Red Rooster.* Patrons came and went, and he was fairly sure he knew which ones he would see again. The lone men walking with intent were easy to spot among the frivolity of college kids and the smugness of well-cashed bankers.

The bike wheel stopped, the fork splitting the white wedge of spokes this time. *Second is Hold.*

Dane watched a portly and extremely mustachioed man with a worn leather satchel enter the bar without looking at either the overhead sign or the pair of trim college girls stepping out. There's one he'd be seeing later.

He spun his wheel yet again. The soft whir of a balanced hub on a tuned bike had the grounding comfort he needed that night. He'd been to the shop the day before, traded weed for after-hours tool use, and restored his bike to respectability. That—his bike—was one thing he could trust.

He watched a tall, thin man enter the bar. He wore a Scottish hat, one of the floppy ones he didn't know the name for. Again, someone with resolve and someone he'd see again that night.

A young, bare-faced cop walked by, his palm resting on his service weapon. Dane watched him crane his neck as he passed an open window, seizing a long, unfettered eyeful of a table full of giggling girls. *That uniform won't get him those numbers.* The cop continued on and Dane exhaled.

He had woken late that morning and told himself that he might die that day. Nothing special about that day in particular—Dane told himself that every morning and had been doing so for years. Keeps things in perspective. Holds emotions in check. Bars the twists of regret and the gnawings of worry from getting in his way.

Later that afternoon, he took a call from one of his regular clients. He was well practiced at masking his emotions but knew his eagerness showed as he jetted downtown to a mirrored skyscraper. Curb exchanges were the quickest, but most of his clientele these days were not people with time to wait on sidewalks, so leaving his bike locked against a planter was a necessary compromise.

He swung through the wide glass doors and into the cavernous lobby. Waterfalls and sconces and well-upholstered furniture welcomed him. The din of the city was quelled as double sets of doors closed behind him, such sounds and smells an unwelcome element in this realm. He found his client on his phone, leaning against a display case full of ugly balding guys. His client cut off his phone call and walked over.

"Damn, Dane, you get quicker every time!"

"This city gets quicker—I just need to keep up. Where to?"

"Address is on top. Leave it with the busty brunette at the desk."

Dane took the stack of folders and buckled them in for the ride. He paused, and his client snapped his fingers.

"Yes, the other thing I promised," he told Dane. "The game is at a bar on Fulton called the *Red Rooster*. Now listen, I'm going to tip you in Canadian." He handed Dane a folded red bill. A fifty. "Buy a drink with this—the barkeep'll show you where to go."

Dane cocked his head in question.

"Money gets bigger and players want more security. More privacy. Plus there's a precinct lieutenant or some such who lost his wife's inheritance at a game last month. She split, so he's got his dick in a twist and has a sudden itch to root out unlicensed gambling in our fair city. Been sending his boys in blue after tables, hence the need to stay low. Just use the bill and play—you'll be fine."

Dane folded the brightly colored bill into his left breast pocket and felt a growing heartbeat behind it. He had floated through the rest of his afternoon on a sharp breeze of anticipation.

In the shadows of the side street, the third spin of his wheel wound down, and the fork split the red wedge. *Third is late.*

He rechecked his pocket for the colorful bill, slung his nearly empty bag, and walked across the street. He grabbed a stool and ordered a martini, which felt appropriate. The barkeep was shaved bald with a long but neatly trimmed red beard. Apparently, the namesake of the establishment.

Dane slid the foreign bill over, attempting discretion while catching the barkeep's eye. He looked at the bill, then back at Dane, shrugged, and leaned in. "Door past the pissers, on the right. You can take your glass."

The barkeep pocketed the bill without giving change. Dane had no idea how much he'd paid for the drink, but it seemed the hall pass was included.

"And good luck," the barkeep added.

The barroom speakers kicked out a familiar melody. He closed his eyes and focused on the reverberations of the bass in his chest. Pounding drums and rumbling subway cars felt the same in there.

He took another sip of what seemed to be a well-poured cocktail and another eyeful of the long-haired patronage behind him before going to the backroom door. It opened to a set of stairs that led to a wide hallway with more closed doors. The gaiety of the voices downstairs faded out, and the music was reduced to dull pulses through the old woodwork.

Upstairs, he crossed into the world of invitation-only New York City poker. Unlicensed gambling in this fair city, as his client and his ticket for tonight had put it. Leather and cigars and cologne and musty fear.

Breathe it all in. He'd earned this.

The room was filled with dark wood paneling and worn leather chairs and framed artwork. Floor lamps filled the corners, and two small chandeliers hung low. The lights were dimmed to a warm glow, draping surfaces and faces in shadow.

The floor lamps were deliberately placed to illuminate the few needed areas. One was a minibar full of uniquely shaped glass bottles, apparently self-service. Another was the money table along an adjacent wall, piled with neat stacks of colored chips. The chandeliers lit the game table, which looked like it could hold a subway car. Stout mahogany with wide curvy legs polished to a sheen that would glare if the room had brighter lights.

At the table sat seven players, five playing and two waiting for the next hand. Among them were the wide-mustache man and the thin guy with the Scottish hat he had seen entering the bar earlier. Names for adversaries helped, so these two would be Monopoly (he had the mustache, if not the top hat), and Haggis.

Going around the table, he quickly assigned monikers to the others:

Librarian (he had the end-of-nose glasses), Capo (he was straight out of a Soprano's casting room, cigar and all), Pirate (he had a squint and the leather skin of decades at sea), Wart, Steroid, and Skunk. The last name went to the lone woman at the table, who had a streak of white down the middle of her thinning hair.

They all looked up when he entered, gave a passing assessment, and turned back to the game without further concern. His youth encouraged the unthreatening impression he needed.

He walked up to the money table. "Buy-in is five thousand, Sir." The man was smartly dressed and had the grace to refrain from questioning the young, unknown player.

Dane unslung his carrier bag and brought out several stacks of rubber-banded bills. If the chip man was accustomed to uniform denominations of crisp bills, he again showed his worth by not reacting to the decidedly non-uniform stacks of bills that hadn't been anywhere close to crisp for a long time. They took a moment to unload and more than a moment to count. Dane received a small brass tray stacked with his chips and grabbed the open seat between Steroid and Skunk. The former shifted his bulk to allow more room, and the latter smelled much better than her namesake. Neither looked directly at him as he sat.

The current hand was ending. Haggis and Wart were waiting along with him for the next hand. All community cards had been played, showing a pair of nines and not much else. Librarian and Monopoly were still in. Librarian raised and Monopoly folded.

Librarian was bluffing. Dane sensed the change in his visage as he raked in the stacks, even in the dim and purposefully focused light. One piece of information gained.

Dane could read people, which is what poker is about. Cards are secondary. Expressions show, regardless of intention. Everyone has a *tell*—something that can alert an observant opponent to the possibility of a bluff, but Dane looked for their *show*, as he termed it. He couldn't really describe the show, not that he would ever do so, but even to himself he struggled to identify what it was that tipped him off. It was a sort of brain tickle or a mental flutter that he'd been able to associate with bluffs. *Spidey sense* sounded better, so he usually went with that.

He had learned time and again that making emotional decisions showed up like a Times Square billboard, so he needed to subdue and confound the message he was sending. His strategy had flipped his meager messenger tips, and a particularly painful twenty-dollar bill, into enough to join bigger and bigger games until he earned his invite here. He'd joined his Wall Street clients in games after trading hours and had massaged those relationships to get more invites across the city. Tonight's buy-in, however, was his entire soul-sucking net worth. That and his bike, hopefully still locked outside.

The rest of these players had probably pulled the cash this afternoon after a round of golf. But they were here to show, and he was here to tell.

He'd heard terms like risk analysis from his finance clients and had adapted techniques to weigh risk and benefit and make emotionless decisions. Emotions are nothing but foul clouds in front of the goal. In life, too, not just games. With the tools at his disposal and his limited understanding of the concept of risk, this usually amounted to giving fate the pedals. Some decisions needed to be random.

For instance, if he needed both to study new opponents at a poker table and not to give them any relevant information about himself, he couldn't let the knowledge of his own hole cards muck that up. So when facing new players, he opted to forfeit any chance of winning the first few hands in favor of gaining—and giving—the information he wanted to share.

Steroid had the dealer chip, so Dane had the small blind. He placed a fifty-dollar chip on the felt, and Skunk placed one hundred. He winced and hoped it didn't show. That's already a few days' earnings. He lifted the corner of his cards but kept his eyes on his opponents. A quick scan gave him a few more bits of information. Capo didn't quite blush, but his reaction tweaked Dane's thoughts in that way he couldn't quite describe. He had something good, most likely a mid-range pair. Librarian, on the other hand, had nothing, but Dane wanted to watch him closely, especially if he didn't fold early.

As poor as people are at concealing emotions and making decisions uninfluenced by them, they are just as bad at creating randomness. The mind, Dane had learned, is structured to see and use and create patterns and simply cannot induce a random sequence. So he had created and refined a strategy to throw noise to his opponents while elevating the signal for himself.

Spinning a bike tire separated into three colored wedges of equal size was his personal wheel of fortune. The results dictated how he would play the first rounds - blue is fold early, red is fold late, and white is hold until the end. He could focus all of his attention on his opponents to learn their tells while throwing up a wall of white noise into which they would expend useless energy trying to read him. Not just useless but actively counterproductive.

And being younger and unknown would bolster their opinion that he was out of his league. None would feel sympathetic, nor would he expect them to. People aren't good at sympathy, either.

He'd refined his methods over time, and although it had worked for him so far, this group was as solid as the expensive table they were sitting at. He'd given himself three spins tonight, all but assuring he'd lose a lot of money early. Risk and reward for himself, and crash and burn for everyone else.

Steroid dealt the flop. Dane checked. His scheme only required him to fold early, and not knowing his hole cards—he hadn't actually looked but pretended that he had—made that easy. He faced a $50 raise when the bet came around to him again, and he dutifully folded. He dealt the next round, which was a white spin, meaning he needed to see it out. It cost him three hundred to do so, and he kept himself grounded as he flipped his hole cards. He didn't even look at them then, either, but rather at the two players still in the hand, Librarian and Haggis.

Their reaction told him that his cards didn't warrant the confidence he was showing. *More information gained.* Haggis took the pot.

The third hand required a late fold so he stayed up to the river, costing him another two hundred. The pain of watching that much go was genuine—no need to hide that emotion. It was cash far beyond what he had coveted for food and a clean place to stay in the recent past. And in the near future, if tonight didn't go his way. But his diligence was paying off. He had received a Times Square ticker amount of clear signal and had given back a subway tunnel worth of useless noise.

Now he could play.

It was his night. He cleaned up, taking every third or fourth hand. He read each and every one of them like a worn book from the New York Public Library. The flutter in his mind told him when they were bluffing, and when they were nervous.

Librarian was the first to go all-in, and he left without buying back. He stopped at the door, turned back, and murmured a quiet "Well played" before leaving. Steroid was the next to go. He stormed out without a glance back. Haggis shook Dane's hand on his way out, and Capo gave him a fresh cigar. Wart grimaced but didn't seem all that perturbed. Five thousand probably wasn't worth someone like him getting bent. Dane wondered why he didn't get the ugly growth on his jawline removed, though.

Monopoly and Skunk were left. On a run of community cards with a pair of jacks and some low cards, they both went all-in. Dane took it. They both bought back in and watched the tide of chips continue to ebb from their side and flow toward Dane's.

The hour had crept into the low numbers when he cashed out—victorious but subdued. Life lesson—celebration isn't worth it. Whatever came his way could all go, and usually did. Money, friends, family, health. They were all transient. To derive joy from any of it is to force inevitable despair when it leaves.

But a shit-eating grin and a celebratory drink can't hurt too much.

Some of the players had cashed out early, but enough of them left empty that Dane walked out of the room with over forty thousand in hundreds neatly bundled in his messenger bag. He took two shots of what must have been expensive whisky from the corner bar before heading downstairs. He tipped the moneyman five hundred. He'd seen that in a movie, and it felt good.

He descended to the bar, his body convulsing with shots of endorphins his brain had held at bay. Like floodgates, sweet chemicals flowed to the point that he nearly stumbled in the narrow stairway. He jittered as his nerves released from hours constrained, and he needed another drink before his ride home. He grabbed a stool and ordered a beer from the red-bearded barkeep.

"It's on me," the red-bearded barkeep said, waiving away Dane's cash. "Congratulations, young sir."

Dane returned a respectable nod, fighting to maintain a dignified air by not grinning as wide as he had in years. People like to buy drinks for celebrities and athletes who don't need the money. An inverted habit, but he could see the appeal more clearly from the other side.

He dowened the drink and walked outside, his messenger bag holding a new life. He couldn't quite conceive the amount of cash bouncing against his hip, all rightfully earned. He wasn't sure how he would have gotten it all out if they weren't mostly bundles of hundreds. He yawned and rubbed his eyes, smiling towards a few tables. There were plenty of girls in there worth buying drinks for, but they'd be back tomorrow night.

He wouldn't, though. That night, he'd bought his exit ticket from the city. He'd dreamed for years and planned for months for a way out, and despite his inexperience at planning anything, it worked.

It appeared to work. Of the many mistakes he had made in his life, strolling outside with a bag full of cash and an alcohol-fueled ego was one he would remember.

4

A **STEP FROM** his bike, Dane's nerves whipped back to full alert, and his euphoria vaporized.

Two men emerged from the shadows. One wiry and tall, one fat with a scrunched face, both with hungry eyes and a sneer of contempt. It didn't matter who had sent these assholes. Dane had carved his life between the unyielding pillars of distrust and betrayal, and there was no reason tonight should be any different.

The pair spread apart and cornered him between the wall and the stacks of scaffolding. Might as well give them names, too, he thought. Rake and Steak would do.

"You made a new friend in there tonight," said Steak, the fat one. "They want to know how you did it."

"How I got numbers from that many girls?" Dane choked the words out, reining in the whipsaw of unhelpful emotions.

"How you managed your cards, kid," said Rake.

A breath. Buy time. "I just played—and now I'm going home."

"Sure, and you've got a couple ways to get there. Tell us your game. Or give us a cut to pass along."

He needed to stall. He anticipated losing his money at some point, but shit, he'd like a chance to burn it his own way. "How much?" Rake and Steak looked at each other, and he saw an opening. They were calling an audible, hoping to get more than whatever they'd been tasked to do. If they had been asked at all.

"Oh, I'd say that would do." Rake said, nodding to the bag.

Dane didn't know who hired these thugs. The guys who left earliest were likely, but the others had taken piss breaks and could have made a call. Could have been the Wall Street guy who gave him the invitation. That lot is certainly not above reproach—they're below reproach, if that's a thing.

But knowing who sent them contributes nothing to the immediate moment. He turned toward the wall with his bag in front of him, hoping it would appear he was opening it.

Bike locks are an essential component of a New York City bike courier's life. If he paid taxes, he could have written off their cost as a business expense. The type of lock and chain were the difference between the bike staying where he left it or not. After a couple of losses, he'd settled on a thick iron padlock with a long braided steel cable. Not too heavy, but strong and flexible. Dane had opened physics book once or twice but would struggle to find an equation for the force an iron padlock swung in a concentric arc from the end of an eighteen-inch cable with the initial velocity gained from uncoiling his torso would deliver.

He knew a girl once who could probably solve that—but she wasn't around, and he hoped to never see her again.

What mattered was that the force was enough to shatter the eye socket of one Steak and fill the immediate area with a lot of blood and noise. The follow-through swing would have been enough to pulverize the nose of one Rake had he not stumbled backward, clearing himself from the arc of the lock but striking his tailbone on the curb and spraining his wrist and adding another burst of noise to the narrow side street.

Dane turned back to Steak, who was blindly groping for something under his jacket with one hand and covering what remained of his eye with the other. He bellowed something about internal organs being removed and reinserted in alternate locations, but through the frothing blood spuming from his gritted teeth, Dane wasn't able to catch the specifics.

He'd been in enough muggings and street fights to know when the goal was something random—where the perpetrators would usually give up when the efforts outweighed the rewards. Cops were the same way. But when the fight was personal, the effort didn't matter and victory was the one and only reward. These were blockhead goons, not professionals, but he had just made this confrontation personal.

He kept them both back with a couple more whips of the lock and then flung it toward them. He grabbed his handlebars and swung onto his bike, pumping into a desperate sprint. A familiar, welcome rush shot in. His nerves knew what to do. He didn't need to think. *Fight or bike.*

One rotation of the wheels, one glorious churn toward the promise of a new life, one deep inhale—and the bike locked up. Hard. He soared over the handlebars and landed cheek-first into a curb. No spidey sense to aid him there.

Another high-pitched scream behind him had accompanied his flight. He glanced back and saw Rake lying prone with fingers mangled between the rear spokes and the seatstay frame. There may have been a finger or two between the chain and the rear sprocket as well. The quick-thinker had dutifully stopped Dane from fleeing, though, whether he recognized his sacrifice at the time or not.

With Steak's one good eye, he either didn't see his associate's hand there or didn't care as he howled into the fray and hoisted the bike upward, degloving the skin from Rake's fingers. Rake's newest shriek cut through the noise of the nearby bars, and shocked onlookers materialized at a safe but recordable distance around the scene.

Dane watched his beloved bike being raised in the sky—dangling bits of flesh—then watched it plummet down at him. The tri-colored spokes spun delicately in the street lights. Stunned from a helmetless face strike on the curb, he couldn't move to avoid it.

Nothing about a bike is comfortable other than riding it, and he felt every sharp angle tear into him with all the rage that a half-blinded and overweight thug could muster. A constellation of pain erupted over every corner of his body.

Verging on shock, he kicked the awkward frame upward with both legs. Steak raised it again, this time jumping on the curb to give himself more leverage. Dane couldn't take another hit like that and stay conscious. As the spinning wheels once again reached their apex, a wooden baseball bat split the center of the frame and Steak stumbled backward.

The barkeep's bald dome reflected streetlights as he stood by entranceway to the *Rooster*, bat in hand, and poised for another swing. His long, red beard twitched.

Dane rolled away and stumbled backward into the growing crowd. The onlookers coordinated their parting to let him collapse once again on the unforgiving concrete. He watched Steak toss aside the remnants of his beloved bike, looking askance at the bat-wielding barkeep.

Dane shifted himself upright and stumbled away until he could manage a trot over piercing ankle pain. Both brutes gave chase, pulling knives to lead their charge. A siren cut through the shouts as a patrol car pulled around the corner.

Disoriented, Dane swerved through oncoming taxis and cut down another street. These assholes were gaining on him. Whatever their damage was, they were more mobile than himself. His ribs burned with each inhale. His right ankle screamed. Curiously, he found blood dripping down his left arm and off his fingertips. He located a slice through the meat of his shoulder that he didn't recall receiving.

He ran—each step and each breath like another cut. He traveled east but lost track of the streets. He'd had years of finding refuge throughout the city, but none presented themselves that night. They were almost on him.

He turned a corner and burst into the first open door in his path. Another bar. He barreled through customers and toppled a waitress who had been balancing an impressive number of beer mugs on her tray. She screamed, and he left blood on everything he touched, including her. He coughed out an apology that no one likely heard.

The two pursuers were a step behind him until Rake rolled his ankle on a fallen mug. Dane grabbed the serving tray from the floor and frisbeed it at Steak's face. He swatted it down—impressive for a guy with rage bubbling through his one working eye.

Dane careened around the room, tripping over and crushing a Styrofoam box filled with ice bags. He grabbed a big chunk of the broken lid and fled to the streets again in the midst of the pandemonium.

Across the road, a wave of nausea hit him like a subway car. He doubled over and vomited. The nerves, the blood, the pain, the martinis—it all came up as an offering to the city streets.

The pair of thugs leaped across the avenue, knives in hand, seeing their prey hobbled. Sirens called from oncoming cop cars. Dane hoisted himself upward and fled, his stomach clear but his head whirling.

The world opened wide as he cleared the confines of lower

Manhattan and beheld the breadth of the East River. Strolling couples and posing tourists took in the iconic scene.

"Nowhere to go, fuckhead!" yelled Rake, holding his knife in his one good hand. "Your balls are fish bait!" Steak gurgled something else through clenched and blood-soaked teeth.

The nowhere to go comment was accurate. Dane was backed against the railing, and everyone nearby had scattered.

Sirens drew near. He had about two seconds to jump or to die, and he really didn't prefer the latter. No use in any further analysis here, he concluded. Over the railing and into the East River he went, the shock of the water and pain from all directions threatening his ability to remain conscious.

His head swam, but his body wasn't quite capable. He submerged and drifted away from the pier, the shouting and sirens fading as the dark, brackish water swollowed him.

5

"SPREADSHEETS IN A bar, how charming," drolled Melanie, and Arin couldn't help but chuckle. "Keep in mind we're about three drinks deep when our rapt attention gets hijacked away from your pie charts."

"I suggested moving to a setting more conducive to an academic lecture," Ross responded. "But the value of my input goes yet unrealized."

Arin had a pair of tickets to see a local indie group, and she and Melanie were pre-flighting at a nearby bar when Ross met them. "Many a wise lesson has been bestowed in taverns," she allowed with an exaggerated flourish. "Please proceed."

"Gladly," Ross replied. "A quick recap on the human eye. Stop me if I'm repeating material you've retained in its entirety from high school biology." Arin tapped her temple and lifted her eyes to the ceiling. Good grades don't always equate to knowledge retention.

"Right, I thought not. The parts of our eyes that are relevant here are the rods and the cones—especially the cones, and one receptor in particular. As humans, including the majority of us at this table, we can see across the spectrum from about 400 to 700 nanometers. That covers the colors of the rainbow from violet to red. Rods receive low light near the middle of that range but don't process color. That's why things are gray at night."

Arin pantomimed jotting notes into her palm. A waiter brought Ross's beer, refills for the girls, and a large basket of fries with a side of mayonnaise. A loud group entered behind them.

"Fries with mayo? If you're going for empty calories, at least make it normal." Ross scrunched his face.

"Got the habit from euro trips growing up," Arin replied. "There's culinary science behind it. Ask your gastro friends."

"And you'd better cliff-notes this explanation," Melanie stated, "You're sinkholing the vibe here."

"As I was saying, I think I was saying anyway, cones are how we perceive color. We have three types corresponding to what we call primary colors, which are..." He opened his hands expectantly, eyes darting between the two women for an answer.

"Red, Green, and Blue!" chirped Arin. "What do I win?"

"How about a dance?"

"Not interested. But you've been staring all night, so please, Sir, tell me what my cones look like." She locked her gaze on his, and Melanie nearly snorted out beer. Ross grimaced with a commendable effort to hold his eyes level.

"The receptors in red cones," he paused for a deep swig and a deeper breath, "in the human eye, are activated at the longer wavelengths in the visible spectrum. They can reach around 700 nanometers, and at the shorter side they overlap a lot with green cones and a little with blue ones. The degree of overlap is how we get all of the color varieties. Your paint store counter would be rather dull otherwise."

"Curiously, *rather dull* is a phrase that just happened to pop into my head," droned Melanie.

"The rancor I put up with for a chance to talk to a couple of beautiful women." Ross gulped down half his glass. "I've got to catch up to have any hope of communicating at your level here. So anyway, that describes the normal human. She," Ross relished the opportunity to lock eyes with Arin again, "is not normal. She's extraordinary."

"Oh, she's that all right," said Melanie, giving her a long kiss on the cheek. Arin let the affection dry on her face.

"She is indeed. She seems to have red cone receptors that stretch the upper limits of what human eyes can usually perceive. Not what she can really see—or process consciously—but somehow perceive. Parts of my test, which I'll remind you I whipped together in barely a couple of days, were to see what would trigger subconscious brain activity. I used infrared images, meaning wavelengths longer than visible red, to see if she would pick them up. Specifically, the receptors in her red cones." He paused for another swig. "Still with me?"

Arin leaned in to hear him over the background bar noise. "So, what did you test on me?"

"I arranged some slides among many that only showed images in infrared wavelengths. You probably saw them as an unchanging gray or black. You didn't click at those points, but your scans showed activity over baseline, indicating your unique gray matter recognized the slides as something other than gray. We went back and forth a few times to verify. I also tried some in the UV range, but those didn't trigger your blue cone receptors in the same way. Lastly, when I turned out the lights and removed your goggles, I plugged in a hair curler and propped it a meter or so above your head."

"In total darkness? No creep factor there at all." She winced.

"Name of science, deal with it. I'm assuming it was far enough away that you didn't feel the gradual increase in heat. And you didn't actively see it, being we were in total *creepy* darkness. But your scans perked right up. Your brain saw that change in heat patterns that I couldn't, Melanie couldn't, and anyone else in this bar couldn't. So, in short, I do believe I've found my thesis. For that, I'll get the next round." He signaled the waiter.

"So, what's next?"

"I think you need to speak with your parents. This seems genetic, somehow, but it could be epigenetic."

"Epi...," Arin started, scraping her current inebriated processing limits to translate. "Above the genes?"

"Close enough. But this bar is getting louder, and you're both flirting with limits of coherence, so I'll save part two for another time. Any questions before I leave you to your revelry?" They sat back, and the sounds of the tavern filled in.

"Yeah, I have a question," Melanie piped up. "Why the hell did you have a hair curler?"

ARIN SPOKE WITH HER PARENTS every few weeks, but per her therapist's guidance, she refrained from any topic that might sound like she was asking for money or any other help. So when she called to learn if either of them had noticed augmented perception or had recognized it in her, she framed it as a research topic for a friend.

That was mostly true, other than the friend part. Ross was an emotional adolescent, but as Melanie had said, he was harmless, and she trusted him. And they were now working together to figure out a bizarre part of her. He sent notes to help her frame the questions she would ask her parents.

Her mother, Holly, expressed no notion of what she was asking about and hadn't heard anything like that from others in her family. No eye exams or other medical appointments from Arin's youth stood out. Her father, Randy, had been raised in an orphanage before being adopted. When she asked the odd question about games like hide and seek, he said he was probably good but didn't really remember. They both asked Arin if she was ok and if she needed anything.

Ross caught Arin on a run along the Charles River when he called to discuss his findings further. She slowed her pace enough to regain conversational breathing. "So I get the genes and DNA thing, but my parents don't seem to have what I have," she huffed. "Pardon the choppy breath."

"Fully pardoned. Keep in mind that you didn't know about this, either, and we only got the first snippet of useful data last weekend. I'm sure your parents are busy, but I'd love the opportunity to test them."

"Doubtful, but I can ask. Even if they do, though, what does that tell us? Neither of them has parents of their own to talk to. What are you thinking about the... what'd you say... epigenetics?"

"That's how our genes are expressed. It has to do with phenotypes and RNA, but I'll try to stay at the level of someone who has had their perfect button nose in more enjoyable books than I have. Think of one of your classical playwrights. Give me a name."

"Aristophanes."

"You couldn't have picked a shorter name? Ok, so he's got his script on paper. That's the hard-coded DNA. How the actors bring that script to life is the expression I'm talking about. There are steps to do so, and there's room for personal style. Options for flair."

"But that expression doesn't get handed down. Just the words do."

"Right! And that's what we've always thought. But what if the methods the actors use to influence the next generation of actors, and so on, even while the words remain the same? My ad-hoc analogy might fail a little here, but I think you're tracking."

She processed that as she ran. The road has always been her best place to think. "You're saying the epigenome can be passed down, too?"

"Maybe. Some studies suggest they do. It's called epigenetic inheritance. Groups who faced periods of hunger long enough to affect their epigenome produced offspring who showed those same markers, even if those kids had ample nutrition. Mice studies show there's germline transmission possible in mammals, but there are a lot of unknowns. In short, we don't know."

Arin was tired of hearing that answer. "Why couldn't this be a random mutation, like other DNA changes?"

"It could. We would need a full DNA panel and new testing techniques. Grants for a controlled, double-blinded..."

"Ok, I get it—that's not happening today. But what do you think?"

"I don't think it's a randomly occurring mutation. Hundreds of generations would have needed to select this trait for some unexplainable reason, and it would have shown up somewhere before with all of the vision studies we've done in the last century or so. We would have discovered and documented a wider spectrum of the human eye's capabilities."

"So you think it's this expression thing? What would cause that? And another *I don't know* will piss me off."

"Oh, believe me, I don't want to do that... but I'm already out of my comfort zone here and don't want to lead you astray, either. All I can say is that abilities like this exist in many animal species. Snakes, bats, frogs. Just not lovely, blonde-haired track stars. But if you're ok with it, I may send out my initial findings to hivemind some answers. Keeping you anonymous, of course." Arin consented, not seeing another option.

"Enjoy your run! It's a bright day—I hope you have UV shades to protect those beauties!"

Her earbuds filled with music again as the call ended. She turned onto Longfellow Bridge to extend her loop by another few miles. That—her running—she could still control.

6

"I LOOKED UP your dad's orphanage," Melanie told her later. "It's not too far, out past Springfield. If there's anything to be found, that's a place to start. What do you say to a quick getaway? I can hone my investigation skills—what is it?" she asked as Arin lowered her eyes.

"Nothing. Sure, I need answers. You booked already, didn't you?"

"We're leaving tomorrow morning. I got a cabin in the Berkshires for us—I know I need the space. You?" Arin nodded, twisting a strand of hair as she looked out the window.

They took Melanie's car, a compact SUV, dark red with roof racks and a few dated campaign stickers. They arrived at the mountain rental and settled on a small porch with oversized tea mugs. A cool breeze filtered through what was left of the leaves. The porch fronted a sloping field and the forest beyond covered the surrounding hills, save for a few scattered cuts for new housing. There must be a number of allowable house holes before the land was no longer considered forested. When control tips to the human side.

They decided to visit the orphanage after lunch. Melanie mentioned a journalism trick where people cooperate more with full bellies. They didn't expect to learn much—there were privacy laws and several decades between them and anything useful, but it would be a start.

Help is what they needed, and Arin herself hadn't provided any. Melanie jotted down questions to ask while Arin watched a small plane buzz overhead. She grabbed a jacket and left the cabin, heading down a narrow trail without a word.

She returned an hour later to find Melanie at her laptop at the kitchen table. She jumped up when she saw Arin's puffy red eyes. "What's wrong?"

"Me. I'm what's wrong. And I can't do anything about it. Everything we're doing here is because of you, and Ross. I'm just a subject here—a patient. I appreciate all you're doing and I want answers, too, but I'm not helping with any of it. At least you're both practicing your areas of study—so glad I can help you with that."

Melanie spread her hands wide, then brought one hand to her chest. "I didn't think about that. There's plenty you can do to get answers, though."

"Like what, Mel? What can I do that you, or that Ross, can't do better? It's my life, my body, but I'm just a passenger." Arin sat and wiped her eyes. "Sorry. You're amazing, really. I'm just feeling helpless."

Melanie pulled up a chair and faced her. "You're amazing. With or without your superwoman eyes. You have so much to offer anyone lucky enough to be a part of your life. I'm doing this for us—not just as a project. And you're contributing more than you think. I don't know where this is going. We'll probably hit a brick wall today, and I'm happy to go back to campus and carry on with life. You can do your parlor tricks at parties if you want. Or forget it all. Whatever happens, I'm here." She wiped away Arin's tears. "Now, let's head over there. You should take the lead. It's your father we're asking about."

The orphanage was an hour's drive through winding, mountainous roads. They arrived at a wide, three-storied brick building surrounded by a garden and apple trees. Arin had called ahead, and they were buzzed into the front office. A middle-aged woman came around the desk and shook their hands.

"Hello, I'm Rose. It's always a pleasure to meet the family of our children," she said. "Of course, I never met your father—I'm not sure if I was even born when he was here." She had a gentle laugh. "As for any records, there's not much we can share without the court's say-so, I'm sure you know. And our records from back then are a little spotty. In your father's case, it was an anonymous delivery, so even he wouldn't be able to get much. So I'm not sure how I can help you."

"I'm just hoping there's something you can tell me about him. Was there anyone here who was working then?"

"There was, in fact. Charlotte is one of our lovely souls who should have retired years ago, but she just loves the children so much that she won't leave. I'll call her down."

An elderly, jovial woman met them a few moments later. "So wonderful of you two young women to visit," Charlotte declared after introductions. "Not many do. It's cookie day here, and the children have a few batches in the oven. They don't always get the recipes quite right, but I'm certain they'll be delicious. You'll stay for them? We can take a stroll in the orchard, and I'll be happy to tell you what I remember of your father."

The older woman pulled on a thick parka and a scarf, and they exited a side door. They strolled through a small grove of apple trees, and Charlotte pointed out which were for eating and which were for pies. She plucked a couple of the former type and handed them over.

"McIntosh has always been my favorite. They snap just so on your first bite. What's your favorite variety?"

"I'm not sure if I've ever thought about that," Arin replied.

"Shame. Everyone should have a favorite apple. That's what I tell all my children here. And the staff, too. Don't let those things leave you when you grow up."

Arin plucked an apple from the nearest tree and took a hearty bite. "They're perfect, thank you," she mumbled around the fruit. "So, do you remember Randall? Or Randy? It would have been a long time ago, early seventies."

"I do—I remember all of my children. Randy was a charming little boy."

"This will seem like a silly question, but do you remember if he was especially good at anything? Maybe games like hide and seek?"

The older woman stopped and gave Arin a quizzical look. "Why, my dear, I don't remember. I suppose so. I do recall a night when several of the boys snuck out after dark, the little demons. They got lost in the woods, and it was Randy who found their way back. And he was younger than the others by a few years, too." Arin exchanged a glance with Melanie.

"Is it true there are no other records for him? I'd like to know who my grandparents were."

Charlotte looked back toward the building. "Rose is a good person and knows the rules. I might have a longer reach. Randy was a closed delivery, so there probably isn't much to find, but I'll look. Things were a little looser back then, but we take in and care for any child we're blessed with." She tilted her head toward the drifting clouds. "Did he tell you about his older sister?"

Both Arin and Melanie stopped mid-stride.

"It seems not. I'm not sure he even knew. I'm not certain, either, but I've been around long enough to get a feeling for these things. They had different last names but were brought to us in the same way, and a few years apart. They had the same eyes. And mouth. I think we all knew, but of course, we raised them just as we raised all of our children."

"Do you have her name or when she was born?" Melanie had been letting Arin ask the questions but jumped in as Arin remained transfixed.

"Gina. I can't recall her last name, but I should be able to find it. We never really used their last names. Dear, did you say your name was Coppertree? Yes, that sounds right for little Randy. Hmm." The old woman's brow creased through the natural wrinkles.

"What is it?"

"Probably nothing—just the cobwebs of an old woman's mind getting crossed. Let me look through the records. My daughter is a waitress at the diner in town. Go get yourselves some dinner there tonight, and I can meet you. But now, the cookies must be ready. Won't you join us?"

ARIN UNDRESSED AND LET THE foamy heat within the antique claw-foot bathtub envelop her. A window hinged outward to let the sharp autumn breeze cool her face and exposed knees, and her arms when they emerged for her wine glass. There is no safe space like a hot bath with a view and a bottle of good Sangiovese.

They had gotten burgers and beers at the lone diner in town. Charlotte stopped by as they were ready to leave and gave them the full name of someone who might be her aunt. Gina Rosewood. She hadn't found any other information about her father, though. She handed them photocopied pictures of both kids, and Arin did see a passing resemblance.

45

Melanie jumped into investigator mode again but quickly hit a dead end. Literally, she said. Gina had died in a psychiatric hospital about a decade earlier. She dug further and found that the facility had been condemned, closed, and sold shortly after. That would have been during the Great Recession of the late aughts, and she didn't get any hits more recent than that. The former hospital was only an hour's drive from their cabin, so they extended their cabin rental through the weekend with a loose hope that a visit might give them something.

Arin could log in for remote classes if she felt a pang of responsibility for her parent's tuition checks. She did, and would, but not right now. She had recently made efforts to distance herself from them. Not out of any sense of them having neglected or mistreated her, but rather the opposite. She was well into college when she realized they had given her too much.

She came north for undergrad on a track scholarship but was now in grad school and no longer competed. She wasn't entirely too old but was old enough to know that she wasn't going pro and needed to focus on the next phase of her life. A life that had been relatively planned, or at least predictable, from the start.

Coming from an exclusive suburb in Maryland, her parents had consistently and persistently reminded her of the value of hard work, personal responsibility, and so on, which was easy to talk about but never really seemed to come up in practice. Sure, her father was raised in an orphanage and got where he was on his own, and she should be expected to do at least as much, considering where she was starting.

She later realized the extent of resources she'd been provided to fill any and all shortcomings. Private tutors for the academic shortcomings, and discrete phone calls or hasty donations for the moral ones. There was always a net to keep her from falling into any real consequences. Her parents loved and provided for her, but she didn't realize until she went away just how much she had been coddled. She vowed to set her own path. Easy to talk about with her therapist but harder to do.

Her father had looked into his own background years ago but hadn't gotten any farther than they had. Even less—he didn't know about the possible sister. Arin had called him when they got back to the cabin. He had a rough memory of an older girl by that name but nothing more. She shared all that she knew, including Gina's passing. He asked her to keep him informed and call if she needed help. As he'd always done.

She was sweating from the bath heat and stretched out her foot to nudge the window open wider. Cold moonlight draped the bare trees.

She could call a halt to all of this if she wanted. Chalk it up to some anomaly worthy of a parlor trick, as Melanie had suggested. She had no real goal in learning more about her unusual ability other than satisfying a curiosity. The family angle wasn't getting them anywhere, and even if they could find others who were the same, that wouldn't answer where the ability came from.

She resigned herself to a quick visit to the former hospital in the morning and then to enjoy the weekend with Melanie. She floated her wine glass in the water, letting it bob and twist as it wanted.

7

DANE'S SKULL THUNDERED. He hunched between shipping containers on a Brooklyn dock. The sun's low angle suggested early morning, and through his pulsing head, he guessed three or four hours had passed since he escaped probable death and certain destitution.

Likely prison as well, if he was keeping count of all the ways the night before could have gone much worse. Dane began to laugh at the thought until it ripped through his torso and doubled him over. The proverbial *it* could have been worse, but it was still remarkably bad.

On a day when the likelihood of the outcome was notably higher than usual, he almost forgot the ritual of telling himself that he might die. The words brought a flicker of continuity to his morning.

He'd been in enough fights and bike crashes to diagnose what was obvious. He had a fractured rib, maybe a few. His ankle was shot but probably not broken. One side of his face was swollen, and he was afraid to move his jaw. The acute knife cut on his shoulder had stopped bleeding and clotted up, but not before taking in the best of the East River's offerings. The water also hadn't done much to wash away the blood covering his clothes and hair. The fever he'd awoken to wasn't abating anytime soon, and his drenched clothing wasn't helping, either. He would get out of this, though. Money can fix just about anything, and he had a lot of it.

His bag. His heart stopped for a beat, two beats, as he looked for his messenger bag. Without it, he couldn't start a new life and would struggle to continue with this one. The months building up to his game the night before would be for nothing. His pain would be uncompensated. His joy would be unfulfilled, which hurt more. His fault for letting such a feeling in.

He had the bag on the pier before he'd passed out. If someone took it. Oh, right. *Idiot.* He eased his beaten body downward and winced as he slung the most expensive and most uncomfortable pillow in New York City over his shoulder.

He checked on the sodden stacks of cash. Probably easier to spend cash looking like this than the crisp type they had been a few hours ago, he figured.

He pulled his phone from the front pocket. There were new phones and expensive cases that do just fine in water. His wasn't one of those. He attempted to fling it off the pier, but a bolt of pain across his torso stopped him short. The phone skittered on the concrete. He shuffled over and kicked it the rest of the way off the edge.

He then took out the broken chunk of Styrofoam he had wedged in the bag before falling in the river. It had kept both him and the bag afloat. Had the bag sunk, he wouldn't have had reason to stay afloat himself.

But that's not true, he told himself. With his transformative haul safely under his arm, his thoughts cleared. He could survive if he lost everything. He'd done it before. The worst that can happen usually

49

doesn't. Even if it seemed so, Dane knew, it was never really the worst if you're still around to judge it. It's one of those paradoxes.

He tried but failed to maintain a stable gait as he walked out past a startled crew of longshoremen. No one stopped him from grabbing a paper cup and splashing in coffee from a dispenser on a folding table. He trundled by and ignored the comments, then pushed himself along a few streets until he came to an outdoor bazaar.

"They're shooting a zombie movie," he said to the vendor. "I got cut."

He grabbed two full sets of clothing and a pair of shoes from the racks and handed over a couple of bills, not waiting for change. He ducked into some bushes behind a church and stripped off what remained of his clothing. He winced as he pulled on a new set, found a trash bin for the blood-stained rags, and then limped a few more blocks to a high school he had once attended.

He had, in fact, attended the school more than once, but not often enough to check the box needed to remain a student. The hasp for the locker room door by the ball field hadn't been fixed, he was glad to see, and he pried it open. The shower room was empty when he entered, but he didn't waste any time. He rushed through a hot shower, scrubbed with some wall-mounted shampoo, and even found a bottle of ibuprofen on the floor between the lockers. The first set of new clothes had already absorbed blood from reopened wounds, so he tossed those and donned the second set.

He bought a new satchel and a ballcap from another street vendor. Ducking behind a van, he transferred the cash to the new bag. With an affectionate caress for the years of service it had provided, he dropped the ruined leather messenger bag into another trash bin. After getting a sandwich and energy drink from a deli, he scarfed down the needed calories as he limped north. He looked torn apart—felt the same—but was now at least presentable enough to walk into a hotel lobby without security turning him around.

He paid for a room in cash, as cash was the only item to his name. His non-driver ID card (he'd never bothered getting a license) was either in a pocket of his old jeans or in his discarded bag or somewhere in a lower Manhattan gutter, but the clerk didn't ask. He found his room, took some more pills, took another shower, and managed to get some food down before crawling into bed. Sleep came in fits as his mind swirled.

DANE COULDN'T REMEMBER A TIME before he rode bikes. Getting him off his wheels was a task no mother would wish to endure, each and every night, with a hope of being spared that burden only in the harshest of rain or the deepest of snow, before the diligent Brooklyn plow trucks would clear his way again. And it was almost always his mother, Gina, tasked with getting him home and cleaned up for a reasonable bedtime. His father, Warren, had worked the late shift with the MTA as a subway motorman, and he only saw him in the quiet early mornings. He would leave after dinner, topping up his insulated coffee mug with bourbon.

He would come home with an exhausted but enduring smile, pour a fresh glass of Evan Williams, watch Dane eat his cornflakes, and then head to bed. His mother would get him ready for the bus with his father snoring in the lone bedroom behind the thin wall.

That was Dane's childhood, until he was old enough to prep for school himself. That was at age seven, it turned out, when his mother left, and it was just him and his father in the cramped walk-up apartment.

As a child, his father brought him along on the job on weekends and sometimes on weekday nights, and he would watch the endless subway tunnels eat up and spit out endless streams of people in the endless city. Riding in the front is like flying warp speed, and he would imagine soaring through the black expanse with lights zipping past. Half of the tunnel lights would be out or flickering, so it looked more like an asteroid field than regulated public transportation. His dad would smile and take a slow sip from his mug. The amount of bourbon he added grew over the years, and soon surpassed the amount of coffee.

They would find a late-night diner for pie and milkshakes before joining the regular passengers for a ride back home.

With his mother gone and his father working the night shift, Dane was on his own. He adored his father, and knew his dad gave him more than he could afford. As a kid, he thought it was cool to share his bedroom with father, until he realized it wasn't. He thought it was cool that his dad was a subway driver, until he was told it wasn't. He thought a bike was the coolest way to get around the city, and years later, he realized it was.

He rode to school and back when he needed to, and rode with friends across the bridge into Manhattan when he could. He'd sail up and down the avenues and cross streets and parks, dodging shoppers and tourists and food carts with a dexterity his friends couldn't match. He knew to swerve before an unwitting pedestrian turned a corner. His friends let him lead, as people and bikes and shopping bags would all end up out of place otherwise.

They learned the city only as kids on bikes can. They knew which bodega clerks would give them expired snacks for free, and which barkeeps would give them beer in plastic cups if they posted flyers for their upcoming live music.

They knew which gates would be open when they needed to flee with a shopping bag or purse or briefcase after "crashing" into an unfortunate pedestrian who had gotten themselves in the way. They knew which streets cop cars would have trouble navigating. Streets with hotels were the best, as tourists and cabs and town cars would be conveniently double parked and blocking all but those on two feet or two wheels.

Dane skirted trouble more than once by finding refuge in subway station offices. Cops expect the miscreants fleeing underground to hop a turnstile in hopes of catching a departing train. They don't expect a kid to see an MTA worker he knows and find welcome refuge in their cramped office. Enough of them still knew Dane as they knew his dad. Not many would have remembered the kid who rode with his dad, though, if not for their last subway ride together.

8

DANE WOKE TO a rising fever and throbbing ache in his ankle, currently his loudest yelling body part. He limped to the bathroom and took another cold shower. Late morning sunlight cut through gaps in the curtain, threatening the extra hour or two of sleep he needed. He was too exhausted to figure out his next move.

The near side of the bed was clammy with cold sweat, so he eased himself into the other side. Closer to the piercing sunlight, but drier. He wrestled with unwanted memories as his body again denied him sound sleep.

ONE SUNDAY NIGHT, WITH A school holiday the next day, Dane went out with his father for the late shift. With his mother gone, he took every chance to go out instead of staying home alone. His ninth birthday had been that week, and a full night on the tracks was as good as a birthday party. He didn't know many friends who would have come to his, anyway.

They packed blankets and pillows and snacks so Dane could sleep in the cab when he'd hit his nocturnal limit. People slept in subway cars all the time, his dad told him. They took the F Train into Manhattan, where they assumed their seats in the front car as usual. The motor car. They traveled several stops, seeing the usual mix of tourists and college kids and Upper East Siders before the train crossed back over toward Queens. Even then, he would watch the countless types of people and know when they were in the right place and when they weren't. Not just by their clothes or what they carried but by their faces and movements. He knew when someone suddenly became lost or worried or fearful. He would point them out to his dad, who would tell him that lots of people get lost down there.

They were a few stops into Queens that night, and they ground and bumped through a long, dark section between stations. Dane was sleepy. One headlight on the car was out, and the other flickered at every jolt. At least half of the wall lights were out. The train knew where to go, though, and that's all Warren had to care about. That, and the drowsy boy on the bench seat next to him, head swaying with the tracks, eyelids heavy.

Until they snapped open. "Stop!" yelled Dane as he jumped from slumber under the blanket, spilling animal crackers and a juice box onto the cab floor. "On the tracks!"

His dad reached out but didn't apply breaks, seeing nothing abnormal through the unsteady illumination. The tunnel curved away to the right, all clear.

"Son? Did you have a nightmare—" Warren's eyes went wide as

the train continued around the curve, and then he jerked the brake handle. The iron wheels let the world know they were not happy. The ungodly screeching didn't slow the train enough to save the errant soul splayed across one of the tracks. The body started to stir at the approaching noise and began to slide away, flopping toward the old stones of the tunnel wall, but one arm and at least one leg were caught by the momentous iron monster, driven capably but beyond the control of Dane's father.

Dane never lost that sound of bones snapping and the subtle bump as the wheels diligently obeyed the laws of physics.

The adjoining stations were shut down from the small hours of the morning well into dawn, interrupting the commuters and families with plans for that holiday weekend. Those on the train were led off and escorted down hundreds of yards of dark, neglected track to the nearest station. It was a funeral march where no one knew the name of the deceased.

Warren spoke quietly to a few different NYPD officers, who took his notes, but there weren't many details he could add to the gruesome scene.

He didn't mention that it was his son who had alerted him, before the bend, to the man on the tracks. They walked home in near silence, plodding along for miles through Queens and Brooklyn. Dane's father asked if he was ok, and he said yes.

Once, Warren began with "How did you know..." then stopped himself, still working through the horror they'd seen. Been part of. Caused. Dane questioned his own memory. His father must be questioning his, as well. A few blocks later, he whispered a soft "I don't know, Dad."

They stopped for pancakes, apple juice, and coffee, which they picked at. The waitress came over to top up Warren's mug. Watching the thick liquid pour from the glass pitcher, Warren suddenly jolted up. He looked around, padding his jacket pockets, and hung his head. "Oh. Oh, shit." That was Dane's last time riding with his father.

After the police found and tested Warren's travel mug and he was sentenced to Riker's Island for manslaughter, Dane was on his own. He went in and out of foster homes and schools around the city. Some days he made friends and lost money. Some days the opposite. He found little room and less reason for any kind of trust.

He learned the city from the bottom up. In the first phase of his young life, he had mastered the underground—the New York City subway. In his second, he ran the streets. His third, he told himself, would be in the realm of gleaming skyscrapers.

He knew as a child that a bike was the best way to get around the city, and there's nothing like a vindication of childhood beliefs. On his way to the train station one Spring night, he did a double-take at a guy slinging a shoulder bag and walking a bike a few paces ahead of him.

"Barry!" Dane called out, skidding to a stop next to one of the few people he called a friend. "Thought that was you, walking your bike just because it got a little dark out."

"Dane, my man! Long time." They chatted for a moment, then he said, "Hey, follow me."

They mounted their bikes for a few blocks and then turned down into a parking garage. Barry waved at the attendant and Dane followed suit. They circled their bikes up a few levels and topped out under the starry night sky with the March wind cutting through their hoodies. Three guys stood in the far corner, beers in hand and bikes against the parapet. Two looked mid-twenties, one Jamaican and one white guy with a backward Mets cap, and one looked closer to 40 with a ratty ponytail and a wispy beard. All had the thin physique of longtime riders. Dane pulled a six-pack from his bag, and all took his offering.

"How's life in the sticks?" Barry asked. Dane's latest housing assignment, given after ignoring rules about curfews and alcohol and girls and school attendance, had been upstate in a quiet town where someone thought he would become something closer to a socially acceptable teenager.

"Slow. Kids go bowling and shit. Video games and weed, that's about it. Cards sometimes, poker, until I took too much of their allowance money and they stopped inviting me. Hey, nice wheels," he said, turning to the tall Jamaican sporting a Rasta hat. "What am I looking at?"

"Theese, my friend, is a feeksie." The Jamaican smiled with big white teeth.

"Where are the gears?"

"A fixie," said the older guy. "Drop that puddle hopper, we'll show you how to ride New York." Dane looked down at the bike he'd saved for months to buy. "I've ridden these streets since I was four." He took a deep swig. "But again, what am I looking at? Can I ride it?"

"Eh, Now! Ride a mon's bike, you might just ride his woo-man!" The Jamaican laughed deeply. "But ya ride Justin's bike, he won't mind. He's small like you. And he has no woman."

The kid in the Mets cap shrugged and handed over his fixed-gear bike. Dane took a few laps down to the lower levels and returned, letting out a low whistle. He appreciated the stark honesty of a bike that locks tire rotation with the pedals, forward and backward. No shifting, no coasting, just full control. "All right. I'm sold." He handed the bike back and cracked another beer. "I don't think I've ever felt the road like that."

The others laughed, raising their drinks.

"We have a courier!" exclaimed Barry.

Dane paused mid-guzzle. "A what? Like the bike mailmen?"

"Messengers, yeah. Dude, keep up. Why else would grown-ass men be hanging out after work with bikes? This is happy hour."

"You all get paid to ride around the city? That's what you do?"

"That's it."

"Faster you are, the more runs, the more pay."

"Best job in the city, unless you care about making actual money."

"Pays like ass..."

"Doesn't come with girls..."

"Everybody needs their shit yesterday, and we make it happen."

"Stop," he grinned wide. "Sign me up."

He worked off the books as a courier on weekends. Barry's dispatcher brought him on and tested him for a few days, sending him on shorter, easier runs. Dane didn't disappoint, and the dispatcher worked him into the schedule whenever he could escape down to the city.

At first it was just weekends until he started skipping school to come down. Classes didn't pay but delivering did. His after-school jobs upstate drained him. Bussing uneaten diner food, spraying foul bowling shoes, cutting grass that just wanted to grow, and kept doing so. That wasn't him. He traded in his 21-speed for an elegant fixed-gear model.

Man and road and destination. He had his duty, and the less in his path, the truer the mission. The simple bike, shorn of unneeded accessories, became part of himself. Sailing down 5th Avenue on two winged wheels, an endless slalom of horseless carriages ahead of him, the precious cargo of time-sensitive legal documents in his backpack, that was him. Manhattan streets were his dominion.

Even when working under the table for the courier company, he had established a reputation for being fast. Speed was the only metric that mattered. Behind the simple timestamps recorded in run logs, though, was a long list of factors. Fitness, dexterity, knowledge of the city, obstacle awareness, bike condition, and dedication. And brazenness. It took a balance of skill and risk to succeed.

He worked through life decisions based on risk assessment. That was a term he learned later from his Wall Street clients, and it clicked for him. Riding was a risk, but if he managed it wisely, he'd make more money. He rode faster than most and still had that knack for knowing when someone was just around a corner or when a car door was about to open, and he could gauge that risk and react by instinct.

He also worked later than anyone else. The most illuminated city in the galaxy had plenty of shadows, and his fellow couriers clocked out when twilight rolled in. Not Dane. He thrived in those hours after sunset. He could still sail down streets and sidewalks, carrying the business of the day, with nary a brush with drunk Texans or rolling peanut carts. He would see taxis and limos before they turned the corner and navigate with aplomb.

Clients, whether Midtown TV execs or downtown traders, were accustomed to the courier service settling down when the sun did. Dane's reputation got around, and the evening TV producers and the Nikkei traders (another term he learned) were eager to use his services for as late as they were on offer. They had his cell number, and he started working off the books again.

He was a young entrepreneur with the pulse of corporate culture shifts, and he was succeeding. Soon he had enough dedicated clients that he left the dispatch company and worked independently. Business was steady and tips were better. He worked late, all night sometimes, and left the daytime duties to the other riders.

He slept in a quiet shared loft during the day while his roommates were out. When they were in, they played poker, which Dane was soaking up. He had the probabilities down—that was easy—but the key was reading each player. There, he had real mastery, even as a teen. He'd always had a sense for someone lying, and poker bluffs were just that. He found a few regular games in backrooms at pubs or artist lofts, and even one after-hours in a library. Most were low stakes, but he honed his skills, worked out some angles, and generally walked away on top. He'd flipped his meager courier earnings into slightly less meager poker winnings but kept his risk within reason.

He managed his life so far by keeping emotions at bay and far from his decision-making. Emotions rarely helped with anything. His parents didn't teach him that outright, but it was one of the few things he learned from them.

He had turned inward when, at seven, he realized his mother wouldn't be a part of his life anymore. She hadn't left for the reasons he'd seen other parents leave, though. As long as he could remember, she had suffered from scorching headaches. They were seemingly triggered by bright lights, but doctors gave no answers, only fleeting treatments.

On sunny days, she was unable to leave the house, and as years went by, even drawn curtains and dark glasses gave her little respite. She visited specialists and spent weekends in darkened treatment rooms.

Dane and his father watched as her condition overtook first her other senses and then her mental faculties. The medical bills clawed through their meager household budget, and she eventually resigned herself to a psychiatric facility out of state where she could live in a well-adorned cave and receive enough medication to give her peace.

He traveled to see her with his father a few times, and once on his own, but the visits were always brief and unproductive. It pained them to see her there, but their sorrow and worry and sympathy didn't help, so the visits tapered off.

She had been at the hospital for a few years when the storm hit. Emergency lights and evacuation horns sounded, and all of the doors opened. That wasn't supposed to happen, Dane was later told.

Gina apparently panicked, and hell-bound to seek relief, she found and consumed enough painkillers to kill her pain for good. In the chaos of accidentally evacuating a psychiatric ward into the thralls of a late-night thunderstorm, her body wasn't found for hours.

9

FOLLOWING A PUMPY morning run through forested snowmobile trails, Arin returned to the rental cabin. She climbed the porch stairs to stretch and found Melanie juggling a deep coffee cup and her laptop.

"Found the obit!" she shouted with a grin. "Had to jump a paywall, but it's in the archives of a local paper. Gina left behind a husband and son. Her married name was Hardy. Not sure why the press notes from the hospital used her maiden name. Anyway, I think I found her in a Gina Rosewood, who lived in Brooklyn, married with a son, but their names aren't noted. My little notebook is filling up!"

"Ok. Might be a red herring, though." Arin toweled off her face and neck before lowering into a hamstring stretch. "I mean, nothing is saying that this woman is my aunt. And if she is, she's still quite dead. And if she has surviving family, then... what?"

"What, exactly!" Melanie nearly bounced. "That's what we're

working on. If we find someone else with your condition..." She tilted her head. "That sounds like a disease. I don't want to say your superpower and let that get to your pretty head. Your *ability*. Someone else with your ability, who happens to be related to you, would be the key we would need."

"A key to what?"

"A lock. Somewhere. One step at a time. The kitchen here has real syrup, so I made pancakes."

Ross called Arin later that morning, and she put him on speakerphone. "Hope you girls are getting some good fresh mountain R&R out there. I can only imagine," he said with an audible sigh. "Anyway, I got an inquiry from the preliminary results I had sent out. The response came in the form of a woman named Linda , who wanted to meet me. Not being a guy who turns down invitations from women, I met her at the cafe.

"Linda, it turns out, works for the US Government. DOJ. Yes, that's the Department of Justice. I was perplexed. Someone had seen my posts and sent it to someone who sent it to someone who sent it to her. More or less. She said a person who can see near-IR with their naked eyes would be very useful. She didn't say how or why. What she did want was your name, which I, of course, did not reveal. Nor did I supply my raw data, which she also requested."

Arin locked her gaze on the ceiling. Melanie twirled a pen across her fingers, considering how to transpose Ross's update into her ever-present notebook.

"So, my friends, any thoughts? Because as you may recall, I am a lowly doctoral candidate, and whatever you have involved me in is well outside my scope of practice. Hey, you there?"

"Ross, I need to think about this," Arin replied. "I'm concerned, but I'm also trying to find answers, and maybe she can help."

"We're chasing down some history here," Melanie added. "Probably nothing useful, but that's our focus right now. Leave this Linda person hanging for now. We'll catch up next week."

THEY DROVE TO THE FORMER hospital site, and Arin's low expectations were met. The sprawling and secluded facility had been abandoned for over a decade. Broken windows and graffiti and scorched walls told of exciting nights for local kids. The No Trespassing signs seemed to be suggestive only. Young trees and brambles competed for space in former lawns and courtyards. Animal-bitten squash and pumpkins sprawled through competing weeds from what must have been a garden.

"Had to be beautiful back then," Arin said. "All this space. So quiet."

"The investors who bought it were looking to make it a resort, but the crash hit and they lost it. Shame no one else stepped in. Lots of history in these walls."

"I am not going in there, Mel. Making that clear right now."

"You'll be fine, it's a sunny day. Ghosts don't like that."

Arin relented, and they roamed the wide halls. Tiled floors, ornate moldings, and remnants of chandeliers indicated the facility's former grandeur. They moved into a large hall with low parapets running along the walls, forming a walkway on each side with the center wide open. A grand staircase filled the far end of the room. After a foray into the upper floors, the creep factor built up, and they wordlessly agreed to escape through a broken doorway and explore the perimeter.

"Looks steep back there," said Melanie, nodding toward a path leading into the forest. "The reports from the night of the storm said another patient died down a ravine. Fell and drowned." They walked the remnants of the trail into the forest, where a brook flowed below a steep hill.

A piercing call sounded from the far side of the ravine. A feral cry, but almost human. Arin pulled her arms close, retracting by instinct.

"Hell was that?" Melanie mouthed, peering into the distant woods.

"A demon cat? What was that you said about ghosts?" Only the wind and the burbling water below answered. Arin shivered, keeping her focus in the direction of the hideous sound. No more sound or movement came, but they turned and hastened their retreat.

"I can't imagine the chaos that night." Arin looked back at the looming building. "I suppose I should feel something more if my aunt died somewhere in there."

"You never knew her. Or even of her. Two deaths that night, no signs of foul play. Why would you mourn one but not the other?"

"Because she's family?"

"Only on paper, and even that's not certain. Don't chastise yourself for not having a kinship with this woman. It's tragic. It was also many years ago."

Melanie took a few photos and jotted down some notes. She had turned her investigative reporter mode on full by that point. They left the grounds down the long driveway, happy to be back in the comfortable confines of their vehicle. After returning to farmland and populated roads, they stopped at a produce stand and bought fresh fruit and pastries for lunch.

"I could live in a place like this," Arin stated, looking across a field full of wrapped hay bales.

"No, you couldn't. I mean, you could live, but you would miss city life too much. You have to do actual work out here. You'd need to learn a whole new set of skills. Most of which aren't in books. You'd struggle and give up within a week."

"I keep forgetting why I like you." Arin narrowed her eyes. "Help me remember."

"Don't get me wrong. I'm right with you. Idyllic place to visit, though."

65

"A little poem or a picture of a rustic place like this. *Idyllic.* Always loved that word."

"I'm sure you'd charm the woolen stockings off some folks out here with your deep pool of arcane knowledge, Arin. Feel free to try it when I'm not around. Anyway, I'm happy to spend money to rent a place with fewer amenities than my own, as backward as that sounds, but I'm also happy to get back home."

Arin watched a hawk circle above the field, then dive for a fresh meal somewhere behind the distant haybales.

"You talk about how it's people who make stories tick," she said. "If they get a chance to tell their tale. What if you were to write a story about people around here?" She opened that day's edition of the local newspaper. The farmstand was in a cellular dead zone, and lacking other input, they had bought one. Melanie subscribed to a few papers out of fealty to her future profession, but Arin couldn't recall a time she'd picked a newspaper up, let alone paid for one. "Here's an obituary about a local resident. He was born nearby and ran a truck repair shop. He enjoyed fishing and football. He is survived by four grandchildren. The piece has a little more, but not much. What if this gentlemen's life story was in your hands? Do only professionals in big cities deserve a dignified send-off?"

"Are you trying to get me to move to the country with you? I know you're not serious. There's not a decent cappuccino within fifty miles."

"No, just ruminating. That's what we're supposed to do out here. *Ruminate.* That means to chew over. I'm still hungry, I think. Go ahead and roll those pretty eyes. I can take it. I know how much you appreciate my etymological—what is it?" Arin stopped as she saw Melanie tilt her head and gaze at the distant ridges. "You've got that look that means you haven't heard the last few minutes of me rambling on."

"What paper is that?" She snapped back and picked up the local rag. "We need to get to cell service. I'll pack up the food. You drive."

SEVERAL MISSED CALLS FROM ROSS accompanied the return of signal bars on their phones. They closed their windows and called him back. "What deep well did you fall in this morning? I've been calling!"

"We see that."

"So I mentioned that I had a meeting with a lady from the Feds, remember."

"The DOJ, you said." Melanie pulled out her notebook. "Different outfit."

"Whatever, lady in a suit who wanted to know all about Arin. Well, guess what. I got a call from another lady. Probably wearing a suit, too. She works for a private medical research company, or works with them, anyway. Super vague but hinted at an employment offer of some type. Contingent on... I'm sure you can guess."

"Me." Arin's voice barely carried over the noise of the road.

"Yes, contingent on my full disclosure of all related data. Which would include you. She wants to fly me to DC for an interview. Or she can meet me in Boston if that's more convenient for me. How generous." Ross's words were growing in pitch and velocity. "This. Is. Wild. I only posted a page or so of preliminary data to a couple of closed message boards. Nobody reads those."

"Her name? The contact from the company?" Melanie was jotting notes again.

"Robin. Didn't get the last name. Or the company. Didn't get the impression she was the sharing of information type, either. Listen.

I pulled all of my notes and squirreled them away. I will not break your confidence, Arin. Firstly, I could punt my career for HIPAA violations. Secondly, I want to help you. And to remain your friend." He paused. "I should have put that last part first."

Arin caught Melanie looking at her. "You're in the driver's seat here," Melanie stated. "Literally and figuratively. You know as much as Ross and I, but it's your life. We can stop anytime. No one knows your name, and he'll keep it that way. I see options, but the choice is yours."

Arin pulled the car onto the shoulder and let it idle. An ancient oak stood sentry in the middle of a rolling pasture. She rubbed her temples. "Those options being what, exactly?"

"Go back to Boston and forget this. Or go back to Boston and allow Ross to share your information. You'll be tested some more, hopefully get some answers, and that'll be it. Or we can take a little more time here, stay away from the campus and anyone looking for you, and see what we can dig up." Melanie twisted a strand of dark hair that had fallen from her hat. "Or stay here and hike and picnic and drink wine."

Arin stepped out of the car and gazed across the field, then turned her nose to the sky. The autumn breeze pulled goosebumps from her bare arms. Melanie followed her outside a moment later.

"I don't want to ask you what I should do. I shouldn't need to ask anyone. But I'm staring into a void."

"You've been following a script your whole life. That's what you told me. That's what your therapist told you." A gust of wind tore some of the few remaining leaves from the oak. "This is what living the other way feels like."

They eased back into the car and sat, silent. The wind complained as it bent around the vehicle. "You were looking at that newspaper." Arin turned to face her and tilted her head. "You've got another itch."

"Like a cat." Melanie produced a cheshire grin and slapped the dashboard. "But I'm driving. It's 3 PM, and places around here close early. Scoot!"

10

BLOOD RETURNED TO Arin's knuckles as she released her grip on the swinging handle above the passenger door. She exhaled as Melanie skidded into the parking lot for the headquarters of the local paper. Headquarters turned out to be all of the quarters. The office complex faced the road, and connected warehouses contained the printers and the archives. She got an audience with a clerk who was helpful but also ready to finish her day.

"I do remember the accident at the hospital out there. Such a shame."

"I read an obituary for a woman who died there that night," Melanie stated. "There was another patient who died outside the facility. He fell down a ravine and drowned in a brook. I pulled up your archives for the weeks following that night, and there was no obituary for that patient. Do you know why the woman might have gotten one, but the man didn't?"

"Well, we usually only print obituaries if someone sends one in. If you have some words for that man, I can get it run next week. More than a little late, but all should get their due, I say."

"That's a sweet thought, but I'm more interested in who sent in the obit for the woman. We think the woman may have been her relative," Melanie said, nodding toward Arin, "and we're assuming that whoever wrote it knew her. We've come to your lovely town on a family research project and are struggling to find much."

"We pride ourselves in our records, but that's a tall order. That's more than a decade ago, and our internal notes are not public, as I'm sure you know."

"It's an important family matter. We won't take or copy anything. If you can show us where to start, we'll be out of your hair."

She pursed her lips. "I suppose so, for a young journalism student helping out her friend. Don't tell the boss, though."

The archives consisted of a large warehouse filled with industrial shelving, which was in turn crowded with boxes, bins, and assorted file cabinets. Melanie had already reviewed the microfiches of the papers from that time, so they dug for any other notes or correspondence that may have survived. The journalist who covered the story had retired and moved south, but they got his number from the clerk.

The rest of the staff had already sent the next day's copy to the printers and left, so the place was quiet. Arin and Melanie rifled through boxes until they had overstayed the first and second fifteen-minute warnings the clerk had given them. They hadn't found anything helpful, and Arin didn't get the feeling they'd be allowed back in another day. The clerk appeared again, her impatience now on full display. "Stay any longer, and I'll need to charge you rent."

"I'm sorry, and I really appreciate your—*charge?*" Melanie perked up. "Where would your financial ledgers from back then be? Someone paid to have the obit printed."

"That's true, printing isn't free. I'll take a quick look, but I really need to lock up."

They returned to the now vacant main office, where the clerk flipped through some file cabinets in a storeroom.

"You're well aware I'm not supposed to share this type of thing." She admonished them with a glare. "But I need to get you both out of here so I can get dinner on. Ah, this should be it. I can't let you see the ledger," she continued with a lowered voice, even though the office was empty, "but I'll jot down a note and leave it unattended while I gather my things." Melanie's eyes sparkled.

"We can't thank you enough," Arin told the clerk. "When she's a famous reporter, she'll stop back and write a few stories about your wonderful town for free."

"I will?"

"Honey, we like journalists who follow the rules."

ARIN NAVIGATED BACK TOWARD THE cabin, and they stopped at a restaurant that seemed likely to have WiFi. Melanie pulled out her laptop. Arin, trying to be useful, left a voicemail with the reporter who had covered the story years earlier. She was glad he didn't answer as she didn't have questions at the ready. Perhaps she would think of some before he called back.

"So, we have a gentleman named Marshall Brock who was gracious enough to write an obituary for your aunt. Possible aunt. We need to find him and ask him why." Melanie jumped between her notebook, her laptop, and a bowl of beef stew.

Arin logged into her school portal and was hit with a deluge of emails and calendar reminders. "Oof, that was a mistake," she sighed, logging off again. She watched Melanie flip through browser tabs with one hand while sipping her drink with the other. How did she still have energy? What could she possibly learn chasing these filaments of nothing? "I'll be happy to get back to the cabin. Honestly, I'll be happy to get back to campus. Are we getting anywhere here? Trespassing into haunted asylums and bothering small-town newspaper clerks is worthy of postcards, but how do you know if it's leading anywhere?"

Melanie gazed up with the distracted look of someone realizing she was being spoken to. "Sorry." She closed the laptop. "I don't know. If we knew, we wouldn't be here. And my chosen career wouldn't exist if answers were easy. Look, maybe working with Ross's endless line of professional suitors won't be as terrible as he's letting on. He gets scared by strong women. You need answers, and someone has the resources to get them." She hesitated, then went on. "It's your life here, and your family. I'm just doing what I can to help. With what I know how to do. But if you don't care, I'll give up, too."

The car ride back to the cabin was quiet, as was the night and the following morning's breakfast. Melanie ventured onto the ice with an update. "So I'm fairly certain I have the right Marshall Brock. He's a retired doctor living near Hartford. Less than two hours." She let the silence linger as she sipped her coffee.

Arin met her gaze with soft eyes. "That's great. Go ahead. I need to catch up on school."

"And leave you stranded here with no car?"

"I'll be fine." She waved a hand around the kitchen. Melanie left. Arin cleaned up and set out for a long run.

The car rolled back late that afternoon. Arin had a pasta dish with garden salad and a decanted pinot noir spread over colorful place settings she'd found in the cupboard. Melanie stopped at the door and then smiled. "Were you tracking me?"

"I didn't want the food cold. Or uncooked. You didn't tell me you were on your way back."

"I wasn't sure if you wanted me to." She set her bag down. "I thought you were working on school."

"I did. Also got in a few good miles on the trails. And did some more thinking. But let's eat." She poured wine as they sat.

"So, Dr. Marshall Brock is kind of an asshole."

"Did you tell him you drove two hours?"

"Didn't get a chance. As soon as I mentioned Gina's name, he stiffened up and then shooed me off his porch like a stray cat. Barely said another word. Not that he was about to offer me tea and biscuits beforehand, but he went from annoyed to downright curmudgeonly, and that was the end of a very short visit. These meatballs are great!"

"Thanks, some of the herbs I used weren't even expired. But he's our guy. People don't write obits for strangers. He was a doctor, so he probably treated her at some point. I'd say that closes that loop?" Melanie forced a slow and hesitant nod, and Arin continued. "Excellent. Because I'm ready to put a *The End* on this *Odyssey*. I want to finish my degree. Another year or two, if my diploma that says Classics on it doesn't have lucrative employers stampeding my way with offer letters, I'll consider talking to one of Ross's contacts. In the meantime, I'll settle for parlor tricks." She watched Melanie bite her tongue. "What, too many loose ends?" She glanced at the plate. "In the meal?"

"It's spaghetti. Loose ends are kinda the deal," Melanie mumbled.

"It's your recipe. I'm in for whatever you make. Whatever you need."

They opened another bottle.

"I have a laptop-sized screen to watch a blockbuster on," Arin said. "Let's light the fireplace and claim the couch before the mice do and have one of those cozy cabin nights they advertise."

An hour into the movie, she saw a missed call from the reporter and sighed as she watched Melanie glance at her notebook. "Go ahead. I'll pause it and call him back."

He answered on the first ring. "I got your message about that story with the hospital. I remember that one, but it has been a while so I dug through some notes. No sign of foul play in the two deaths, so not much reason to look deeper. There were a few things that didn't make the story, but that's always the case. Some minor injuries, the power company's recovery efforts, things like that. There was a parked truck they clipped in the dark as they rushed to get up there. The utility company, I mean. That was a good mile or so from the place, though. Guy picked it up from the tow yard the next day. Claimed he got lost and the truck broke down. Little odd, that's why I noted it, but again, no foul play, so no need to question him further at the time."

"Do you have his name? The kind of truck?"

"Didn't note the truck, but the guy was a local physician. Dr. Brock is what I have here, but the police might be able to double-check that for you."

Melanie squared off to face Arin. Arin locked her gaze straight ahead, avoiding Melanie. The standoff held until a log snapped in the fireplace, loud enough that they both blinked.

"I suppose..." Arin drew out her answer, "that we could take a detour on our way back."

11

D **ANE WOKE TO** tangled bedsheets. His fever had surged back, and his wounds needed care. None looked infected yet, but he needed a robust dose of antibiotics. His ribs and face would heal. He struggled to shove his swollen foot into his shoe.

Some clinics didn't require IDs or ask too many questions, especially if the patient paid in cash. And with no gunshot wound involved, they didn't need to report it. Dane knew where those places were.

He doubted any cops were looking for him. The city is big, and his infractions against the things they care about were forgettable. The fight was self-defense, and despite how the other two must look right now, there were plenty of witnesses on Fulton Street to back that up. For gambling, most cops wouldn't bother, except for that lieutenant who was supposedly cracking down. The issue there, though, was that Dane would lose his winnings. His ticket out. That wasn't going to happen.

He didn't want any blowback on the barkeep, either. He'd likely saved his life last night. The guy had crushed his bike, though. That was one piece tying Dane to the scene. The cops would gather up the mangled bicycle with bits of finger still wedged in the sprocket, and show that around to the couriers. They all knew who had the tri-colored spokes. His concern wasn't about any minor charges themselves, but those charges would keep him in the city.

He'd never been a planner, but the looming stacks of cash were the one ticket he needed to leave New York and start a new life. One goal and nothing else mattered.

He bought and consumed as much over-the-counter medication as he felt appropriate, followed it with a few pepperoni slices, and sought out a clinic. A few lies and a few hours later, he headed to the train station with fresh bandages and prescription antibiotics.

He had one more stop before leaving the area. Warren, his father, had finished his prison sentence and talked his way back into an administration job with the Port Authority. He wasn't allowed near anything that moved passengers after the vehicular homicide rap, though. Dane visited him a few times in his small apartment in New Jersey. He seemed content, by all appearances sober, and was dating a cheerful woman from work named Mandy. Dane wrote him a note and left it in an envelope with a thousand in cash. He didn't owe him anything, but a parting gift would ease his father's worries.

Dane didn't want to speak to him or anyone, not for a while. A clean break and a new life where he'd have time and space to think. To plan and to dream. In the note, he said he'd contact him when he'd settled somewhere and asked him to dig up his birth certificate, as he'd lost his ID.

Dane settled onto the next train out of state. A pair of cops strolled up the aisle, talking baseball, and passed by without a glance his way. Skyscrapers faded away behind him. One tower, in particular, caught his eye, and the memory brought him a bitter smile on his way to sleep.

COPS, LIKE ANY OTHER PEOPLE, will put in no more than a nominal effort at their jobs. Dane learned that most would give up when the effort of the chase outweighed the value of the target. A simple equation. He'd always kept his apprehension value just under the effort required to catch a fast teenage biker. Calculated risk, although before he learned that term, he would have called it common sense. Street smarts. Whatever the name, it was hard-earned.

His lessons outside of school were more painful than those inside. Over the years, he'd broken an arm and a wrist and had been forced to ditch a few bikes while fleeing police. He was usually able to find unattended bikes to replace them. He'd found a couple of poorly attended and poorly locked bikes as well, although taking those never felt right. If he had to pick a people that were his people, they would be bikers. There was no shortage of other lucrative targets on the streets, though.

In his waning teenage years, he'd found one of those targets in an Upper West Side cafe on a weekday morning. He was splurging on good coffee after a casual ride through the park, interjecting a few hours of what he imagined was a more stable life into the tumult of his own. He'd gotten a haircut from a friend and was wearing a new button-up shirt. A rare day on the town.

He could pose for a morning, but his real life and real needs beaconed. Two tables over were a pair of middle-aged women. Designer purses, coiffed hair, and botox meant they had husbands who would buy them things and buy them twice if needed. One showed the other a shallow black case covered in felt with a polished hinge. Only one type of thing came in those, and it could keep him above water for months. The women cawed together, and the case went back into a purse. Snatch and grab wasn't his favorite style, but it was effective.

There are always unknown factors to anticipate, though. The challenge is that it's damned hard to anticipate what, by definition, isn't known. And Dane found himself soaking in the comfort of an Upper West Side brunch, which clouded his instincts.

He hadn't considered how strong a couple of middle-aged women could be. He also hadn't noticed that the pair of men at the counter had short hair and mustaches. The latter was out of trend for gay couples, but not for cops.

Following these two miscalculations, Dane found himself pumping down Fifth Avenue with a ketchup-bottle-shaped bruise on his head while under pursuit by an unmarked cruiser driven by two cops who left their breakfasts half-finished.

He hoped that they hadn't gotten a good look at him. He was wearing a hat and a sweatshirt, both of which needed to go at the first opportunity. That chance came a few blocks later when the big lions in front of the New York Public Library welcomed him.

He glanced back and saw the cruiser held up behind delivery vans a block away. He tossed his bike over a fence and sent his hat and sweatshirt after it. He snapped his phone to his ear and did his best impression of a college kid headed to a study session.

Once inside, he stood at an intersection of hallways. Adrenaline pumped, clouding his reason, and he needed a random factor to guide him. He grabbed a pencil from a nearby desk and flipped it in the air. It landed and pointed to a reading room off to the right. He entered it and promptly sat across from a pretty young brunette. He tucked his bag under the table, hoping his sweat wasn't showing.

"Excuse me?" She looked up from notes and an open textbook.

"I'm really hoping you can help me." He gave her his best toothy smile. "I see you're working on..." he started as his eyes flicked to the open textbook. "Statistics," he noted. "So am I."

"Do I know you?"

"Dane. Good to see you, miss...?"

"Molly. Are you in my class?"

"No, but I'm very interested in," he pointed with an exaggerated arm at her book, "statistics. And I would be most appreciative if you would let me help you study in the very near future. Like, right now."

Molly looked around, her lips scrunched to the side as if waiting for a punchline. The two cops hustled into the study room, short of breath. Dane laughed louder than necessary, saying, "No, Molly, the probability of me being wrong can't be that high!" He swiveled the textbook toward himself and began flipping through it.

"Excuse me, Miss," said one of the cops as they approached the table. "Is he here with you?"

Molly looked at Dane, then back at the cops. "He's not that bright, and I don't think he'll ever get it, but I've been asked to help him."

"So he's been here studying with you?"

"He's been studying with me as long as I've known him." The cops turned and moved to the next room without a word.

"I am in awe, Molly."

"You are in trouble, Dane."

"I owe you for this. How about dinner?"

The young woman laughed. "How about you go now."

"I will. But I'll write down an address here, and I'll take you to one of the most exclusive dinner spots in the city. I'll be waiting there at 6 pm tonight. I am forever indebted." Dane bowed with a flourish, leaving behind a bewildered college freshman.

AT THE APPOINTED HOUR, HE stood against the weathered stone of a park wall, resting a foot on his bike with his shoulder bag slung in front. He did not expect her to show, so he nearly floated when she turned the corner and made apprehensive eye contact.

"I'm only here because I'm curious what the most exclusive restaurant in the city is, and how someone like yourself manages to get a table. Also, I have mace."

"Use it to flavor your food if you'd like. It's good, but probably nothing exquisite. And I didn't mention a restaurant. I said dinner. Shall we?" He held out his arm, and after a short hesitation and through some fortuitous intervention from unknowable forces, she took it.

They crossed the street, arm in arm, Dane wheeling his bike with his free hand. They walked along a fenced construction zone, a half-finished tower looming within it. Dane pulled aside part of the tarped fence and ducked in with his bike and a wide-eyed girl.

"We're surely not supposed to be here."

"It's okay. I work here. Sort of." Molly raised an eyebrow. "I deliver blueprints from print shops to the contractors." He locked his bike to the side, and they walked over gravel and dirt to an alcove of steel beams and temporary lighting that would someday be a grand lobby. "And the foreman, he got tired of riding down the elevator to get the rolls from me, so he made me an access card." Dane held it up like a trophy, beaming.

"I'm intrigued, and I'm also pretty sure I should be running for my life. Please tell me where we're going."

"Do you trust me?"

"Not really."

"It's a yes or no question. I'll sit here with great sadness and watch you walk away. And then I'll need to eat all that food myself." She didn't answer, but she didn't leave, either, which was an answer.

"This way." He walked through another unfinished room to a freight elevator. The badge reader beeped and opened to a large industrial car. "This is the only one active at the moment. No mirrors and show posters, but it does the job." He selected floor 58, and the car jerked to life. "It's also a bit slower than the passenger elevators."

"And big enough to haul out a body," Molly said. "You're dragging out the suspense here. Most of the floors didn't even look closed in yet."

Dane smiled. The car stopped, and the doors opened to a sleek office with carpets, lights, and glass-walled conference rooms. "This is the show floor. They finish one area first to have something for buyers to look at." He took her hand and walked her to a large conference room with an expansive view of the sun setting behind the city skyline. On the table were boxes of takeout containers and a six-pack of beer. Molly gasped at the sight, then laughed when she saw the meal.

"Exclusive dinner. Killer views. Breaking and entering." Her eyes were alight. "This may be the best date I've been on for a while, Dane."

"Hey, we didn't break anything to enter. Details matter." He popped two beers and handed one over. They sat and dug into the still-warm Thai takeout. "Place on Lex. Great stuff. Hot enough, or do you need the mace?"

"We'll see. Do you bring girls here a lot?"

"I've never been here before. Not past the elevator. I came up with the food and beer half an hour ago for the first time. I sat in the corner office and claimed it."

"Is that how it works?"

"Sure does. I'll show you." They walked into a sprawling executive office on the southwest corner of the floor. The lights were off, and the evening cityscape bristled through the windows. Bright, wide veins of the avenues split and rejoined. They pulled a sofa around to face outward and opened another beer.

"I don't know if I'd ever get tired of this," Molly stated, looking between the view and Dane.

He pulled a joint from his shirt pocket and lit it. Took a drag and handed it over. "Smoke detectors aren't wired in yet." She took it, puffed, and handed it back without breaking eye contact.

"You're lucky I was studying statistics when you barged in," she said, exhaling with a gentle cough. "I knew the probability of you being a serial killer was exceedingly small, even as someone with cops in tow. If I'd been studying my criminal justice course, I probably would have turned you over right there. If I were studying women's rights, I might have flipped the table on you."

"I didn't realize until now how much I loved statistics." He'd been with girls before, but this was the first time he felt he'd earned it. "What about gender studies? Why aren't there more women in chairs like that?"

She looked at the black leather executive chair. "There will be. More now than there were before. But for now, I'm good here on the couch. The chair doesn't have the view. Or the company."

She put down her beer and leaned into him, kicking off her shoes. He didn't need his unique sense to see the heat rising in her cheeks. The orange brilliance of the city lit the office suite as they kissed and pulled at each other's clothes.

They woke early and walked to the floor's east side, which was carpeted but otherwise unfinished. They dragged the sofa over, ate cold leftovers, and split the last beer. Then they went down again, together, as the sun rose.

After his childhood in the subways and adolescence on the streets, Dane had told himself that the next part of his life would be among the towers of the city. A vague plan of three phases and no solid intentions.

But if that night with Molly culminated his aspiration, it was god-damned good enough. He strode out of that building like a CEO, his hand in hers, through a crew of shocked contractors milling about before their shift. The two teenagers stared ahead and walked with purpose. Confusion ceded to grins and chuckles. A deep laugh and a few hoots rang out, coffee cups raised high and steaming in the morning air.

HE NEVER GOT HER NUMBER or even her full name. Didn't matter, he told himself. He knew he was nothing but a night out slumming that she would regale to her friends after a few drinks. He passed her outside a club queue a month or so later and laid out his essence for her with a smile and a confident approach. She shot him a double-take, then abruptly turned away and said something to her friends. Something witty, apparently.

Then, as he approached, she turned again and handed him a twenty, accompanied by another laugh and some words about helping the less fortunate. He was too stunned to refuse the bill. He diverted his course and walked long, aimless miles that night.

He expected nothing more. Not from her, the job, his father, or the city itself. He wouldn't let the streets grind away at him until he was a balding messager, fretting about how much longer his body could sustain that work.

Deciding to leave the city was the first long-term plan he'd ever acted on. The only real factor was getting enough money while keeping his name clean for a fresh start. The poker game he'd barely escaped from was his last chance, one he'd built up for months to earn. He'd started the plan at a low-stakes game with the same twenty-dollar bill Molly had given him.

Now, with a cash-laden note for his father delivered, Dane fulfilled the final phase of that plan. He pulled out a folding map he'd purchased from a tourist stand and spread it on the empty seat beside him. A pen rolled against his foot from the seat in front. He picked up the pen, flipped the map upside down, and stabbed it through an advertisement for an eyeglass company. He flipped the map back over. He'd struck a town in the northwest corner of Massachusetts. Pittsfield.

He allowed a low chuckle at the name. Of course it would be a place that sounded like a country joke. Like a PG version of East Bumfuck. Far from New York City in distance and in spirit. At the next stop, he departed the train and looked up his new home.

12

ARIN WATCHED THE For Sale sign creak back and forth in the breeze as Melanie walked to the door and knocked, knowing there would be no answer.

"I was here yesterday morning."

"You said you barely spoke with him."

"And he fled."

They peered through windows and over the backyard fence before turning to leave. A neighbor walked over.

"He left last night. Not sure where to. Didn't say anything. Not that he said much anyway, keeps to himself. Drove in with a camper yesterday, one of the big new ones. Thought he was just traveling until the realtor showed up with the sign this morning."

The neighbor didn't have any more to share about Marshall. They sat in the idling car, and Melanie drummed her fingers on her closed notebook.

A call from Ross broke the silence. "Don't come back. I think I'm being followed. Both of those contacts have called me again, trying to get to you, Arin. I feel like I shouldn't even be calling you from my phone. What kind of operation did you sign me up for here?"

With no satisfactory answer for Ross, nor one for themselves, they drove away from the house. They drove because moving was better than not moving. Aimless driving wasn't the same as running, but it had a similar way of clearing the chaff and sifting order from chaos.

Arin inhaled with intention. When other people make the decision for you, she thought, sometimes you need to go with it. "Mel, what time did you leave his place yesterday?"

"One-thirty, maybe two. Early afternoon." She cocked her head, and a wolfish grin crept in. "Are you getting sleuthy on me?"

"I'm pretty sure that's not a word. I need a word for when someone who might have a connection to an unknown family member who died over a decade ago decides to upend his life and flee instead of talk to you."

"There might be something in German for that, but I'll stick with sleuthy." She laughed. "Welcome back, my love, let's dig!"

They arrived at the only RV dealership close enough that Marshall could have gotten there, purchased a camper, and returned to his home within a few hours. Melanie peeked through the showroom window, and then came back to the car. She removed her cap and glasses, ruffled her auburn hair loose, and undid the top two buttons of her shirt. Arin raised an eyebrow and bit her lower lip.

"Follow me," Melanie said with a wink. The teenage kid at the counter pushed aside his phone and offered his most attentive customer service all week.

"We're really hoping you can help us." intoned Melanie with a high, pleading voice that Arin couldn't recall having heard before. "There was an RV purchased yesterday. My friend here, her grandfather came in, but he gets confused." She leaned forward over the counter. Arin watched the poor kid try and fail to keep his eyes upward.

"You see," Melanie continued, "we're afraid he's lost and we need to find him. If you can show us what he bought, we'd be so thankful." She draped her fingers over his on the counter and leaned forward a little more.

"I... wasn't here yesterday, but the paperwork probably hasn't been filed away yet." He peeled his gaze away to a wall file and grabbed a stack of papers. "What was his name?"

"YOU ARE UTTERLY SHAMELESS!" LAUGHED Arin as they drove away with photos of the RV's registration documents.

"I'm efficient." She grinned, tucking her hair back into her cap. "Call it another journalism trick. But I'm still not sure how we'll find him."

She flipped through her notes as Arin looked for a lunch spot. They ate hearty grilled sandwiches from a lunch counter at a quaint country store. In their efforts to get answers, they were once again stuck. The RV information wasn't helpful unless it happened to drive up next to them, and the only name they had for anyone they hadn't spoken to was Warren, Gina's husband.

Her widower. The male gets the active version of that word, thought Arin. It makes it sound like he's done something to earn that title, whereas *widow* is more passive. That's often accurate, the husband playing the active role in such situations, Arin suspected. No known bearing on her supposed aunt and uncle, just her etymological mind drifting for want of something more purposeful to do.

Without a better afternoon pursuit, they decided to call Ross and console him. And they would have done so if he hadn't called first. From an unsaved number.

"They've got your name, Arin. Well, one of them did. The government one, Linda. Who knows how, maybe phone records or the logbook from the Medical Center. Doesn't matter, but she doesn't need me to get to you anymore. She still insists that she wants to talk to you about some way you could be very helpful to an ongoing investigation. Not a single detail would she share beyond that, and believe me, I asked.

"Now, for Mystery Woman Number Two. And by way of oversharing, I've envisioned plenty of scenarios where multiple mystery women are seeking me out, and absolutely none of those scenarios was anything close to whatever freakshow this is. So the second one is nearly shoving job offers at me, and I can't say I'm entirely uninterested. I do, after all, intend to make enough money to repay my loans someday. And her hints indicate that could be a lot sooner than planned."

"Please skip the footnotes and get to the goddamn point," Melanie requested.

"The point is that I got a photo of her. I agreed to meet, although she was disappointed I didn't bring my lovely little test subject. I was positively sweating when I panned my phone her way while pretending to check a text. Whatever she read in my nervousness was genuine on many levels, I assure you, so I don't think she suspected my clever deception."

"Again with the editorials, when all we need is the headline."

"Lovely speaking with you, too. Glad you could find the time. I'm calling from a friend's phone, by the way, as a reminder of the life you've put me in. Stand by for a photo."

He sent a still of a professional-looking woman, maybe early sixties with skin treatments and dyed hair taken into account.

"I thought I recognized her but had to ask around. Now, I'll let the budding journalist show her worth. Go!" Arin pictured him leaning back, positively smug, looking at his watch.

"Seems familiar, but can't place her," Melanie said, "Oh! It's that congresswoman from a while back. The one the feds are looking into. Carmine."

"The Feds?" Ross asked. "I don't know anything about that, but it's her. Robin Carmine. No idea what she's doing now, other than being super secretive."

A quick internet search showed that the one-term congresswoman and failed senate candidate had found employment with a K-Street lobbying firm a decade ago. Then nothing of note seemed to surface until her recent interest by the FBI. Her most cited event was during an old campaign stop at a power plant where she was promoting an infrastructure funding bill. The electrical transformers near her exploded while she was on the makeshift stage. She escaped harm, but a few rallygoers received minor injuries. No foul play was suspected, and inspectors deemed it a poorly timed accident. Media sensationalism defined her by that incident, which didn't hurt or help her campaign, as her polling remained in low single digits before and after.

Arin asked Melanie what it meant. Why this former politician had an interest in her. She watched her flip through notes, stalling. She conceded that she had no idea, and noted that a good journalist doesn't speculate—something she said only when she was utterly clueless.

They got a hotel room and spent the evening deep in notes and questions and fruitless internet queries. They ate spaghetti and chased loose ends. They drank wine and let their questions ferment.

The following morning they met Linda.

13

THE REARVIEW MIRRORS of Melanie's car filled with the dreaded kaleidoscope of flashing red and blue. Arin and Melanie had left their breakfast spot and were contemplating their next destination until the local cruiser behind them decided it would be the narrow shoulder of a forested road.

"I was barely over the limit," Melanie stated. "He must be picking on out-of-towners."

They waited. The cop kept his lights flashing while he remained in his cruiser for several minutes. "Why isn't he getting out?"

The officer finally left his car and approached them. He took a long look at them and at their backseat before taking their IDs. He was back in his cruiser before Arin thought to question why he'd asked for Melanie's ID as well, as she wasn't driving. "Aren't they supposed to say why they pulled you over?"

The next wait was even longer. Their omelets were well digested before they saw further movement from the officer behind them.

A tractor and a delivery van passed them. A sleek, dark blue sedan didn't. The car pulled in front of them and parked, trapping them between it and the idling cruiser.

"Mel, am I more worried than I should be?" Arin whispered, lips barely moving. "How's the offroad package in your car?"

"Let us not find out, please." She recorded the license plate of the dark sedan in her notebook, then did the same for the cruiser.

A woman in creased business attire left the vehicle and gave them a friendly wave as she walked by. Arin returned a blank stare. The woman continued past them to the patrol car, where her exchange was quick, and the officer pulled out from behind them. He cut off his flashing lights and allowed himself a backward glance as he drove off.

"I apologize for the theatrics," stated the woman as she approached and leaned toward the open driver's window. She was early fifties, Arin guessed, and accustomed to getting her way. She wore her dark hair short and had quick but not unkind eyes.

"I would have called you, but didn't. For reasons. The local PD was happy to assist, as they usually are. Do you mind if I sit?" She gestured to the back seat, currently filled with travel bags and some empty takeout wrappers. There was probably an empty wine bottle or two, Arin realized, a remnant of their last picnic. The officer must have ignored them.

The woman took their baffled silence as a yes and climbed in, moving some loose clothing to make room. "Much obliged. The mountain air stays cold this time of year."

Arin couldn't find a response, and apparently, neither could Melanie. They twisted around to face the peculiar intruder in the back seat.

"I'm Linda. I'm certain your friend mentioned me, so I'll try not to bother you any longer than necessary. And no need to introduce yourselves. Here are your licenses back. You," she intoned, pointing at Arin, "are quite the remarkable person if your initial evaluation holds merit. We will, of course, need to verify."

"Do you have ID?" questioned Melanie, regaining her composure.

"Of course," and she handed over a badge. It looked real enough to be DOJ. "Now, I'll be clear from the onset. You are under no obligation to help us. Legal, moral, or otherwise. You can kick me out of your car right now and drive off. I'm a big girl and I won't hold it against you. Nor will the Department of Justice." She let the statement linger.

Arin looked forward. She hadn't stretched that morning, and holding her neck craned toward the rear seat was adding to the palpable tension building there.

"However," Linda continued, "you could be useful in confronting a current challenge in our judicial system. I apologize for my obfuscation, but it is necessary to state things as general as possible. For reasons."

"I'll bet you write the most endearing birthday cards," Melanie stated. She seemed to be regaining herself.

"Oh, I do, Miss Hobbes," she chirped.

Arin couldn't read her. She might be sincere about that.

"And I never forget a birthday. Or much else, either. I have no intention of further disrupting your pleasant retreat in the mountains. But I need to emphasize that there is a valuable service in the pursuit of truth that you may be able to provide to your country. You would, of course, be compensated."

"In the pursuit of truth? Can you please clarify what the fuck you're asking me to do?" Arin demanded.

"Everything we do is in the pursuit of truth. And that's getting harder every day. We're the good guys out there, and you can help us." At this, she put her hand on Arin's shoulder. "Come back to Boston, and I'll explain how."

She handed over a business card and left the vehicle, gently closing the door. She paused at the open window. "You were driving twelve miles over the speed limit, according to the officer. He was kind enough to give you a warning, but be watchful for wildlife around here. Someone spotted a bobcat this week." She gave a double tap on the top of the car before walking back to hers.

They sat until Linda's vehicle was well out of sight. And then sat awhile longer. Arin looked at Melanie, twirling Linda's card in her hand. "I'm apprehensive. I'm confused. I'm also dying for answers over a cup of real coffee."

ARIN FACED THE IMPOSING CURVED glass facade of Boston's US District Courthouse. The sharp sea breeze at her back drove her into its clutches. She overcame a last pang of doubt and entered. After security, she was led to an upper-floor conference room where she met Linda and her colleague, Jeremy. He was tall, thin, and had a trace of a flat accent from somewhere in flyover country.

"Your results are unique, Miss Coppertree," Jeremy said. "I'm eager to move forward with your evaluation as a potential consultant."

"Consultant. Can you shed some light?" She asked and was predictably rebuffed.

"Well now, let's pump the brakes a smidge. We need to see if you're the right wrench for the stubborn little nut we have. I'm going to ask you to join me in the room next door, but first, the Non-Disclosure Agreement. We need you to sign this NDA, which says you'll not talk about what you see or do here—no funny business. I know you have some questions, but we'll get that all straightened out here in no time. After me."

She signed the long form and followed him into another room where several monitors of various technological generations were set up. They ranged from the newest, flattest LED screens to older plasmas and much older projection types. She didn't know what to call those other than museum exhibits.

"Arin, we appreciate your time and your signature, and we can now convey specifics around what you can do for us. Have you heard the term *deepfake*?" Linda asked.

"The doctored videos?"

"That's them. Bad actors are making these videos at levels beyond what the casual viewer can perceive as real or not. That's not new. What's new is that the latest generation of deepfakes is beating even what our programs can detect. We have no quick way to determine if a video sent to us is real or not, and that's a problem."

"The videos sent out on the internet will impact the court of public opinion," Jeremy added, "but that's someone else's problem. We here at the DOJ care about the real court. We can't rely on video evidence anymore."

"You can't prove a fake?" Arin asked. She had no idea where she fit into the situation but needed to show she was listening.

"We usually can," stated Linda, "But in most cases, it consumes resources we don't have. Time and talent. We can take any specific video and send it to the lab to dissect, but unless we have models nearly identical to the sample, we need to create new ones. Lighting, spacing, ambiance, granularity—the number of factors is endless. And temperature. That's the factor we're exploring to beat the fraud."

"Temperature?" Arin could feel hers rising as she began to surmise why her ass was in that chair.

"The fancy cameras we buy, even phone cameras, pick up a lot we don't see," answered Jeremy. "People like to pay extra money for bigger numbers. Doesn't matter a lick if that changes what they see or not, long as it sells. That helps us here. New cameras pick up light ranges outside of what we see and record it along with the rest that we can. Do you get what I'm rambling on about? Cause if you do, I may need you to explain it back as it's honestly not fully tracking myself."

"I've had a recent refresher on the topic," Arin replied.

"Thermal adds a whole layer of complexity to a video," Linda began. "The way the heat from your face reflects on your glasses, your hair, your shirt collar. The heat pattern in your face changes as you speak and squint and roll your eyes. The fake videos don't account for that because they don't need to if they're attempting to deceive human eyes. Our infrared analysis software is improving, but it's not capable of knowing where heat gradients should be, let alone how they should change frame by frame in any given environment."

Arin stood as they evaluated her. She gave what she felt was a solid impression of someone taking it all in. Considering her role. But she wasn't prepared for something like this.

"The time and effort needed to conduct a thermal analysis on a short video clip is impractical, especially if the need is urgent. This is where we're hoping someone like you can help."

"We want to sit you down in front of a whole slew of videos," said Jeremy. "We think you might be able to sort the reals from the fakes. We have different monitors and different recording formats." He grinned, showing large white teeth. "It'll be like one of those film festivals! Except instead of pretty celebrities, you get us. Coffee?"

"Uh, yes, please." Arin collected her thoughts as he left the room. "Why me?" She asked Linda.

"Do you have a group of like-minded and like-eyed friends you could suggest?"

"What if I can't see anything that helps? I really don't know what I should be looking for."

"Nor do we. Hence, the testing." She lowered her shoulders. "Look, you may be right, and we'll thank you for your cooperation, and we won't bother you again. But we're hoping that's not the case. You could help us win this battle for authenticity. For truth."

Jeremy returned with a tray of drinks. They spent the next hour watching short clips of seemingly random scenes. People talking, eating, arguing. Dancing and working out. Some inside, some under the sun and clouds. Arin watched some of the same scenes on different monitors. They didn't ask her anything.

"All of the videos up to now have been real," Linda stated. "We're going to order lunch and then show you some fakes. Some of these we made, and some are real-world examples we pulled in. You'll need to let us know if you sense anything different."

"And if I can detect something amiss, that would be permissible evidence in a trial?" Arin was pleased that her question garnered a glance between Linda and Jeremy.

"Absolutely not," Linda admitted. "But in a preliminary hearing or a request for a warrant, it may. If a video impacts a trial, we would have the time for a complete analysis."

After a lunch of mediocre pizza (leave it to the government to find such a thing in Boston), Arin sat down again for part two of the worst film festival she'd ever attended.

"So, we're trying to hone in on what you may be able to perceive. Take your time. Relax. This next clip is a mix of real and fake. Two people in the same setting, talking to each other. The guy on the left is real, but the guy on the right isn't. The face was superimposed."

The video played first on the old TV, which Jeremy said was a CRT. She couldn't detect or feel anything abnormal through the heat on the glass and told them so. The next was the same video on a plasma screen, with the same result. Then, they brought up the same video on an OLED screen.

Arin noticed that fleeting buzz in her mind as she concentrated on the guy to the right. She blinked and sat up straighter, gasped, and pointed. The two officials perked up and exchanged glances.

"SO THEY BROUGHT ME BACK for round two the next day and stopped telling me which ones were fake." Arin walked with Melanie and Ross along the river. "But I got them all right. Linda and her team were all business but barely seemed to stifle how pleased they were."

"Even on a TV you could tell?" asked Ross. He veered as a jogger passed closer than was warranted on the spacious Esplanade. "Take off your sunglasses and you might see where you're going," he whispered in complaint after the toned guy was well out of earshot.

"Only the LED screens," Arin replied. "The older ones emit too much heat and wash out whatever nuances in the heat patterns would have been recorded."

Melanie gave her a sideways glance.

"I've learned some new terminology. Again, I can't actually see anything you can't or that they couldn't. But once they told me what to look for, I could recognize... I don't know, like a flutter in my mind that told me something was off."

"So what do they want from you next?" asked Melanie.

"I guess I'm a consultant, now? A few higher-ups came during the final round to watch me do my thing, and it seemed I got put on the good-enough-to-use list. They'll give me a call when they need my help." Arin explained what she could about the legal weight of any consulting she did, which was narrow in scope and shady in execution.

The jogger returned and gave them a wider berth. He faced straight forward, but behind his dark glasses Arin saw the unmistakable crinkle indicating his eyes swiveled their way as he passed. Not uncommon, but he seemed to take more than a passing glance.

"I also asked Linda for a favor," Arin said, getting Melanie's attention. "Help with locating the surviving family of my long-lost aunt. Her reply was along official lines of not prying into private citizens without due cause. I may ask again, but I don't think your shirt trick will work with her."

Ross cocked his head.

"Don't ask."

Lacking other plans, they returned to campus with mutual intentions to refocus on overdue schoolwork. In her dorm, Arin spread books out and logged into the BU portal. She cracked a beer. She sighed, then opened another tab and looked into studies on epigenetic inheritance while envisioning a long, unhurried run the next morning.

14

THOUGHTS OF HER long run burned on as Arin thumbed on her playlist, speeding through a just-red-enough-to-get-pulled-over light outside the campus. Music should subdue her racing pulse if not her driving awareness. How would she explain the urgency to a cop? A call to her new friends at the DOJ would help, but there wasn't time for that. Not when they didn't give her time for a shower or a change.

She'd been relishing that overdue jog in the crisp early air when Linda called. She had left the courthouse building the previous afternoon with the notion that she'd have time to settle back into classes and passing normalcy before they called again. Whatever she'd heard about the wheels of justice moving slowly didn't apply here. Didn't apply to her.

Arin realized she was wearing her worn-through leggings with the frayed hem. She'd meant to replace them, but her life of late hadn't left time for shopping trips. Sipping the warm dregs of a smoothie while changing lanes, she checked navigation. Three miles to the address they'd given her. A gift shop. Not the large courthouse this time, but somewhere in a quiet strip mall outside the city. She didn't bother guessing why they needed the change of venue.

A call came in, flashing "Mel" and cutting out her music.

"Hey, thought you'd call."

"They're trying to find you, but your voice tells me they did."

"Inconsiderate douches cut my run short. Do you know what this is?"

"Of course not. You're on your own here. Stop by my place after, heroine of mine!"

Arin pulled into the sparse parking lot outside city limits, sweat drying but pulse revving as she paced to the shop door. Pulling a band from the small pocket in her running leggings, she snapped her blonde hair into a ponytail.

Could she still back out? She could, right? Go back to campus and dig into a neglected project or three, and forget the last couple of weeks had happened. Linda had been deliberately obtuse about her role here, and Arin hadn't asked enough questions. Had she even signed any papers other than the NDA? Too late now.

Her quaint research project into her family history had morphed into a life-altering diversion she didn't understand. Didn't control. She saw a gaping black hole of the unknown ahead and told herself that she wouldn't turn away.

It was an opportunity to fulfill the shake-up her therapist had suggested. To embark on a boundary-pushing move away from the predictable script her parents had written. Speeding to a clandestine government office to demonstrate a dubious ability while hoping her armpits didn't drip wine sweat might not have been on the brainstorming list she'd worked up, but she could pencil it in later.

Her parents were on a sailing trip deep in the Atlantic blue and wouldn't be available for help, anyway. They'd made that clear. Her therapist said that would be good.

The sign on the gift shop door was flipped to CLOSED, but the door was unlocked. She entered, passing racks of gift cards, pilgrim souvenirs, and Patriots gear when Jeremy popped his head out of a back room and beaconed her.

"Arin, thank you for the quick response."

He looked exhausted. He stood up to shake her hand, and if her sweat felt clammy to him, he didn't react. Linda and a pudgy, balding guy with glasses glanced up from computers. They also refrained from judging her disheveled look and well-worn running attire.

She stood in a makeshift conference room with a large flatscreen monitor against one wall and a few desks along each side. A donut box and coffee sat on a folding table in the back. It looked like a temporary office setup that had been used for a while but hadn't been planned for that. Even tired, Jeremy didn't miss much, and he didn't miss the extra second her eyes lingered on the coffee.

"Henry, a cup for the witness, please. One cream, one sugar, right?" The balding man obliged, a quick smile showing through fatigue.

Linda chirped, "Arin, we thank you for your prompt response today. Let's get to it." She seemed more rested than the other two and remained standing while they sat. The woman was responsible for her life's recent derailment. She didn't get the sense she would stop long enough to care.

All attention turned to the wall-mounted monitor. The Department of Justice logo filled the screen, including the motto "Qui Pro Domina Justitia Sequitur," which Arin translated internally. She felt her pulse in her temples—a marker more typical of tough exams or romantically daring phone calls, but there it was.

The screen cut to a stern older woman in red-framed glasses, silver hair, and a judge's robe. Or gown? Frock? She would look that up later. The Judge's voice pierced the digital divide. "Good morning, my name is Judge Wittmer, and I'll be conducting this morning's business on behalf of the United States. Arin Coppertree, I presume?"

"Yes, Ma'am. Your Honor." Arin mumbled. *Get to the point where they tell her why the hell she was here,* she thought. Surely there are others better suited for... whatever was needed. Could she get a cooldown stretch first? "Grad student at BU. Classics with a focus on linguistics."

"Wonderful, but please confine your answer to the given question," the Judge replied. "You will be giving testimony this morning under oath. This is not a conventional courtroom as you would recognize it, but it carries the full legal authority of the United States judicial system. Do you understand?"

"Uh, I do. Sorry, I'm-"

"Don't stress," said Judge Wittmer, cutting her off and not quite helping with the stress thing. "We just ask you to focus."

No problem. She stood, hoping her knees would hold. The Judge proceeded with a truncated version of the swearing-in oath, during which Arin had time for a hand-trembling sip of coffee, hoping that wouldn't negate the sacred phrases. Everyone looked at her. Professional and focused, even through fatigue.

Arin was a sweaty mess struggling to hide how lost she was. Last night's wine seeped through her pores and permeated the small room. No one commented on that, either. She looked up and squared her shoulders. She could outrun any of them. It was a mental device she used to feel less inferior in a group. She figured it was probably true in this one.

Linda briefed the room, but Arin was sure she was the only one getting news at that point. "We received this video last night. It appears to have been recorded within the last week." Linda paused to lock eyes with her, "We're going to show you thirty seconds of this video. We need you to tell us what you see, and what you don't. Do you understand?"

She nodded.

"We need a yes, Miss Coppertree," directed the Judge from her virtual bench.

"Yes, your Honor."

"Great," continued Linda. "Please center yourself."

She shifted, setting her coffee aside, and then struggled with her hand placement. She settled on clasping them in front. The stance seemed polite and as serious a bearing as she could pull off in sweaty running gear at nine in the morning.

Henry clicked around on his computer, and the Judge's screen minimized to the lower corner, but her presence didn't recede. A video appeared. A boat, deep at sea, with an older woman on a bench and a young man at the wheel, both shaded by a canopy. He was young, fit, and wore sunglasses and a light-colored visor. She had oversized sunglasses and a head tilted into a book. A drone from the engine, the whoosh of waves, and sporadic gusts of wind filled out the audio. Seemed to be footage from a boat version of a dash cam. A prow cam?

The man sparked a passing familiarity, but she couldn't place him and couldn't divert her focus to dig. She didn't recognize the woman obscured by a sun hat and oversized glasses.

Nothing changed for about ten seconds until a sharp bang cut through the background noise of the wind and waves. Both heads snapped toward the back of the boat, and the older woman put her book down. The low drone of the engine was gone, replaced by shouts and frantic scrambling. The man jammed some buttons on the instrument panel and wiped his face. The woman hunched into the middle of the boat, behind the benches.

A fire sprung up from the rear deck of the boat. Wind blew thick, black smoke of burning gasoline to the side, then to the front and into the camera as the crippled boat drifted and spun. Both occupants shouted, then began flipping seats to find PFDs. A flash of orange and black filled the screen before the feed went dark.

Arin stared at the screen, processing. She knew what they wanted her to see, and she'd seen it. Sensed it. That's why she was here.

Linda spoke, breaking the silence. "A charter boat company sent this footage to local police a few days ago. They record all outings, and when this boat didn't make it back, they pulled footage from the cloud. The video made it to us yesterday evening when someone realized who was on that boat. That doesn't concern you. What concerns you—why you're here—is the authenticity."

Arin just watched people die, and lives would be affected by her answer. Not in a positive, random-act-of-kindness type of way. She wasn't ready to be someone who cast detriment on others. Her next sip of coffee was manageable only by imbued muscle memory. She forced a shaky breath and rocked her knees to keep the blood moving.

"Like Dolos and his clay." Her mind's tendency to drift under pressure could be aggravating to her. And to others, except Melanie, who Arin knew found it secretly charming.

"Like... what?" Linda recoiled, with a thinly-veiled sneer, at the non-sequitur.

"Prometheus's apprentice. The one who made the false statue of Veritas. *Truth.* He ran out of clay at the feet. Pseudologos stumbles." She faced the ancient spirit of deception in the converted back room of a closed gift chop, and her own stance wavered.

"Miss Coppertree." The Judge on the screen huffed. "Please focus. Would you care to comment on the video, or would you like to see it again?"

She blinked and looked around at her expectant and annoyed

audience. "Yes, please, and can you slow it down when the fire appears?" She didn't need to see the video again. She had her answer but wanted to buy time. And the repercussions here... who knows how many people this would affect? At a minimum, everyone on the screen and everyone in the room, besides herself. No, she realized, including herself.

Henry obliged her request to slow the framerate down in the middle of the video. The scene played again. There it is. Clear as day. Or night. For her, it didn't matter.

"Thanks," she said as the Judge's face returned to full-screen size.

"Arin," encouraged Linda, adopting her matronly, commanding tone. "Tell us what you see."

"It's off—It's not real," she stated before she could give it any more thought.

"Please elaborate, Miss Coppertree," the Judge requested.

"The beginning is good. That's real. But when the fire starts? It's not right."

The Judge tilted her head forward, awaiting more.

"It's deepfaked. Is that how you say it? The faces and clothes near the flames are wrong. The boat itself lines up, though. It clicks for me. There was a fire on that boat. But those two people weren't on it. At least not during the explosion and subsequent fire."

Linda pressed her lips together and allowed a slight nod. Henry stared at his computer, his focus boring through it, and Jeremy placed an avuncular hand on Arin's shoulder. The Judge's gaze suggested an attempt to breach the digital boundary and assess the unconventional testimony in the flesh.

"They were probably there before the flames but not after. I'm sorry, I really don't have anything else to add. But it's not real."

"Very well," intoned the Judge while maintaining her countenance.

"Miss Coppertree, the People of the United States thank you for your testimony today. You are dismissed. And I'll remind you that this is not a public court and no details of your testimony or anything you saw or heard or said today may be divulged."

15

THAT EVENING, AS she divulged all of what she saw and heard and said over a bottle of cab franc from Melanie's balcony overlooking Boston Harbor, she bolted up.

"Hey, did you hear about any boat explosions recently? I need to know what I just pulled today."

"I haven't, but I don't believe I subscribe to many nautical disaster publications. Where was it?"

"That's a question for you to *journal*, my favorite journalist student."

"I thought we agreed to pause school tonight, my favorite *classics* student. Now please, continue with your *Epic*."

"More of a yarn than any coherent thread." Arin continued unspooling the narrative of her perplexing day. She saw Melanie itching to jot down notes but settling with refilling her glass.

She did ask good questions, as she is wont. The setting, the people. Mostly the people and their reactions. That's how a story goes somewhere, she says. Otherwise, it's just an encyclopedia entry. Arin wrapped up her recount of the morning with being dismissed from the trial, if that's what it was, and being dismissed all the way to her car with the shop door promptly locked behind her.

"They were friendly, thanked me and all, but were eager for the next shady step. Urgency all around." She drained and refilled her glass. "What am I doing? I missed another research session and don't have a sharable excuse."

Melanie let her eyes drift across the bay below them. "I'd say you did something good today." Her soft words floated in the autumn air.

"You don't know that."

"You don't know it's not true. So drop Occam's Razor and let it be."

"That's probably a millennium past my era of study, but I'll take it," she said. "I have no reason to doubt their authenticity. Linda and her team. I'd rather work with her than whoever Ross's other suitor is."

They watched the bustle on the streets and in the harbor below as the sun set behind them. A small jet descended towards Logan Airport. Arin continued to process her day, and the last week, but conceded that she would never know what her testimony did.

"Qui Pro Domina Justitia Sequitur," she pronounced, breaking the silence and intentionally irking Melanie. Behind her glasses, Melanie raised an eyebrow, but Arin couldn't drag the obvious question out of her.

"You know, you could be more supportive of my deep well of knowledge of dubious practicality." She waited, but Melanie still wouldn't cave.

"Fine, I'll tell you. It's the DOJ motto. They had it as their screensaver. It means they prosecute for Lady Justice, or on her behalf, I think. Cool phrase. I've grown to appreciate that our country uses Latin when they want to ground their words. The language of our former rulers doesn't ring the same. So when we broke off, starting with feeding tea leaves to the fishes down there somewhere," she said, waving at the harbor below with her wine glass and splashing a non-trivial amount over the rail to the street below, "we adopted older and wiser language to use where we could. Gives it *gravitas*...." Arin relished Melanie's eye roll as she dragged out the second *a* for a good three seconds.

She sucked the spilled wine off her fingers as she checked her phone, then blinked away the autumn-and-alcohol-induced haze. "What the hell does she want? My roommate's blowing me up. Something about pizza delivery. She says she was sleeping—doubtful—but they woke her up. And they had my name? That's..."

"Odd, for sure," Melanie finished.

"I don't think I've ever had pizza delivered there. Whatever, home-girl gets free food. She'll get over it." Arin sat back again but couldn't settle herself. "If today weren't today, I'd ignore it, but I'm... Shit, I'm on edge right now."

"I'm sure it's nothing—but, hey, stay here tonight."

"But you're not sure it's nothing. I don't need your journalistic instincts. It pains me, but I might need to call my parents. Wherever they're off galavanting to these days."

"How much have you told them?"

"Not a lot, just that I was involved in a research project that had some connection to the government. I kept it vague, and they didn't press. They probably assumed it was about grants."

"I don't know what they could do, anyway. And you've shared your intentions to keep your distance from them. From their penchant for fixing everything for you—that's admirable. Even for an, ahem, twenty-six-year-old grad student."

Arin replied with four fingers on her glass and the fifth and longest one extended in full rebuttal.

"You can move on," Melanie advised. "I don't know what Linda needed from you for with this video, but maybe it's just another test. Maybe you so thoroughly underwhelmed them that they'll give up on you, and you can return to your life."

"Um, thanks? What hearty endorsements you give."

"You're a rock star at so many things, Arin, and maybe you should stick to being good at the types of things a privileged white suburban girl should be good at."

"Again, with the stellar endorsements. Remind me not to ask you for help with my CV."

"You know what I mean, and you've said it yourself. Your parents gave you the opportunity to thrive wherever, and if earning liberal arts degrees at prestigious schools is within the realm of what they imagined, so be it. There's nothing wrong with meeting expectations, and you enjoy the work. You can reset anytime. Forget this diversion. Whatever's best for you, I'm there."

"Maybe I can. But your journalistic feelers are clawing apart your advice, aren't they? And I'm not clear on the bounds of my role here. Can I just tell them I'm unavailable the next time they call?"

"You didn't sign a contract, right? You don't work for them. You can't be expected to drop your obligations at their beck and call. Whatever the hell a *beck* is."

"I'll need to look that one up." She sighed. "I just want to know if I'm helping. Or who I'm helping. Or hurting." She pulled a sweater on as the breeze picked up and the remnants of dusk faded. "Mel, what do your instincts say? I know you're not yet a renowned investigative reporter, but you have suspicions."

"I chide you, and you respond by giving me too much credit. Your parents did raise you well. Girl, I have no idea what the DOJ has involved you in. But truth is nearly always a good thing, and you're working towards that."

"Nearly always?"

"There are exceptions, of course. And matters of privacy and so on. But if you're exposing someone trying to deceive someone else, I can't see how that would be a bad thing."

"I hope so. I need to go. I'm not getting any answers sitting up here, and it seems I have some cold pizza waiting for me." She stood on the balcony, looking out over the harbor.

Melanie pulled up her phone and scrolled for a moment. "Hey," she said, her eyes widening. "A hunch, but any chance this was her?"

Arin took the phone and almost fumbled it over the balcony. The face staring at her was the woman on the boat. The one in the mid-ocean explosion, if the video were to be believed. Ross's other contact. The congresswoman. Doff the hat and sunglasses, and it was her.

"Mel, what's happening?"

"Those instincts of mine you mentioned just got hot-wired. Read it."

Arin read the bulletin aloud: "Robin Carmine Arrested. Former Congresswoman and Senate candidate, Ms. Carmine was arrested on unspecified charges. She was apprehended at Dulles airport this afternoon by Capitol Police. Her K-Street office, her home in Virginia, and her vehicles were searched. Multiple boxes of records were confiscated." Arin looked up, her face ashen, as she started to hand the phone back.

"Read past the ad," intoned Melanie, fixing her eyes on the horizon.

Arin continued. "An arrest warrant was also issued for Ms. Carmine's son, Troy. He was a decorated Special Forces soldier and is now employed as a private security contractor in New York. His whereabouts are unknown, per a statement from the NYPD." The face accompanying that paragraph was the younger man on the boat video. She groped for the chair as she slumped back, nearly spilling more wine.

"I'll stay here tonight." She cradled her head.

ARIN WANTED TO CRAWL INTO a shell. A small, dark one. She hadn't asked for and didn't want any of this. The ancient myths she studied all featured deities forcing unpleasant chaos on unsuspecting and usually undeserving mortals. She admonished herself for the irrational comparison to the likes of Persephone or Eurydice, but her mind, under stress, did what it did.

"Lachesis is fucking with me," she told Melanie the following morning.

"Who's doing what now?" she replied in pre-coffee grogginess.

"One of the Fates. The one that steers our lives. Too early for dusty Greek references?"

"It's never not too early for that. Spare me."

"I just don't understand my life right now. Someone's pulling strings I can't even see." She paused. "Despite my super-whatever eyes."

"Your eyes are just as lovely as always. Green, luscious. Mesmerizing."

"It's definitely too early for that."

Arin found a pan and cracked some eggs. "What am I involved in here? I have a newly discovered but long-dead aunt. The only guy who knew her punted his entire life to the curb and fled rather than speak with us. I've testified that a video showing a former congresswoman and her son being blown up in the middle of the ocean was fake, and the same day, she gets arrested. And someone ordered pizza for me, which is the opposite of generosity if they were trying to see if I was home. I've missed more classes than I can count, and all I got was a thank you card."

"That's all? Thank that Fate you mentioned for not casting any more your way, or you might have overcooked the eggs." Melanie laughed, without mirth, as Arin looked down and flipped them. "Wait, who gave you a thank you card?"

"Linda did, as she escorted me out yesterday. I did say we were tucked in a back room behind a gift shop, right? She pulled a card from the rack and handed it to me as we walked out. The place was closed, so she either stole it or charged it to the taxpayer fund later."

"That's it, there? She took an envelope for it, too?" Melanie took the card off her counter and opened it. Her eyes widened. "Arin, I assume you haven't looked at this yet."

"No, she just grabbed it off the shelf. I didn't read it. I don't need tacky platitudes right now."

"It wasn't a random card." Melanie handed it over. "This Linda woman might be a bitch, but she can also deliver."

16

DANE COUNTED A stack of weatherproof signs printed with bold blue arrows on a white background. He figured they'd do fine if he again needed a random direction to flee. He hoped he wouldn't.

"Nail the signs to trees with ribbons, got it. How do I know which way the arrows face?"

"Use the map," replied the bike shop owner, his new boss. "Make sure to orient it right. And it'll usually be the more ridden trail, except for a few runs farther up that we just cut." He handed Dane a folded map, wax-coated for rain protection.

"I'm more used to city blocks, but I'll figure it out."

He had secured an apartment and a job the day after the bus dropped him off in the postcard town of Pittsfield, Massachusetts. The town's name set low expectations, so Dane found reality encouraging. A well-kept green centered old brick buildings and stone churches and offered views of surrounding mountains. Bars and bike shops gave him familiar anchors for his transition to his new and hard-earned opportunity.

He was prepared to bribe his way in, but cash doesn't help to smooth out questions in a small town as well as he was used to. No one asked him for a detailed history. He found the inherent trust unsettling.

After his wounds had diminished to a concealable size and his gait healed to passably normal, he walked into the first bike shop he saw. He demonstrated his acumen over a few repairs and secured gainful employment from the kindly owner, a long-haired, soft-spoken, mildly tattooed guy in his fifties.

A fellow employee caught his eye the day he walked in. The tone and tan of biking legs in biking shorts was a sight worth staying for. Her name was Trish, and on the day he got himself a job, he also got himself a date.

Well, more like a coffee date, which wasn't something he did in New York, but he knew the level of significance fell below that of a real date.

No, not even a coffee-level date, although coffee was involved. He found his emotions driving the narrative and checked himself. He and Trish walked down to the art supply store to get signage materials for a race they were sponsoring over the coming weekend. They brought along cups of coffee from the aged pot behind the bike store counter.

He was thinking about extending his near-date with Trish into a genuine one as he stacked race day signs when a couple of customers walked in. Good-looking girls, one blonde and unfairly fit—an athlete, he guessed—and one brunette with a Red Sox cap and glasses. The blonde kept her shades on as she walked inside. Everything about these two said city girls. Trish was a local. He hadn't been in town long enough to form a preference.

When the brunette asked for him by name, he returned a stupefied stare. He wasn't exactly hiding out in the old mining town but also hadn't told a soul where he was going, either. His heart jumped a little from the shock but also because it had been a while since he'd heard his name come from lips like that.

The blonde continued with another question that shattered Dane's flailing grasp on the situation. She mentioned his mother. That name he hadn't heard for years, from any type of lips. He braced himself on the counter and then rubbed his forehead. "Uh, yes, Gina was my mother. She's been gone awhile. What's this about?"

The blonde repeated something about a research project for college. He missed a beat in what she said, but somehow his mother was a subject that came up in their work. He circled his head to stretch out a growing tension in his neck.

His day had gone off the wheels. He wasn't seeing himself asking either of these girls out, which was disappointing enough, but now they had dredged a horrid part of his past into his new life. He looked at them. The pretty ones are always trouble, but this was just odd.

The blond pushed her shades to the top of her head, and Dane hesitated as he caught her eyes. Sharp green, almond-shaped. Enticing. And something more, but he pushed the thought away. "Hey, listen. I've got to get to work. There's a race this weekend I need to prep for. But I'll help you if I can. Come back at six? We lock up around then, and I've got nowhere to be."

"Of course," said the brunette. "Sorry to bother you. You must think we're a little whacked. We are, but we're hoping to learn more about your mother."

He remained silent but pushed a smile forward. "How about a ride in the meantime? I'm guessing you've had a few hours in the car today and need some air. Plenty of trees and rocks out there for you. Rental bikes are over there."

"We didn't exactly dress for that."

Dane pointed to the clothing racks on the other side of the store.

"Well, I do need some new gear," said the blond.

"HOLD UP, THERE'S A WASH station out back." The girls started rolling their mud-streaked rental bikes back into the carpeted shop a few hours later. Six o'clock had come and gone, and the sun was setting. They weren't the type to flee with rentals, so he had waited. "Feel free to hose yourselves off, too. Looks like you found some dirt. It was Melanie and Arin, right? Sorry, you threw me off a bit earlier."

"That's us. And lately, I throw myself off."

Dane kept himself almost busy enough to avoid watching them hose each other off through the rear window of the shop.

"We ran out of drinking water out there, and I think we got lost," Arin said as they came back inside, toweling cold water off their arms and legs. "A couple times. Or maybe it was just a single long time of being lost. Not sure how you count that."

"I'm used to street signs myself. Not many of those out there. I assume you're hungry, so I ordered burritos and beer." He held up a delivery bag. "Post-ride staples, and by the scratches and mud you've brought back, I say you've earned it. All the tables are packed up for the race, but I'll flip over a box here if you don't mind sitting on carpet."

"I'm ravenous, and that's perfect," Melanie said as they all sat cross-legged and tucked into oversized burritos and cold local lagers.

"First, intriguing guests of mine, how the hell did you find me? I moved out of New York barely a week ago. In a hurry, and I didn't exactly leave a forwarding address."

Melanie looked at Arin, who couldn't speak around a full mouth, so she began. "Short version, we have an associate who gave us a name in a secret gift card. Two names, actually, a father and a son. Then that son's name popped up on a social feed for a bike shop in Pittsfield, Mass. New part of the team, the post said," she waved her hand around the shop, "and helping to prep for their big race."

Arin washed down her mouthful with a swig of beer. "Long version later." She attacked a fresh corner of the burrito.

Dane rubbed his temples. "So, Arin?" he started, guessing at the crux of their visit. "I know this isn't just a research project. You have her eyes."

She paused mid-bite, looked at him, then swallowed without breaking eye contact. He didn't know what to expect, but her next question was about as far off the grid as it gets.

"Dane, were you good at hide and seek? Like, really good?"

He furrowed his eyebrows. Then he relaxed his face and sat back, bracing himself on his hands, his mind cycling. Clicks of understanding came together as Arin awaited his answer.

Could that be? Did that question just explain so many of his own long-standing questions? On the rare occasions as a kid when he had others to play with, he'd win. He assumed he was just good. He was good at other things he couldn't explain, too. His bike riding at night, where he sensed what was around corners. His poker insights, where a good bluffer won't turn visibly red but may still have subtle heat rise into their face or around their collar. As a child, the still living but fated body he saw around the bend of the subway tunnel. This girl may have just solved his life.

But he wasn't ready for this. "Maybe," he replied. "Not something I remember."

They sat and talked in the closed bike shop late enough into the night that they ordered more food and drinks. The girls talked, mostly, and he was happy to listen. Dane hoped his new employers wouldn't chastise him for using the space for the impromptu meeting, but he wasn't going to take them to his low-rent apartment and he didn't feel comfortable enough around town to go to a restaurant for a personal conversation.

Arin shared her family history. She described times when she noticed that inkling of an awareness. Her ability. *Their* ability. She and Melanie walked Dane through her search for family and for an explanation. She had taken some tests with a medical student friend of theirs. Some guy named Ross.

Dane listened. He'd never been a talker and didn't have much to add. Not about family history. When she spoke of the visit to the orphanage and then of the abandoned hospital, he retracted. His new life, as of that night, was no longer fresh. No longer open. No longer full of opportunity. He'd been gone less than a week before his past had found him.

"We didn't intend to bring up these memories for you," Melanie intoned. Dane didn't realize his withdrawal from the conversation was that apparent. "Sorry. I've only read about her in an old paper," she continued. "I didn't know her. But she was your mother."

Dane inspected the ceiling tiles. He didn't want to relive any of it but wanted to give them something. "Only until I was seven, really. She died soon after, and she didn't do much mothering in the last few years."

They sat in silence, nursing beers. Dane's legs cramped from sitting on the carpet, so he stood and meandered around the shop. His visitors stood up as well, stretching their long legs.

"Do you know what Aristotle said about seven-year-olds?" Arin asked.

He saw Melanie give her a look of admonishment. "Excuse her, that's something she does," Melanie stated. "Tell her off. You have my permission."

Dane shrugged. He didn't know the name Aristotle, let alone anything he's said.

"'Show me a seven-year-old, and I'll show you the man," he said. Basically, people are formed around that age, shaping the rest of their lives." She looked downward. "I realize that's not helpful. Sorry. But I'd love to hear anything you'd like to share about Gina. Or about your childhood."

Dane wasn't going to share his life. Not like she had shared hers. He didn't know if he could. He'd never tried or even wanted to and couldn't remember ever being asked. The grit of his existence didn't fare well against the postcards of their experiences.

"I just moved here last week," he replied. "Had some complications back in the city, and I wanted to try a place like this. Fresh start and all."

Skipping his story gave them plenty of room for conjecture. That was fine. He didn't need to relive the pain or share his rare triumphs. And he didn't want sympathy from these girls. The hour was late, and he reminded them he needed to get up early. They got the hint.

"One more question, if you don't mind, then we'll be out of your hair," Melanie said. "Do you know a Dr. Brock? Marshall Brock? He may have been someone who saw your mother."

"No. Name doesn't sound familiar. Sorry." He pulled a trash can around and began picking up bottles and wrappers. The girls stooped to help.

"I don't know what to make of finding a cousin at this point in my life," he admitted. "I was never a kid with a family, so I don't know what that's supposed to mean. It was great meeting you both. Stop by the next time you're in town. We'll go biking and get some more beer."

He ushered them out of the shop and locked up. Memories intruding to his surface were rare. Most of them hurt, and the better ones only made him long for times when he had control of his life. He walked to his apartment. To his home that should have been the start of a new life if these two girls hadn't just dragged decayed remnants of the old one onto his doormat.

17

"**A**RIN, WHAT DID you think of your cousin?" Melanie inquired, with caution, the following morning. They had booked a room at an old country inn after leaving the bike shop and fell asleep as soon as they hit the bed.

"Assuming he is that. We're from different backgrounds. I don't know, the kid's had a rough life. I want to spend more time with him, though. Even if he doesn't have information that would help me figure out my family history, I'd love to hear more about his story."

"Would you, though? I mean, he's a stranger, and he wasn't quite breaking out his journal for us to read. I hope he has some useful info, too, but he might not."

She lowered her head. "But he's family. I guess. I don't know what he's running from, but I want to help him."

"Arin, I can tell you that help is the last thing he wants. He was being polite hearing about your life in manicured suburbia, but people who have made it on their own don't want charity from people like us." She sighed. "Give him time. I think we turned his life sideways just by showing up, and it seems he's still trying to right it from whatever the last turn was."

"He's family, and he has whatever I have." She felt her voice pitch higher. "One other person in the world I can talk to about this vision shit, and you're telling me to stay away?"

"You'll scare him off. He's just run from something, and he'll do it again. I want to hear his story, too. The journalist in me wants to wring every detail from him and fill my notebook. The part of me who thinks—knows—he's your family wants to care for him. But that's not happening today."

"I need answers, Mel. We're chasing shadows again, except now I'm in the middle of something that's making headlines. People died on that video, and I testified under solemn oath that it was faked. Someone is still looking for me. If I say I wish it were only the US Department of goddamned Justice who wants to track my whereabouts, would that be reasonable? No, it wouldn't because none of this is!"

She looked out the window, her breath swelling. The street was empty of people and cars and anything else to break the tension. "Linda gave us his father's name, too. In the card. We should find him and call him."

"Then Dane will absolutely run. Two psycho chicks stalking him along with his father will scare him to distant shores. Didn't you pick up on any of that last night? He doesn't want to talk. He wants to leave his old life and start again, and we pissed all over that vision last night."

The quaint kitchen attached to their room became unbearably small. Arin left for the bedroom and returned a moment later in running gear. She guzzled the last of her coffee and left the inn without a word.

She navigated out of the village to a long stretch of empty country road. Miles passed before she could scrape aside the muddle and frustration and worry that had built up over the last few weeks. With the beat of each step and each regulated breath, she saw a clearer image of what still worked in her life.

She had her health. Her school semester could still be salvaged. Her relationship with Melanie would heal. Her fretting about being able to live something other than a blanched life was both distant and ludicrous. She'd tell her therapist so if she had any inclination to go back.

The roadside opened into wide fields, and the wind picked up. Arin kept running. She had no place else to be. Maybe she'd run back to Boston. It's the same state, and she could get there in a few days. No one would miss her other than Melanie, but she'd get over it.

Back to Boston just long enough to leave again. Call the DOJ and say she wouldn't be available as a consultant anymore. Skip a semester and fly somewhere with warm rain and no cell service. Settle into a deep armchair with a stack of paperbacks and a crate of wine and give not a single shit if anyone says that's what a stereotypical rich white girl would do.

Her thoughts returned to running across the state. The notion was enticing. A couple hours' drive would be about... doesn't matter how many miles. It was doable. She would find accommodation and meals where she needed them. Take breaks if she found a quiet town to rest for a day. Give up if she wanted to. There was no benefit to judging herself. But she would try. She needed something spontaneous and challenging and under her control, and at that moment she could picture nothing better.

That's it then. That's what she'd do—keep running. Forrest Gump was a philosopher she hadn't studied yet.

She almost called Melanie to share her plans but decided to text instead. She didn't need her or anyone else to talk her out of this. She put her phone on airplane mode after the text went through. No replies needed.

Was she doing this? Without vocalizing a definite *yes,* she continued pumping one leg in front of the other. Her pace evened out. Her spirit needed this, and her body would deliver, as it always did. She welcomed the beckon of the road as it descended into a forested valley.

A bridge crossed a small stream at the base of the valley, and the road forward rose over the hill beyond. She slowed at the bridge to catch her breath. A wide but shallow stream bubbled underneath. She braced her hands on the upstream guardrail, watching the water flow toward her. She inhaled slowly. Then, she walked to the other side and exhaled, watching the water churn away from her over the rocks. *Let it all go.*

Her idea was ridiculous. Running across the width of the Commonwealth to prove what? That she could make a decision? It wasn't a sound one. And her problems would be stacked even higher at the end of the road. She stood near the side of the bridge, listening to the water. To the wind and the birds. None of them had answers. She ran on.

She crested a hill and ran down the other side, approaching another narrow bridge in the undulating landscape. She sought out the quietest roads whenever she could, and few cars passed. Every vehicle was an unwelcome jolt to her rhythm and scraped a bit from her hard-earned flow state.

As she approached the next bridge, a sleek beige sedan slowed down behind her. She jogged to the side of the road and gave an appreciative wave as she did for considerate drivers. The car slowed further but didn't give her berth. She jogged fully off the road into the gravel edge, her appreciation changing to annoyance.

The car neared. She looked back, and her heart skipped. Her knees buckled, the edge of her foot caught, and she tripped, her forearms breaking her fall into the sharp gravel.

The man driving the car was dead.

He wasn't truly dead, but she had seen him blown up on a boat two days before. And—she now realized—she had seen him running on the Espanades in Boston the week before. That's why he was familiar. He was the jogger who nearly collided with her and Melanie and Ross.

Arin scrambled backward on her hands as the car stopped. Her elbow and wrist were scraped raw, and blood trickled down her arm.

The driver exited the vehicle and walked toward her. A throbbing pulse in her head vacated rational thought. Her stomach went hollow, and her vision blurred. "I'm not going to hurt you." His tone was level. Professional. He stopped about ten feet away. "But you'll need to come with me."

The man was rugged, fit, and no more than a few years older than her. If she was fresh, she might be able to outrun him. Maybe. But she was more than an hour into her run and was panicking. A deep breath became a cough, then she tasted bile and vomited up what remained of her morning coffee.

Her vision blurred further as tears welled in her eyes. She drew an arm across her chin to clean it and regained enough breath to blurt out a question. She wasn't sure what she asked, and it didn't matter as it went unanswered. He stepped closer, clasping his hands loosely in front of his chest and staggering his stance. He remained calm but looked ready to move if he needed to.

"You need to take out your phone," he directed.

She gasped. She hadn't even thought of her phone. The worthless thing was still in airplane mode.

The man glanced up both sides of the valley road, which remained devoid of any other cars. She stood and spread her arms to regain her balance, then brought out her phone.

"Toss it in the brook."

After a painful hesitation, she did. She knew the jokes about phones existing like a bodily appendage for her generation. She watched it slide into the babbling water and wink through the refracted sunlight. The loss she felt was unreasonable, but that's where her mind was. Not on escape. Not on her future.

He opened the back door and gestured inside. "Here or the trunk, it's up to you."

She saw heavy black mesh installed between the back and front seats. Like a police vehicle. Surely, the rear locks were disabled as well. The back seat would be better, she knew, but she was utterly unable to make any decisions.

The man hesitated before opening the front door and tossing her a water bottle. "Rinse out your mouth and clean off your arm."

She saw that the water bottle was sealed, which felt relevant to know. She swished out the regurgitated coffee and doused her scraped arm. She chugged the remainder and attempted a discrete glance at her surroundings. She knew she had failed at the discretion part when the man rebuffed her with a quick head shake.

A thousand chase scenes from movies flashed through her mind. She could flee into the woods. She could jump off the bridge to the other side of the brook. It was low enough that she probably wouldn't sprain an ankle. She could stall until another car came, but the bliss of the quiet road she'd chosen had become a terror devoid of any chance of a savior. The only thought she could process was that no blue light stations were in sight.

She could... but she didn't. None of those things. The choice was made. She moved her feet toward the car as her world swam and her pulse thudded in her ears. She let him ease her into the back seat, her face ashen and her breath shallow.

He closed the door and climbed in front. "There's a cuff in the seat pocket. Put it on your ankle." She found a thick, heavy device she recognized as a tracker. A friend from years ago had one for probation and had to deal with endless ribbing, but no humor came to mind now. She couldn't even process which ankle to put it on. Such was the extent of her decision-making paralysis.

"Left ankle."

She almost thanked him for making that choice for her. She may have thanked him aloud but wasn't sure. She clicked it closed, keeping it comfortable.

"Another click," he stated.

She complied.

"And one more."

She closed it another click, and it was no longer comfortable.

An eighteen-wheeler crested the hill in front of them.

"If you do anything other than sit quietly," he intoned, "your day will get much worse."

She choked out an involuntary laugh. She supposed any day could get worse, but he'd need to work to beat this one. He pressed a button on the console, and the window tint darkened to a near-blackout level. *Fancy*, she thought. The truck cruised by without slowing. Her captor eased the car into the road and over the bridge and looked in the rearview. "Seatbelt."

She complied. The car sped over the hill and down the desolate country road.

18

DANE HAMMERED THE directional sign into a tree near a trail fork. He gulped water and then pulled out his map to double-check the arrow's orientation. The forest was quiet, and his task was solitary. He appreciated both aspects as he needed time to run the previous night through his mind. He had been dismissive when the girls asked about his life. They understood. He hoped they did.

His past wouldn't help anyone. Not himself. Not the girls and their questions. He'd eat and drink and talk with a couple of good-looking girls anytime, even if one of them was apparently family, but he'd come to this hole in the woods for a reset. That—his reset—could still happen if he made the boundaries clear with his attractive intruders. They were risky, those women with their traveling and notes and incessant digging, and he worked his hands literally bloody to carve out a new, low-risk life.

Arin and Melanie were still in town. He'd call and postpone their next meetup. Plan for another one at some indeterminate time down the line. Such were his intentions until Melanie herself spun around a bend in the trail on another rental bike, red-faced and wide-eyed.

"They told me where to find you." She huffed as she jumped off the bike. "She's gone! And something's wrong. Severely wrong. I'm scared." She looked up and pulled off her cap to brush matted clumps of auburn hair out of her face. Whoever had lent her the bike hadn't given her the mandatory helmet. Or she just hadn't waited for it, nor changed out of her jeans.

Dane remained silent as he slipped the map back into his pack.

"There are some things we didn't get to last night," Melanie continued. "Arin's involved in... a lot. She testified for the DOJ about a video where two people were on a boat that exploded. Except it didn't. Or, the boat did explode, but the people weren't on it. And there's a recruiter for a medical company that's been hounding Ross and trying to contact her. That woman used to be in Congress, now she's been arrested, and we think it's because of Arin's testimony. And the only guy who might know enough to sort out this shitshow sold his house and bought an RV and fled within a day of me talking to him."

Dane realized he was gripping the hammer at his side. He slid it back into the bag as Melanie caught her breath.

"Yes, I sound whacked. I assure you I am not."

He searched for words to form a reply but asking her to sit down on a nearby stump was the best he could do. "All right. I'll need some context and probably some edibles to understand the rest of that, but start with where Arin is, or where you think she is."

Melanie shared the text his cousin had sent about running across the state. She then showed her multiple unanswered replies and calls. She'd driven out to the last shared location and then a few more miles in every direction but didn't see anything.

"I don't know how I can help," Dane admitted. "But I'm sure she's all right. She's crazy bright. Strong as hell. Probably looking for a place to charge her phone."

"It's not like her. She might make a wild boast about running across the state, but she wouldn't actually do it, and she damned sure wouldn't cut off communication." Melanie paused. "We did have a little tiff, but no way she wouldn't call by now."

Dane pondered. "Speaking for myself, I haven't had many positive interactions with police, but I'm told they can be helpful in situations like this. Missing Young White Female is APB-worthy."

"Yes, that's next," Melanie replied. "I wanted to make sure she hadn't contacted you. I know we just met, but thanks."

"Give me a call when she shows back up. And I was a bit of an ass last night. I don't know how to talk about childhood and all that. And it's not a story you want to hear."

"You're wrong. I do." She looked at him. "I care for her. And her family—including you. I'll keep you posted."

Dane watched her churn down the trail in her jeans and ballcap. He felt an inner pang imagining Arin hurt. The day before, he didn't know she existed, and if he hadn't seen his mother in her, he probably wouldn't have cared.

He continued with the race preparations. He had a real job and intentions of keeping it. But an afternoon of trail work didn't shake his thoughts of Arin. Of his mother and father. Of the life he'd risked everything to escape.

Melanie called him that afternoon without any meaningful updates and they agreed to meet. Dane entered the Irish bar by the town green and they got a partially secluded table behind an arched wooden wall. As they sat, Dane shed the absurd notion that he could drive his past away. He said as much as they waited for beers.

"I got a summons in the mail today for a court appearance in southern Manhattan," he added, drawing Melanie's attention from her phone. "Nothing severe. A little misunderstanding on a busy street turned into a misdemeanor charge for me. They care when things happen in front of tourists."

It could have been worse. He'd said that a few times recently.

"Point is, I can't just start a new life here and ignore my past, try as I might. And Arin? She's cool. I'm glad to know her." He leaned back on the bench, stretching out his trail-work aches. "So what did my friends in blue do for you?"

"They told me to shove an APB up my ass. In a cordial New England way." She sighed. "We argued in the morning, and I have a text saying she wanted to disappear on a spontaneous week-long run, then she turned her phone off. I see where the cops are coming from." She tapped her fingers on an untouched glass of beer. "But they're wrong. She would have shown up back at the inn, or at least called by now."

Dane let the silence linger as he sipped his beer. She eventually drank hers, too. Her eyes were distant, and he knew she was chewing herself apart with worry. "What did you argue about?"

"You."

The answer was immediate, startling him. "I'm not used to two girls arguing over me. Maybe at me. What was it about?"

"Arin wanted to ask more questions. To dig. She's scared and looking for reasons why her life is going batshit. I told her you didn't seem keen on a therapy session about your childhood and your mom, and doubted that anything you could share would be helpful anyway. No offense." She chewed some fries and took another pull to wash them down. Dane watched her pulse lower. Saw the heat ebb from her cheeks.

"Funny thing," she continued, "I'm the journalist inclined to push for answers. Arin's been ready to fold and bury herself back in school and ignore whatever this ability is. After the last couple of days, though, that option to back out seems to be off the table." She lowered her eyes and let out a low exhale. "And I think she may have been right to want to let it go. She's not equipped for this. I turned her life into a journalism project, and now she's disappeared."

Dane sighed. "I still don't know what I can do. If I thought rehashing my life growing up on city streets would do a damned thing to help find her, I'd share it all. But I don't see how it would, and I don't want to depress this scene any further."

He spun a coaster on the table. He was back on that cold concrete pier in Brooklyn and facing a painful choice. His health was considerably better this time, but his mental state was roiling like a bloodstained chunk of styrofoam in the East River. He saw a path here in this quiet town that could lead to a life he was proud of. A new history that he could idly banter about, unguarded and unconcerned about scaring people away. That could be him, he thought, looking around at other patrons in the bar. But he couldn't live that life and send birthday cards to this woman—this cousin—if he brushed her off like a stranger.

Everything he did, once locked in, he did with abandon, or not at all. His last poker game was all in. The night following that game, he was done with the city, and he was all out. What was his risk here, he asked himself, and how would he evaluate it? Could chance help?

He looked at the coaster he was spinning under his fingers. One side had the logo of a local brewery. The other side was blank. Unknown and uncontrollable. He could spin it and let beer-soaked chance drop him an answer. At one point, recently, he would have done just that.

He downed the remainder of his drink and slapped the coaster down in front of him, blank side up.

He held Melanie's eyes. "Let's find her."

19

ARIN'S NEWLY PURCHASED performance running gear failed its wick-away claims as her sweat gelled cold over her body. Someday, she'd finish a run where she'd have time to shower and change afterward.

Salt rings formed around her legs and back on the dark leather seats. She squirmed against them to ensure a costly cleaning bill. She almost wiped her abundant cool-weather jogging mucous on them as well but saw a tissue dispenser and decided to maintain some dignity. She'd see how the rest of the ride went.

On the abductee spectrum, she conceded she was on the I'm-probably-not-going-to-be-dismembered-today side. Other than the virtual dismemberment of her phone. Without that appendage, she was incomplete.

The sedan was spacious and equipped with all of the luxury trim options she knew about and some that she didn't, such as the tint control on the windows. *All the better to not see you with, my dear.* Her upscale prisoner transport ride was smoother than any she'd known on frost-scarred New England roads, and the engine's acceleration power pasted her and her salt into the leather. The mesh cage separating her from the silent driver was ancient technology but wasn't a feature she was accustomed to. She hadn't tested it, but it looked more solid than what she'd seen in police movies. And once as a teenager after a misunderstanding that her parents had helped to clear up.

She found a storage console stocked with convenience store snacks and bottled drinks. After a few miles on the road, her panic subsided, and hunger filled the gap. She helped herself to an energy bar and a bottle of green tea.

Her captor hadn't said a word since they left the bridge. She hadn't asked any questions, either, but was working on a good icebreaker. After refilling her belly and passing a quiet thirty minutes in a leather seat and a controlled climate, she could once again process rational thought.

He had ample opportunity to hurt her. Or to drag her into the woods and attempt what men do to lone women. He hadn't, and that was the raft of sanity she clung to. He had a military bearing about him. Professional, assertive, somber. The type of guy who doesn't wake up and decide to abduct girls for fun.

Had Melanie snooped into Troy's background yet? What was it, two days ago when his name surfaced? If so, she hadn't shared anything. Melanie didn't know he was the jogger stalking them on the Esplanade near campus. She probably dug into his background. She's thorough, but they hadn't had a chance to recap. Maybe that was on the agenda for today.

Arin hadn't cried. She hadn't pleaded or begged. She'd been in an asphyxiating and blinding panic and vomited, but that would happen to anyone. And she recovered to a passable imitation of stability in a reasonable time. Whatever was planned, she'd get through this.

They wanted to test her, right? She could do that again. She'd prefer agency in such a decision, but if they ran her through another MRI before she had a chance to escape, and if that ended up being the worst thing that happened in her life thus far, she could rationalize this away and bore her therapist to tears of her own in weeks to come.

She would, of course, try to escape at her earliest convenience. The digital shackle on her leg wasn't a chain. So, if the tracker led this grunt to chase her into a police station or a semicircle of backwoods gun enthusiasts who have trained for years to protect young women from government agents (she would describe her driver as such), then the device would be useful to keep on, anyway. The former scenario would be more likely, but the latter more rewarding.

She needed to focus, envision the flight, and be ready to seize the next opportunity without hesitation. She closed her eyes and attempted deep breaths. She drew from years of yoga practice to center her inner core, set her intentions, and accept with gratitude the first opportunity to get the fuck out of there.

She thought of her mindfulness app and instinctively reached for the phone holder on her arm. *Shit.* She'd never been without it for this long. Turning it off in a lecture hall is anxiety-inducing. Knowing it was a shiny fish lure miles away was enough to send her pulse northward again.

Nomophobia. The word injected itself, unbidden and unwelcome, into her churning mind. Language evolution fascinated Arin. New words—she even brought to mind the new word for new words, *neologism*—spoke to the needs of a culture. What Arin needed was her mobile phone, and nomophobia is the fear of being without one. She diligently studied such new additions to the language. But she preferred they stay in the abstract. Loss of a phone being on a level of being kidnapped was something she couldn't reconcile. No, *abducted.* She wasn't a goddamned kid, and hadn't been one for a while.

Her watery phone's logged activity was literally waterlogged, so she focused on recalling her last communication. It was informing Melanie of a spontaneous solo cross-state run. Effectively disappearing for a week—a threat she was fulfilling in spades.

Her focus veered, and she tried to think what was meant by *in spades*. The shovel or the card suit? If she had her phone, she would look it up. Maybe the guy in front of her would know. She'd find out.

"Hey Troy, what does *in spades* mean?" She asked, hoping her first words since entering the car would carry a confident tone. Her voice cracked, but she got through it and watched his eyes in the rearview. To her satisfaction, he jolted a little and swerved the car, though if it was at the sudden voice behind him, the freak question, or her admission that she knew his name, she wasn't sure. Other than correcting the car back into the lane, he didn't respond.

Actually, the car corrected itself, she realized. That could be helpful to know. For escape plans and such. Now that he was listening and she'd found her voice again, she decided to ask some questions. Not relevant ones. She knew he wasn't going to answer those.

"Nice *sedan*. Did you know that the earliest ones were chairs on poles used to carry people who imagined themselves to be important around?"

Through his sunglasses, he met her eyes in the rearview, then looked back to the road.

"That's right, just like the sedan we're sitting in now. That's where we get the word *sedentary*. Do you sit a lot, Mr. Carmine?" He grimaced but kept his eyes forward.

"Not a car guy? What about roads? Towns? I'm taking my topic inspiration from my limited surroundings, so your path of travel might influence what we talk about." She was running on fumes and struggled to shove coherent thoughts together. But if she could keep him on edge—or at least keep him annoyed—then... what? Some potential to fit into a plan. The rest of the scheme would need to come later.

"*Counties.* Why do we have counties here but no Dutchies or Baronies? We don't appoint counts to oversee them. We don't have dukes or barons either, but their nominal parcels of land didn't make the hop across the pond. Thoughts on that?"

He apparently didn't have any thoughts on that. And whatever impact Arin may have had on her situation was diminished, as he showed no further interest. Did she just waste one of the limited tools she had access to? She should have saved her knowledge of his name, at least. She was sure that's what had startled him. She wasn't very good at this.

She needed to pee and told him so. He nodded. He had stuck to state roads so far and had been traveling south. She determined that from the position of the sun, the moss on the trees, and also from the road signs labeled South.

Was his aversion to highways to avoid toll gate tracking? Maybe there was a statewide manhunt underway. She should drop something for them to find. *Manhunt* needs an update, but *personhunt* lacks force and *womanhunt* sounds dreadful.

Arin blinked to refocus. Was she going to see this day through? Maybe they were headed for a nearby farm where she would be locked in a barn, and all her initial, irrational fears would be fully warranted. These were some of the questions she didn't bother asking.

He pulled the car into a weedy dirt lot across the road from a diner, stopped behind a pair of parked backhoes, and cut the engine. It was a construction site with a portable toilet tucked into long grass at the far end.

He turned around and spoke for the first time since they'd been on the road. "I'm going to order some food." His tone was even and direct. He nodded towards the outhouse. "I'll unlock the door, and you can go while we wait."

He then pointed to her ankle. "You'll feel a vibration when you leave the vicinity of the car. If you choose to go farther than the toilet, that buzz will turn into a small shock and then into a larger and more painful shock. After that, if you continue to move away from the vehicle, you'll be subject to a voltage high enough to alter your cardiovascular rhythm to the point that you will struggle to move. It will be indescribably painful. If you feel brave and somehow manage to continue even further, the cuff will inject your leg with a fast-acting tranquilizer." He finished by unlocking the doors.

Arin's throat constricted, and her vision tunneled again. Her stomach went sour as she struggled to keep the energy bar and green tea down. Her door was unlocked, but she couldn't assemble the muscle sequence needed to open it.

Troy scrolled through a menu on his phone, ignoring her. He placed a call to the diner.

She steadied herself enough to pull on the handle and step out without falling. She'd wasted energy and hope planning an escape. The beastly thing on her ankle killed that chance.

He wasn't bluffing about the cuff. At least not about the first stage. It vibrated like a dog fence collar as she inched towards the outhouse. Then the light tingle became obnoxious pins and needles. She was quick about her task, then moved briskly and with increasing relief back toward the car.

With Arin secure again in the back, Troy left the car to cross the road and retrieve their lunch. She watched diner patrons come and go, but they might as well have been miles away.

They ate on the road. The club sandwich looked flavorful, but Arin didn't taste much.

20

ARIN'S EFFORTS TRACKING their route had been in vain. She knew of only one George Washington Bridge, and they crossed it. No isolated barn or musty basement or remote cave in her near future, she conceded.

But why are isolated places more feared? She was snatched and transported in daylight through public areas. Empty roads and dark forests would be better. They don't encourage hope, that fickle, dangerous ingredient. She despaired as she passed within lunging distance of thousands of people she coudln't reach. She passed police cars and paramedics who could have helped if she wasn't constricted to silence and window-tinted obscurity. The proximity to freedom was a maddening window in her level of hell.

Was there an APB out yet? She told Melanie she wanted to disappear for an impromptu run across the state. In a text message, which would be evidence if she went to the police. Now she was truly and completely disappeared. Case closed. If she were six or sixteen, they would send an alert immediately. But at twenty-six, the authorities wouldn't lift a pencil for at least a few days.

Knowing she was helplessly bound by a sleek control device seemed worse than rusty chains or duct tape. Illusionary control. Door locks and an ankle bracelet in place of Sisyphus's rock. He, too, was bound through obligation and not physical restraints. She threw on psychological chains of her own, which was a heavier set.

She regretted not running at the bridge. She was a runner, a track star since childhood—it's what she did. Until the time she needed to. She froze, and her inability to commit cost her her freedom.

And that, the planning of her life by others, was the mental mill-stone that continued to roll her over and wear her down. Her parents paving her academic career is a different bucket than Melanie guiding her family research trips and an entirely different realm than this asshole abducting her and bringing her to god knows where, but the foundation is the same. She lets others make decisions. It's the only thing she does. That was the heaviest chain.

She saw skyscrapers pass as they traveled south. She'd done the city tourist thing a few times but couldn't orient herself if her life depended on it. And here, now, it just may. They were somewhere in Midtown, which was all she knew.

Her driver turned down into an underground parking lot. She missed the avenue or cross street they were on. The gates lifted, and a sleepy attendant looked up from the window. An arm's reach away but an uncrossable gulf for the helpless captive in the back seat.

Troy parked the car in a quiet corner of the garage and turned around to face her. She had remained quiet for the last leg of the journey, assuming this was the end of it.

"I shouldn't need to use it, but on the cuff, I can activate the injector immediately. I won't need to use it, will I?"

"Probably not." She felt an ambiguous response would show

confidence and keep a little of her dignity intact. He held her gaze for a moment. She couldn't think of anything worth adding.

"Stay near me, and stay quiet." He unlocked the doors and they both stepped out. She looked at the car and then her cuff. No, *his* cuff that he was lending to her. Semantics are important, especially when nothing else is under control.

"The proximity to me matters, not to the car."

So, she learned, the tracker was on his person now and not fixed to the car. Another piece of information that she would probably never take advantage of. They walked to an elevator in the corner, and the doors closed on the two of them. She could smell her dried sweat in the enclosed space. Last night's wine seeped from her pores. The car must have excellent ventilation as she didn't notice how much she reeked until then.

The elevator car didn't have buttons or any floor indicators that she could see. Troy passed a blank card over a black box and the car ascended. The lift was smooth and quick, and she didn't venture a guess at how high they went. After fifteen seconds or so, the car slowed to a gentle stop, and the doors opened to a narrow hallway with nondescript white walls and a gray carpet. He nodded to the right, and she moved down the hallway.

The floor was exceptionally quiet for a Midtown office tower. She focused but couldn't even hear the muffled sounds from adjacent floors or outside that she would have expected.

Troy directed her to open an unmarked door at the end of the short hallway. She did, and walked into what looked like an office waiting room. A plush armchair with a floor lamp and a stack of outdated periodicals sat on one side, and a computer terminal filled the other corner. With further direction from Troy, she opened the inner door.

Inside appeared to be a small apartment. Small by normal standards but perfectly respectable by her understanding of Manhattan square footage costs. A large window faced the door. She guessed they were somewhere in the forties or fifties, floor-wise. A kitchenette and bathroom filled the space to her right, and another closed door stood to her left. A two-seat sofa and a wooden coffee table in front of her completed the space. The sofa faced the window with the skyline view, and a neat stack of paperbacks sat on the table.

"Sit down."

She did. He took her ankle with the cuff.

"Turn on your side."

She complied and immediately found herself in a martial arts leg lock. Judo, maybe. She had freely subjected herself to a submission hold.

He pulled a blocky implement from his pocket. A key of sorts, which he turned in the side of the cuff and rendered her unshackled. Her ankle floated in relief, but his grip kept her from any quick movements. From any movement at all.

"I'll let you go. You'll need to sit when I do. Understood?"

"Sure." Her options were limited to the point where the only one she had was to oblige. He released her leg and stepped out of reach. She turned and settled into the sofa. Anticipation, worry and anger all clashed for dominance.

Tell me what you want from me, she pleaded in thought but wouldn't satisfy him by begging aloud. An answer wasn't likely.

"The walls and floors are sound insulated. The fire alarm pull station isn't connected." He turned and left her with those helpful tips like rental home sticky notes. The porch door sticks when closing. The kayak paddles are in the shed. You'll be hurt if you attempt to escape.

Arin stared at the closed door for several moments. She curled into the sofa. Her upscale cell was surely equipped with surveillance. She didn't care.

She cried until exhaustion dragged her to sleep.

ARIN WOKE AS THE SUN was setting. Her window faced east and long orange shadows across the city suggested the time. She'd slept the afternoon away on the sofa.

She was hungry. Thirsty. Salty with dried sweat.

She rose and explored the apartment. The kitchen was stocked with fresh food and cookware. The bathroom and shower were stocked as well. Department store shampoo and fresh towels. Everything was new.

She'd never been frightened by the sight of an empty laundry hamper before and wondered if anyone had, ever. Someone had bought a new hamper, meaning she wouldn't be leaving anytime soon. She nudged it with her foot, just in case it might not be real. It was.

The bedroom contained a neatly made twin bed, a nightstand, and a small closet. In the closet were folded sets of clothing. Simple loungewear of various stock colors. Sweats, socks, t-shirts. Bras and underwear. A pair of sneakers. All in her size.

That shook her. She shuddered and felt goosebumps rise and pulled her arms around herself. Everyone's buying habits are out there on corporate data clouds. Privacy is a suggestion, a quaint concept of times past. She knew that. But her purchase history logged on a distant server is an abstraction not worthy of practical concern. The folded pile of panties in her right fucking size was an intrusion that shredded any facade of remaining control.

She felt filthy. The blatant affront to her privacy layered on the dried sweat and clinging fear.

Someone could have broken into her dorm to get her clothing size.

Another pizza delivery guy who found her roommate gone, or high, and picked through her drawers. It didn't matter how. She didn't want to know.

She stood in the bedroom, transfixed. She didn't want to lie down. She didn't want to touch anything. She didn't want to look for cameras in the ceiling.

She needed Melanie. She needed her parents. She needed help from Linda or Jeremy or anyone. She needed out. The life she complained about to her therapist and her friends was bountiful. Safe. Predictable, but that's what she needed. She couldn't deal with the questions about her and her family and the unknown people who wouldn't stick around to answer them. She couldn't handle the total loss of agency over her own goddamned life.

Arin didn't touch the clothing, but she needed a shower. She walked across the small apartment and turned the water on. She didn't see any cameras but knew there wasn't anything she could do about them anyway. She peeled off the running gear she had donned what felt like days ago. But it was that same morning, in the cramped kitchen with Melanie, where she had downed her coffee and peaced out without a word. Her leggings and shirt were stiff and caked with rims of dried salt. She threw them on the floor. Next to the hamper, not in it.

She stepped under the cold water, not waiting for heat. The shock took her breathing from the uncontrolled gasps that preceded sobbing to the arrested inhale of frigid water. She forced herself to stand under it until the warm water blended in. She watched dust pool around her feet. She tasted salt as it cascaded over her lips.

Her friends made decisions for her. Her family did. Her coaches and teachers did, too. She'd thought that was a problem she needed to work out until she'd had her life ripped from under her, been imprisoned, and began to see how ludicrous her former complaints were.

All she needed was to do things for herself. Not just run for miles and think about it, but to tell people and act on it. Shit, she didn't even know what that would be. Travel, paint, start a track club for kids? Find something to actually do with her degree? She'd stayed in school to kick decisions like that off to her future self.

The water heated and she scrubbed herself until she couldn't go any deeper. Her body could get a fresh start if nothing else. The scab on her forearm reopened and fresh blood went down the drain before she realized it. She sat in the stall, hugged her knees, and let the water continue to inundate her and steam everything into obscurity. Whoever owned this place could afford the water bill.

She dried off and wrapped the towel to head to the bedroom. She did need clothes. She tried to push down images of Troy or some other stranger picking them off a rack and pushing the shopping cart through a busy checkout lane. Maybe her captors ordered them online to give themselves more separation from their task. She didn't want to know how long ago her new wardrobe had been purchased.

The enviable view from her window caught her eye as she passed. Her window? The window of her cell? The pane of unopenable glass that she was adjacent to but trapped behind? Perspective matters.

Epictetus lived as a slave and then in exile, but found contentment throughout it all and even shared his teachings with others. Those ancient bastards were tougher. She had a microwave and laundry service and nothing to teach anyone.

She dressed and went back to the central room. The living room. She sat and looked over the darkening cityscape and then picked through the stack of paperbacks. There was a mix of genres. Sci-fi, romance, mystery, biography. A couple of them she'd read. None seemed to be the type that would provide suggestions for how to break out of a high-rise prison cell.

A book about a family and their dog on a lake was in her hand when she stopped looking through the stack. That's what the cover showed, anyway, but she forgot the title as soon as she opened it. She glazed over the small black print before putting it down again.

She watched people below her, unaware of their freedom and just how tenuous it is. The visible corner of a park filled with people and then emptied and filled again. Lights went on and off in the adjacent but far too distant buildings. She couldn't see inside any of them, just like they couldn't see inside hers. She wouldn't know how to signal to them if she could. Like the forested houses on the distant hills she'd seen in the Berkshires, they were neighbors without contact.

There was no way to communicate. Her captors had made sure of that. *Captors,* plural. She assumed there was a team of asshole kidnappers and not just Troy.

The room outside had a computer station. But that was outside. She tested the door it was indeed locked from the other side, a blatant fire code violation. That and the disconnected pull station were major infractions. She could end up killing herself if she attempted to incinerate a fork in the microwave. Maybe she'd try that tomorrow.

The room was silent. No TV or radio to change that. Muffled sounds from the city below were the only external noises. She stopped counting how many times she reached for her phantom phone. Her new loungewear pants had deep pockets that remained empty. She paced and rubbed her arms and pulled at her hair.

It was like a sick, inverted zoo. She was caged, and no one was looking at her. It really wasn't like a zoo at all, then. Maybe she was Rapunzel and needed to grow fifty stories of hair. It was... it didn't matter. She had no one to share bad metaphors with. She went to the bedroom and curled under the sheets. There was no alarm to set and nothing to set it for.

21

DANE AND MELANIE closed down the local bar. Not as impressive in small-town Massachusetts as in downtown Manhattan, but the hour was still late at last bell. She recounted in detail her and Arin's persistent digging and desperate visits over the last week. She shared what she knew about a sketchy closed-door testimony Arin had just given for a federal court. One that relied on the ability she and Dane shared. The former politician she outed in the deepfake video was arrested later that day.

Holy hell, what were these latte-sipping chicks involved in? Dane admitted they were more formidable than his first impression had allowed. Melanie had a notebook she referenced a few times and seemed to leave nothing out. Dane listened in awe.

"I called her contact at the DOJ, too. Linda. No answer. Not the second or third or fourth time, either."

They walked along the quiet streets. Dane stopped where their paths home split. "So this older doctor guy, he's got the answers?"

"He jettisoned his life to avoid seeing me again. Makes a girl feel special. Arin never met him and all we have is his RV plate."

Dane perked up. "So you just got my name yesterday morning, right? From that government woman's *Thank You* card? And you got my dad's name at the same time, so you probably haven't stalked him yet? I'll save you the clicks. He works for the New York Transit Authority." He watched her light up. "I bet he could get EZ Pass logs. I don't know how this works, though. Should I call him?"

"Yes." Melanie smiled. Dane guessed it was the first time she smiled that day, and he was fortunate to be the one receiving it.

"Yes, you should call him. That's how this works."

DANE DREADED GOING TO THE bike shop the following morning. He had a legitimate job, one where he was happy enough. First in years, and now he had to demand time off. The shop had the race weekend coming up, and the owner was counting on him.

If he were them, he'd fire himself. But he'd never been in a hiring or firing position, so wasn't sure how that worked. *Family emergency* was a concept his father had used for getting out of work, and Dane supposed it was the one to use now. It was true enough. He delayed that meeting with a call to his father.

"I found your birth certificate," Warren said. "You should see it in the mail the next day or two. And the cash you left, I never thanked you for that, but I'll send it back when I'm caught up on a few bills."

"That was a gift. You need it more than I do." He paused. He wanted this conversation with his father to be about the new life he was starting. Away from the city and away from his past. Their past.

"What I do need from you is help with something that might be a little on the murky side of things. But I wouldn't ask if it wasn't important. And it has to do with Mom." His father was silent. "It's important. I can't go into it all now. Partly because I just got the full story last night in a bar and I'm not sure I remember it all. But I'll explain the next time I see you."

"About Gina? Dane, what do you need?"

"Dad, did you know someone named Marshall? He was a doctor. Last name Brock. He wrote mom's obituary."

Warren let the question linger for a moment before answering. "I had my problems, and we struggled with money and her headaches. And you, at times. But I never suspected her of stepping out on me. Is that what this guy did?" His voice wavered at the end.

"I don't think so. No, nothing like that. Was he one of her doctors?"

"Name isn't familiar. Did you talk to him?"

"No, that's the problem. He won't talk to anyone, and he fled as soon as someone asked him about her. I don't have time to recap what's going on right now, and it's not a phone type of conversation, but I need to find him and talk to him. Along with a new friend. I'm asking you to look up a tag for me." Another pause. "It's not only important, but it's urgent."

"Christ, Dane, what are you into up there?"

"I told you I moved out to get uninvolved in things. And I'm trying. But I'm not in trouble." He was excellent at bluffing. "And I have a full-time job at a bike shop." *For now.* "I'm good, Dad. I just need that little favor. Tollbooth logs. We need to know where he is."

"I don't have access to records like that."

"I'm sure you know who to ask, though. This guy knew Mom. And he wrote the only obituary she ever got. Anywhere." It hurt him to twist a little guilt toward his father. In their limited interaction since he left prison, Dane never blamed his father for his life's direction. That kind of thing was never helpful and never useful. Until it was.

"I'll see what I can do, Son. But I can't risk this job. And you'll need to tell me what the hell you're up to."

DANE ASKED THE SHOP OWNER for the rest of the day off. His boss accepted the family emergency angle but was clear that they needed him for the race over the weekend. Dane said that shouldn't be a problem and was excited to help. That was true, and he hoped to keep that promise. The little town had already grown on him.

Melanie offered her car to ride down to New Jersey to see his father. He didn't have a car or a license, so he accepted. She had a compact but smooth-riding SUV. Dark red with mandatory New England roof racks.

They arrived at his dad's place and spoke for hours. Warren remained quiet, his eyes soft and deep as he glanced at wall photos of his late wife. He showed concern about Arin missing. Dane knew the sentiment, which was why they were here. A family member resembling Gina appeared in his life, and had just as quickly disappeared.

They joined Warren on an evening walk with his new dog, a six-year-old rescue mutt who filled a gap in his life. Dane hadn't seen his father smile as he did at that dog for a long time, since before Gina started getting her headaches when Dane was a child. He'd been spending more time with his coworker Mandy, too.

Warren was content and seemed to find pockets of joy after a hard life. Dane wondered what his own life would have been with two happy parents.

Dane and Melanie had intended to return that evening, but after traffic delays on the trip down and long hours talking, they decided to return in the morning. He stayed on the pullout sofa in the apartment, and Melanie got a room at a hotel a few blocks away. He offered the reverse, but she declined, and he didn't want to make it more awkward.

She and Arin hadn't spelled out their relationship for him, and he didn't ask, but it was easier to assume that there was nothing for a single guy like him to be working on. His life was already more frantic than it should be—no need to throw more rocks in front of his wheels.

Melanie picked him up in the morning. They got breakfast, and she talked Dane into a quick drive-by of his old house in Brooklyn. He explained that going from here to there would involve crossing Manhattan and would not be quick. She insisted and he relented. Skills like that, she'll be a solid reporter.

They took Lincoln Tunnel into the city. His past dredged itself against his will, and revisiting those streets so soon after a nearly fatal flight away from them was verging on masochism.

He felt like an out-of-body tourist as he traveled his familiar haunts inside his new acquaintance's car. Sheltered from the smell and the noise and the city soundtrack. No one would recognize him inside a vehicle, and though running into people he knew in a city of millions was rare, Dane had crossed paths with a lot of them.

The gap of barely a week had done more than he realized. Not just the noise and the smell, but the hustle of the people and the grime of every surface and the determined and exhausted looks on faces. It all seemed more than he remembered.

How much of all of that energy was necessary? He'd had time to think and observe in his quiet new town up north—until those two beautiful young women showed up. He saw how much hustle was wasteful and how much the city itself pushed people to do more and be bigger and faster and tougher to some indeterminable end.

It's all he had known. He'd seen the frame of a different life during his brief stay at a foster home upstate, but he'd been young and filled that time as bored teenagers do, which didn't allow time for reflection. That time and his couple of trips to see his mother at the psych ward were his only prior departures from the city.

His whimsical goal of learning the subway and then the streets and finally the towers was construed from the racing heartbeat of the city and constrained by his limited exposure to anything else. He'd fulfilled that promise to himself, but the promise of leaving for good was proving elusive. He hid his frustration as Melanie pointed out city landmarks.

They passed a library he'd spent time in. He read a lot. More than most of his friends, at least. He'd pass idle hours in public libraries. They were free and warm in the winter and cool in the summer. He escaped to distant times and foreign lands—anywhere outside early aughts New York City. He wandered and dreamed but always stepped back onto his streets at the end.

He didn't check books out as libraries don't like group homes as a permanent address. Too many aren't returned, they had said, and the effort to track down kids like him was on the wrong side of the cost-benefit line. The effort outweighed the value of the target, which was his evaluation of cops and teachers and other kids when managing his decisions. And now his decisions had brought him back to the city.

But just for a day as a tourist. Low risk, and despite his displacement as he viewed his streets through the windshield of a college girl's car, he felt a sense of control he hadn't known in years. Control of his life, as he had options. He didn't feel a pull from the familiar steel and concrete. Partly because he could feel lingering pain from where his recent interactions with that very steel and concrete had driven him out, but he also knew his time here had done all it could to shape him, and he could leave, again, without regret.

Passing through was low risk, but he didn't know where to begin evaluating where he was with the two girls and the pursuit of this doctor who knew his mother. He was throwing down raises at an unknown table without knowing his hole cards.

This Arin chick didn't seem like one to simply go dark. Even if she said she would. He'd only spoken to her for a few hours, but he knew people like her, and they would be posting photos and live-streaming their transformative and amazing adventures within the hour.

She was bright. Stong. She had resources and money. Statistically, there's nothing she couldn't get out of. But statistics sometimes stayed in textbooks. The exceptions made the news. As the hours went on with no word from her, he saw Melanie fade. She grew quiet as she drove, looking at the cityscape without interest. Dane realized her request to visit his old home was a distraction to keep her from the fact that the person in the passenger seat wasn't Arin.

He pointed out a few landmarks from notable events from his youth, but her questions were minimal and only came from rote journalistic instincts. He let the silence inside the car grow. The familiar din of the city carried on.

Dane's instincts were still in place, though. They were a few blocks from leaving Manhattan when he directed Melanie to ignore her GPS and take an alternate route. After a few turns, she looked at him in question.

He saw her expression match his own, and although he didn't believe she knew why, her knuckles whitened on the wheel.

Dane pointed out which car was following them.

22

"THE BEIGE CAR** with the dark windows?" Melanie asked as she spent too long looking in her mirrors while approaching the next cross street. When biking, Dane had swerved from drivers like her. He refrained from comment. "Are you sure?"

"You took three left turns and he followed. No one does that by mistake. But look—no, keep your eyes on the road—he's turning away now. He knows we've made him."

On a bike or on foot, alone, Dane could flee anyone. But he was a passenger in a car driven by someone who'd probably never fled or chased anyone. Might as well ask. "Have you ever had to outrun another car?"

Her expression said no.

"I don't see him now," Dane noted. "Any idea who he was?" He didn't recall any characters from their story that fit this guy's description. Late twenties, short dark hair, clean shaven. Fit as a movie star but a hard stare that showed he wasn't acting.

"I didn't get a good look. Happend to be driving through midtown at the moment and didn't have a free eye. He must have been tracking us. These streets are a rat maze, and I was already jumpy."

"I noticed," Dane replied, trying to put himself in her place. "If he was tracking you—or me—then why bother following us? Maybe he lost us in the tunnel awhile ago and was getting reconnected. Could have our phones or maybe the car. Main question—what does he want? If they already have Arin..."

"Stop, Dane. I can't think about that. I need a place to get out. Need air."

"I don't know if leaving the car is a good idea." He'd rather be on foot as well but didn't know who was after them. And didn't know Melanie's capabilities well enough to make that call. The car's mobility might be safer, but this girl was tough enough to adapt.

"Fuck me, there he is!" She yelled and swerved right, nearly cutting off a biker. If the biker gave the response Dane would have, he missed it as they sped on. The driver had circled around a block and was in oncoming traffic when Melanie spotted him. She sped up and took another tight corner.

"This guy didn't give up," Dane said, giving a needless update. "I'm turning off my phone. Give me yours." She gestured at the center console, but her eyes didn't leave the road. She took two more turns and found a relatively empty stretch of Lexington Avenue. She gunned through a few blocks and then swerved west. The driver reappeared a block behind them.

Dane scrambled to think of a hole they could find. Car-sized holes are harder to find, and this guy seemed to know the city as well as he did. Melanie spun through a few more turns but couldn't lose him. The driver was only two cars back.

They needed to go on foot. He needed to convince Melanie to ditch the car to lose this guy. He'd earned a name by then, and Dane, constricted to the useless passenger seat, had time to give him one. From the brief glances they'd gotten, he was driven, focused, and emotionless. Military type, for sure. In other circumstances, he would have been impressed. He was impressed, really, and he hoped the guy's abilities stopped at the wheel. Wishful thinking, but he doubted it. He'd call him *Limit* in hopes that he had one.

He looked at Melanie. She was good under pressure—rugged, grim. He noticed a fierceness under her ballcap and glasses he hadn't seen before. Old books called women handsome. That described Melanie.

He turned forward and resumed looking for a way out. *Got it.* He started giving directions to his happy hour parking garage. The place with the open top level where he'd decided to become a bike messenger years before. He knew the gate guys, and if Melanie got enough of a lead, they could disappear before Limit turned the corner. If he did see them, they'd rush to the top level and ditch the car. Park it sideways and block this son of a bitch in the lower levels. He had the code for the rooftop stairwell, and one of the floors connected to an office building. Which would lead to another street exit and then to wherever they'd decide to hole up.

He guided Melanie through a few turns to carve out more breathing room, but Limit was better. Dane saw sweat beading under Melanie's cap as she pushed where she could. Her shoulders hunched and her breath quickened. She was learning on the fly, and he wasn't a driver. Four wheels were twice what he wanted.

Dane snapped his attention forward as a red light and steady cross traffic barred their way.

"Hold on!" Melanie's voice pitched high as she wrenched the wheel, screeching out a 180-degree turn that cut two lanes and brought them halfway up the opposite sidewalk. Crazy chick nearly clipped a news cart. Horns blared and middle fingers flew. A bigger car would have crushed someone or hit the adjacent building, but she straightened out and sent the gas pedal home—almost comically with her leg straight and her back arched—and peeled out in the opposite direction.

They both glared into the window of their pursuer's car as they passed. Dane wasn't sure if he or Limit was more shocked.

"That dick runner!" Melanie yelled. She apparently recognized the driver now now. Dane would ask later.

The sedan was locked inside a row of cars patiently awaiting the light. The sidewalk was dotted with trees. He was stuck and they were free.

Until he plowed aside the inconvenient motorists next to him. He reversed his vehicle between two cars, scraping and grinding them both askew and earning himself his own fingers and horns. Dane turned and watched through the back window. He didn't know reverse gears had power like that.

They were under pursuit once more. Melanie visibly shook now, and Dane couldn't claim his nerves were anywhere near settled.

Cars were coffins. He needed a bike. Or feet.

They got back on course to the garage, and she focused enough to navigate. Limit kept pace. She gunned toward a red light at the next intersection. Dane felt his throat constrict as the familiar mental pang kicked in. The one that told him something warm was approaching, fast, just out of view.

He yelled for her to stop, but not in time. An ambulance popped out from the cross street. Both vehicles swerved, neither successfully.

"Shit!shit!shit!" Melanie yelled as she threw her meager body-weight into the turn. The car lifted onto two wheels. *Not what I meant by wanting to be on two wheels*, Dane thought in the slowed-down time that exists during a crash. The ambulance swerved the other way, but not enough.

The two vehicles collided and the SUV careened off the heavier ambulance.

Their world blew asunder as the car tipped to the driver's side and skidded along the street until it slammed into a post.

Airbags and violent scraping and shattered glass assaulted them.

Dane punched down his airbags and clawed at his seatbelt to get free. He kicked open his door and then pulled Melanie up through his side, now on top. Blood ran down her face. He dragged her across the street past gaping onlookers.

They ran. This was too familiar. Dane's mind clicked into street mode. He knew when people and cars were around the corner. He knew how to flee.

They sprinted around a few blocks, her huffing and him searching. And huffing as well. He pulled her along and kept her from swinging into anything that would slow them down.

He didn't look back. He didn't want to know if they were clear yet. He was pretty sure he knew that answer.

They sprung through the door of a deli. He knew the owner and got help with a towel and water to clean the cut on Melanie's head. She'd lost her cap, but her glasses were still intact, if a little skewed. Dane hunted for bandaids until he saw Limit running toward them from the other side of the street. Not surprising—but the sight kick-started his nerves again. He lept to the deli door and locked it. Their eyes met again before he fled out the back door, grabbing his lovely but stunned and bleeding companion as he went.

"Do you still have your phone?" Dane panted as they darted down another street. A small dog park bordered their path. "Throw it over there."

She tossed her phone into the park. It probably landed in dog shit. She was moving on pure adrenaline, he could see, and would need to rest before she went into shock. He pulled her across the street into a clothing store and climbed to the second-level mezzanine. Windows overlooked the park.

They waited. A moment later, Limit arrived on the corner. He looked at his phone, then surveyed the area. He was calm—not panting like they were. Not frantic. He walked along the fence and scanned the area.

"It was your phone. You were tagged."

"His name is Troy," Melanie blurted out between gasps. "It was him and his mother on that boat that blew up. Also, he was a runner near campus—that's where I saw him first. Feels like forever ago. Nearly ran us over. That was him."

"He needed to get close. Proximity hacking. Must have dumped a tracking program on your phone. Maybe the others, too, but I'm not sure how that works." Dane gripped the second-story railing they were standing behind. A siren blared below them as a patrol car sped toward the crash scene. More sirens sounded in the distance.

"My car, it's gone—I just fled the scene of the accident," Melanie whispered, her face ashen. She swayed as the terror of the past few moments caught up. He needed to help her. And himself. One way. One option.

"Go." He held her eyes, willing her to understand.

She didn't hear him. Or didn't understand. He needed to explain his plan. As soon as he had one. He turned back toward the park and his heart skipped. Limit—Troy—was standing in the park, holding her phone. Looking directly at them through the storefront window.

Melanie looked at her feet and tried to catch her breath. She hadn't seen him. Yet. That might push her over the edge, and he knew she was done with running. Limit knew that, too.

It was a standoff. He spoke to her without breaking eye contact with Troy.

"Listen. He wants me. Not you. He had you pinned and could have gotten to you anytime. Like Arin, but he didn't. He didn't need to chase someone he was tracking, but he wasn't tracking me. Doesn't know who I am but is tearing up the city to find out. I'll let him. But you need to go back to your car."

She looked up and shrieked when she saw Troy, startling the shoppers around them. Troy tensed. He was ready to run if they did, but the standoff held.

"Walk to your car. Talk to the cops. Describe a guy who looks like me who jumped into your passenger seat and forced you to drive away. You were trying to escape and crashed. You ran and lost him. Got it?"

She nodded.

"Girl like you, they'll believe it. Now repeat back to me where you'll go."

"To my car." Her voice was thin. Eyes unfocused. She wouldn't need to convince the responding officers she was traumatized.

"I'll find you later. Call my father."

He left her on the balcony as he spun and bounded down the shop stairs three at a time. Breaking the standoff, he caught a moment's hesitation from Troy. He hadn't expected them to split. Dane forced his hand—called his bluff—but he hoped to hell he'd read him right. If not, he had just left a girl in shock to be freely abducted.

He always said that the worst things never happen, but sometimes they do. That would be the case if he were wrong. He would walk to the Brooklyn Bridge and surrender what remained of himself to the filth of the East River.

He darted out of the shop and for the first time in his life was relieved to find himself under full pursuit.

23

ARIN WOKE TO a grumbling, unsettled belly. She hadn't eaten anything since the sandwich her captor had ordered from the out of bounds diner the day before. She wasn't sure she would have held much down once she'd been escorted to her cell. She located and assembled the two ingredients needed for a bowl of granola and milk, found a terrible impression of coffee in the form of plastic pods, filled a mug anyway, and moved to the sofa with the enviable view.

Tiny cars and tinier people scuttled about in the early sunlight below her as the city woke up. She finished breakfast and gave herself enough space for her yoga practice. She'd already eaten—not ideal—but she could make exceptions.

What she couldn't do and what she craved now more than she ever had before was to run. Let her legs pump through the glory of a long, steady stride over endless miles with no destination nor time constraint. She watched the joggers below and pointed a finger gun at each one. *Namaste,* bitches.

She settled onto the open carpet and drew through her poses and envisioned herself on a weekend getaway to the city. Which meant the only element of her situation to repress was the locked door.

And lack of communication.

And privacy.

The more she pushed herself, the easier it was to let everything else fade back. She churned through the routine and transitioned into push-ups and sit-ups and lunges until she was panting, sweaty and sore.

She showered again, which required another set of fresh clothing. She used the hamper this time. After changing, she turned off the lights, drew the curtains, and reassessed her tower prison.

She hadn't had much time to practice, but with an informed understanding of what her eyes were capable of, she felt she could glean a little bit of signal from the influx of light, or noise, her brain was constantly processing. That, or she was trying hard enough to imagine things that weren't there. Either way, she couldn't think of a better way to occupy her time.

She looked around at the walls and ceiling. She knew where the lights were, and even off, they would still be warm. LEDs lose heat quickly, but she concentrated as she looked toward and away from them. She may have been imagining—or trying too hard—but she felt she could recognize that little flag in her mind.

With the kids getting their temp checks and the cup of tea at the cafe, she didn't think about what she was seeing. She knew when something was different and went by an instinct she had all along. Now that she understood some of what was happening, noticing those anomalies was harder.

She practiced meditation, being that type of girl. Occasionally practiced meditation, being honest. That process brings the flurry of random monkey-mind thoughts to the surface, making focusing on a mantra or a clear mind even harder than before. This felt similar. Now that she was working to pull that signal from the noise, she was more aware of the rest of the noise that got in the way.

That's why they call things like this practice. She had time—and none of those unhelpful everyday distractions someone not imprisoned would need to deal with.

She perceived something lining the walls. Likely electrical wires or hot water pipes that shed their heat outward. She walked to the bathroom where she knew the water pipes would be and saw similar, but not identical, patterns.

Unless she was trying too hard again. She looked at the ceilings in each room. She detected something in opposite corners of the middle room but nothing leading to or from them. She felt a headache building and turned the lights back on.

She opened the drapes and made a cup of tea. She'd need to have a word with someone about the coffee. This was New York City, for Christ's sake. It's got to be hard to find coffee that bad.

She settled into the sofa to give the book about the family on the lake another try. After a moment, she peeked up into the corner. She had tried to be discreet earlier but needed to know. There it was, a little shiny bulb behind the molding, nearly blending in. She stood, stretched, and saw the other one in the opposite corner. She hadn't seen any in the bathroom or bedroom. She supposed she should be relieved by that. It was a hollow consolation.

ARIN JUMPED AT A KNOCK on the door behind her and nearly dropped her book. She was a few chapters in and was eager to learn if the teenage daughter's boyfriend would show up and disrupt the family's plans with the charter boat. They hadn't reserved enough seats for the family plus him. It was that kind of high-stakes drama that she nearly dropped to the floor.

She didn't respond to the knock. She couldn't open the door if she wanted to. Which, of course, she wanted to. The knock came again, and a male voice—older, not Troy—came through.

"Miss Coppertree, I'll open the door unless you need me to wait a moment."

They had live video and would know she wasn't in the bathroom or sleeping. She was tempted to give a come-on-in wave but was banking on the value of concealing information. She regretted imparting her knowledge that she knew Troy's name the day before and was trying to learn prisoner strategy as she went.

"I'm here," she mumbled while standing up. She faced the door, ready for... ready for nothing. She had no idea. A middle-aged man, portly and balding, entered her cell. He wheeled a small bag behind him. Carry-on sized. Did he fly here?

Seeing the room outside her door sent an unexpected jolt. She'd been contained—in ostensible comfort—for less than twenty-four hours, but simply seeing the waiting room shocked her. It was a new realm. One door closer to freedom. And there was a computer. There was hope—she didn't expect that. Again, perspective, and its viscissitudes.

Seeing that open door filled her with a hope she knew would be shattered as soon as it closed again. She studied Greeks like Epictetus and thought she understood and even tried to practice some of those teachings. To not rest one's well-being on aspects beyond control. But that open door swung her.

The man was alone. She was nearly offended that Troy or a burly guy in riot gear wasn't standing behind him. This guy looked like he spent more time in a chair than out of one. She could outrun him with her feet bound. Were they testing her? The next door would be locked and staffed with someone more formidable, she assumed. She remained stationary. Silent.

"I'm going to need you to sit down for a few moments."

He seemed nervous. *Why?* He opened his case, and she saw a neat collection of medical devices and instruments. Like an old-time traveling doctor doing house visits.

"I assume you haven't fasted today?"

She glared at him. He recoiled.

"I... I'll assume not, then." He laid out a syringe, a rack of small tubes, and some cotton pads and tape. His hands trembled. "That's not a problem. I'll make a note."

Was this shaky old guy going to draw blood? Her arm tensed at the thought. Maybe she should stop scaring him with dire facial expressions. Or go the other way—she could push him over and try to walk out. Or grab that scalpal she saw in his bag and take him hostage. Stroll outside and down the elevator and into the street with the blade at his jugular. She let that fantasy play out for a healthy moment.

"Where's the medical authorization form?" she asked. They were her first words since the traveling doctor entered. She was loud and direct. The guy jumped and nearly dropped the specimen collection bags he was holding.

"Uh... I'm here to get some samples. I'm not supposed to discuss anything else."

"Who do you work for? What do you need from me?"

He wouldn't meet her eyes. "I'm here for samples. That's all." He tried to restore some confidence to his voice. "Please. I'll be gone as soon as I'm done."

He looked up and met her eyes. His brow furrowed a little. It may have been genuine sympathy. Was he under their control as well? A fellow prisoner, but one who could walk out?

She lowered her voice to test him. "Will I leave when we're done?"

He blinked, averted his gaze again, and returned to his prep work.

"You know that I'm being held here, right?" She hadn't said that out loud, and her breath caught. "Look at me."

He did, briefly, then returned to his work. She couldn't get any more out of him. He started with an eye exam and then took a saliva sample. By then, his hands were more settled, and she wasn't quite as worried about him bleeding her out during a series of blood samples.

Arin closed her eyes and willed herself away. The intrusion clawed away her grip on the remaining strands of herself.

Was it worse than the bras and underwear? Sickening violations all, but this was a different realm. It was a further loss of control and bodily autonomy that all drained together into a murky pool of despair. When he left and closed the door behind him, she showered again. She did her best to strain the hot water budget.

HER WINDOW FRAMED THE BUSY city beyond like a museum display. Contrived but inaccessible examples of life, curated for her viewing pleasure. She envisioned vicarious freedom through those below her—unconcerned and unaware as they scampered about, hauling briefcases and guitars and groceries on their chosen paths.

She settled back into her book about the family by the lake. The boyfriend didn't show up, and this must have been before social media and cell phones because not showing up was tantamount to breaking up. At least for that summer. The young girl got over it, though. She claimed she needed repeat visits to the outfitter in town for gear, which the long-haired boy behind the counter was happy not only to supply and help her try on but also to provide thorough instruction. Arin hadn't read a book that sappy for years but was getting into it.

Flashing lights and dull sirens permeated the window of her lofty cell. Not unusual, but she felt compelled to see if someone else was having a worse day than she was. Perspective matters.

She watched an ambulance and a pair of patrol cars block off an intersection. No, two ambulances. One responding and one that seemed to be involved in the crash. Another vehicle showed her its underbelly as it lay on its side. Rough accident, but she didn't see anyone being pulled from the vehicle or otherwise treated. Odd. Even if the driver were ok, they'd be evaluated for shock. Perhaps that happened already. Her distance was too great for detail. But no gurneys there. No inbound medivac flights.

She watched until a tow truck entered the scene, and the driver took steps to right the vehicle. The winch tipped it back onto four wheels, and it bounced before settling, glittering the road with shattered glass and hanging deflated airbags out of the windows. She almost didn't recognize it until she saw the roof racks.

Melanie had told her recently—quite recently, but she wasn't in a state to measure time—that they were beyond coincidences. Her car's model and color were common enough that Arin might have convinced herself this wasn't the same vehicle she'd traveled countless miles in.

But she dropped to her knees and her breath cut short when she saw the racks. She clawed—slowly at first—against the window.

"Mel," she croaked, her voice breaking as her eyes blurred and the walls constricted around her.

24

DANE TOLD HIMSELF he could lose Troy. *Limit.* He'd do his damnedest to find his.

With Melanie and her crash scene behind him, he sprinted away, hoping his risk evaluation held. He'd given Melanie a chance to escape, but Troy was there, tracking each turn and gaining. Quickly.

He swerved through a group of shoppers and around a construction barricade. His lungs burned. The streets blurred. He darted through an intersection and pushed off the hood of a cab that braked and swerved the wrong way. All he accomplished was clearing a path through the crowd for Troy to follow, unimpeded.

To snag any real shot at getting away, Dane needed to change the rules. A few blocks away and his pursuer had closed half the distance between them. He saw a young couple getting rental bikes from the ubiquitous kiosks that line the midtown sidewalks.

He shouted to get their attention as he closed in, then snatched the bike from the girl and left them with a hasty but sincere apology. As unchivalrous as it goes, but the boyfriend was bigger and might give Troy a little more hassle when he tried to take his bike. And judging from the stream of profanity that followed him down the sidewalk, the affronted boyfriend was ready to give all the hassle he had. Let them sort it out. Dane churned away.

The sorting happened too quickly. He glanced back and watched Troy strong-arm the puffed-chest guy to the side and grab the handlebars with his free hand in one fluid motion. He barely slowed as he mounted the rental bike and continued to close the gap.

The guy was relentless, and Dane grew worried. Grew very short of breath. The rental bikes were clunky and poorly maintained, but he ripped around blocks and across a park, scattering birds and fallen leaves.

He had no destination. Hadn't thought that far ahead. Should have lost the asshole by then.

But if he could keep this guy occupied long enough, Dane thought, Melanie would have time to get to the cops. Her story—if she stuck to it—would get her the help that comes with female victimhood. Damned sure a female looking like her. The fabricated story about Dane being the carjacker would pass the sniff test. They could worry about later, later.

And Dane wanted a chance to talk to Troy. The guy didn't look like the sharing type—he could recognize that—but anything he could get would shed light on what these girls were involved with.

And Arin. He couldn't lose Troy before he asked him where she was. But he needed to keep him running for Melanie's safety. He had to get to familiar ground.

Underground.

He wasn't gaining distance on wheels. Wasn't losing much, either, but Troy would win on stamina. Dane spun toward the nearest subway entrance and clattered down the risers and toward the turnstiles.

Dane's mood sang as he saw his pursuer bail on the lower steps and sail ass over handlebars. Then his relief turned sour as the machine of a guy tucked into a recovery roll and sprang up again, barely losing momentum. He was now on foot, but Dane didn't waste time heaving a bike over the turnstiles. He jumped them—he hadn't had a subway card since he left the city—and pumped desperately, willing his legs to keep pace with his growing panic.

Troy hopped the turnstile behind him. The station was quiet, and the few waiting passengers barely looked up from their phones as they shifted to avoid the two sprinters.

The station was also small, and Dane was running out of platform. He could only go lower.

He reached the end and bounded down to track level. Foul air blew against him as he plunged forward. The dusty dark swallowed him whole, and he heard heavy shoes hit the gravel behind him.

Lights flickered as he plunged down the tunnel, hugging the wall to seek stable footing. Dane knew to avoid the third rail, and so did Troy. Hidden pipes and wayward planks and broken concrete would end the chase as soon as a wayward foot found them, but somehow none did.

Troy's pace was quicker than Dane's on open sidewalks, and the difference was starker over the treacherous footing and inconsistent lighting. He was paces behind. Dane knew he wouldn't make it to the next station. His lungs sucked in filth and burned for fresh oxygen.

He needed an out. He saw one.

A slight alcove jutted ahead on the opposite side of the track, and Dane lunged for it. Maintenance access doors were rarely locked. Too many guys forget their keys, and no one wants to trudge back to their truck. He pushed out a final sprint and pulled at the door.

Locked. *Shit.*

Probably the only locked door on the line, and that's the one he found. But most doors had a spare key tucked somewhere nearby. He ran his fingers over the frame but came away with nothing besides a nicked finger from a poorly welded seam.

His panic swelled. The chase would end here. He picked up a loose brick to turn and fight.

A glint behind the brick caught his eye.

Dane lunged and sent the brick flying into Troy's path. Before seeing if the throw connected, he turned and grabbed the key hidden behind the brick. The door shrieked as he tore it open and jumped through, yanking the handle and turning with momentum to slam it closed.

A pincer hand clamped his arm. He spun to brace his feet against the door frame, straining to pull the door closed against the intruding hand. The arm didn't relent. The grip scorched, digging into the meat of his bicep.

Troy braced himself chest-deep into the doorframe and didn't budge. His grip was unreal, and Dane strained to hold the door handle. Sitting in the filth of the access doorway, he needed both legs and his one free hand to hold his stance.

He would lose his balance and be pulled outward toward the tracks if he tried to thrash the intruding arm away. For Troy's part, he was wedged into a steel door frame. Dane hoped he was equally low on options.

They locked eyes. Dane had found his pursuer's limit and had his chance to talk. In ragged breaths and between coughs.

"Where is she?" He snarled. He didn't specify which *she* he meant, but he didn't need to.

"Safe." His breath was short as well, but he hid it better.

"Why do you need her?"

"Come. I'll show you. Open the door and we'll walk out. I don't need to hurt you."

Dane strained and pulled the door tighter to the frame. Troy winced and coughed. More of a choke with his ribcage compressed. He seemed to accept the answer.

A familiar rumble echoed down the tunnel. A light beam lit up Dane's grimacing face through the narrow doorframe. Dust swirled in the light as he yelled through gritted teeth.

"Why? What is she to you?" His voice carried over the sound of the approaching train.

"She's a solution to an old problem. She can help us." Troy turned to look at the oncoming train, then back to Dane. "So can you!"

Dane squinted against it all. *What?*

Seconds remained until the train reached them. Troy could press against the wall and stay clear of the unyielding steel beast. If Dane didn't interfere, and if Troy were in control. But one push from Dane and Troy would be another dismembered body on the tracks. Dane needed him alive. And despite it all, he didn't want his return to the city to end with another subway victim.

Or, Dane realized, Troy could pivot, rip him from the doorway, and whip him downward into the passing cars. Risk off the charts for both of them, and they both knew it.

The train approached. It didn't slow, meaning the motorman hadn't seen them—not that there was time now to make a difference. Dane knew stopping distances well.

The lights of the train brightened through the crack of the door. They illuminated grime and sweat and exasperation in a harsh band on Dane's face. He saw blood covering the side of Troy's face, which shadows had concealed. His brick must have flown true and given him that invaluable extra second.

The train reached them.

"You won't find her again!" Troy yelled, then the acute pain on Dane's arm vanished.

Troy's arm flashed away into the tunnel. The door slammed shut as Dane's coiled energy released. In the last glimpse before the steel door closed and separated them, he saw Troy career off the side of the train.

Dane tumbled back into a heap of dust and discarded pipes. Swirling and stumbling, he fled up the nearest stairs and shouldered open another door. He emerged into the far end of another station, startling the passengers who bothered to look up from their phones. He raced on what remained of his endorphin load through the exit turnstiles and up to street level.

Sunlight beamed and assaulted his constricted pupils. He gulped crisp fall air deep into his burning lungs. He would pass out if he stopped, so he didn't. A few more blocks. A few more corners.

He slowed to a walk as his lungs went flat and his legs went to rubber, then slumped against the side of a building. Checked for wounds. A few scrapes and what would become ugly purple bruises on his bicep—that grip was something else—but he'd clean up all right. He'd seen worse. The worst never happened.

Logistically, though, he was a disaster. He'd lost Melanie and was no closer to finding Arin. No phone. No ride. No bike. His face was probably on NYPD alerts already, either from street cameras or from Melanie's description.

He was working on his planning-ahead skills, and that day gave him plenty of practice. He'd told Melanie to describe himself as a carjacker for two reasons. First, the cameras. Her story had to seem realistic, or the cops wouldn't buy it. Second, he wasn't sure if she could have fabricated a fake story in her state of panic.

So he couldn't walk into a cop shop and ask about her. He still had his wallet, though. *Right?* He patted his back pocket and felt the familiar wedge. He looked around and let a low, pained chuckle escape when he realized where he'd ended up.

He walked across the street and through the swinging double doors of the *Red Rooster*.

THE HOUR WAS THE QUIET one that preceded happy hour when suited asses were still warming plush office chairs and the day drinkers had gone off to nap or do whatever they do. The barkeep—with his long red beard—froze when he saw Dane.

"Why, hello. Are you bringing trouble with you this time?"

"No. I left it a few blocks away. Ignore the dirt." Dane splayed his hand on the polished wood. "I never thanked you for stepping in. You saved me." He tilted his head and gave him a scolding look. "You did crack my bike in half, though."

"I assume you can afford another one. Unless you blew through all that already." He raised a bushy red eyebrow.

"No. Tried to leave the city. Start fresh. But would you believe it, here the fuck I sit." He scanned the shelves behind the bar and found a squat bottle to point at. "Double, please."

He got his drink and watched the mirror for passers-by on the street outside. If Troy somehow managed to find him here, though, Dane would buy the bastard a drink and then let him walk him out to wherever the hell he wanted to take him. That's all he'd be worth.

The double of Knob Creek burned and soothed and calmed. His heart rate descended from orbit level to somewhere in the mere stratosphere.

"I had to answer some questions about that night," the barkeep allowed. "Not sure I'm in the clear from the altercation yet, and any other activities that may have been going on," he said as he lifted his eyes toward the second floor, "are halted. Attention from the law

176

is piss on a nice fire. People don't gather." The barkeep crossed his arms and looked at Dane. "I like you, kid, wouldn't have stepped out if I didn't. But you still look like the kind of trouble I don't need any more of."

Dane didn't have a good response, so didn't offer any.

He used the bar phone to call his father. Warren said he hadn't heard from Melanie, but would pass along a message. Dane didn't have a message to give. He needed to think. He asked the barkeep if he'd seen local news about a crash that afternoon.

"Saw something. Car rolled against an ambulance? That was you? Shit, kid, you ok?"

Dane raised his tumbler in response.

"They didn't report any injuries but were looking for the driver. You sure you're not bringing more trouble my way?" His fingers drummed on the bar.

"I'm not," Dane replied. "The driver was—per the news, that is—a woman with a Red Sox cap and glasses. Mid 20's, dark hair."

"Huh. Didn't catch that detail on the news. I hope she's ok."

Dane nodded with mutual hope and swirled his drink for a moment. He ran back his brief exchange of words with Troy. Something about what the guy had said just before his hasty retreat back into the tunnel irked him.

Troy said he'd never find her again. The thing is, he'd never found her in the first place. He hadn't even lost her—nor had Melanie, not really. Is that what Troy was saying? He seemed to be the type that didn't say much at all, and when he did, he chose his words carefully. Like himself.

He let that thought stew as he looked up at the TV mounted above the far end of the bar. The news had moved on from local topics to national affairs. He tuned it out as he attempted to sort out what little he knew over slow sips of whiskey.

He needed to make some assumptions. First, he had to assume that Troy had taken Arin the morning before. Him or someone he works with. Second, he'd been tracking Melanie but not himself. If he were tracking her, there was no need to follow her. But she was driving with someone unknown. Himself.

So what? There are a thousand reasons people travel together. Troy wouldn't risk his life for a random guy who might be no more than a ride-share. Did he know he was related to Arin? That he was like her?

He'd barely met the girls and hadn't shared much from his past. If Troy or someone else was eavesdropping, what would they have heard? The bike shop was closed when they met and shared burritos. The bar where he'd spoken to Melanie the day before was nearly empty. By then, Arin had disappeared. It didn't make sense.

He downed his drink and tapped the bar for another. Then perked up.

Arin.

They—Troy and his gang—were holding her somewhere, and it was vital that she stay there. What would alert them to send their task guy after a driver they were already tracking? What if that driver were nearing their valuable hostage? And transporting an unknown passenger?

Troy suspected a rescue attempt. He saw Dane and Melanie as an urgent threat. That meant one thing.

Arin was in the city.

25

ARIN RAKED HER fingernails against the unyielding windowpane as she watched what remained of Melanie's loyal ride winched onto a flatbed truck. The carpet bit into her knees as she rocked back and forth. Her eyes burned hot.

Pedestrians below gawked but walked along. Police took statements. Arin didn't sense an urgency on the scene that would surround a critical victim. So Melanie wasn't there.

Or was already... no, even in that unthinkable case, EMTs would rush the patient to a hospital. The best trauma care centers in the world were within screaming distance. Maybe she was already there. The questions ripped through her.

The people at the scene were mere specs, but she watched them all. The witnesses and their statements. The police photographer and the tire mark expert. The streets were loaded with surveillance cameras already, but protocol rules the day. Sanitation arrived and cleared out the glass, plastic, and twisted bits of memory.

Hours passed. The scene devolved until the last of the emergency personnel left, and the crowds seeped back in. Cold humanity filled the void. The machine churned on. An inconvenient hiccup in the day of the city that didn't stop. She watched it all.

She sat back on the floor and held her head. She needed recovery. She needed a plan—anything—to get out.

She needed Melanie.

She needed a distraction. She needed to eat. The fridge and cabinets were stocked well enough for a decent chicken and pasta dinner. Fresh basil and a chunk of good parmesan. Red wine vinegar to marinate the chicken and crushed pine nuts to crust it. Her gracious hosts had even stocked a few bottles of wine. She ate enough for herself and for Melanie twice over and didn't bother recorking the wine bottle.

Arin paced the confines of her three-roomed cell. Melanie was hurt. Or lost. Or taken, like herself. She needed to get out, and not just for her own sake anymore.

The walls encroached further each time she paced between them. She was imprisoned and under constant surveillance. No communication. No way to signal for help that wouldn't alert her captors first. No knowledge of why she was there or for how long.

The wine flowed, the couch beckoned, and she settled into the novel about the family at the lake. She reread the same page half a dozen times before she could focus, but she needed the escape.

In the story, the long-haired boy from the outfitters invites the young protagonist on a moonlit canoe trip through the marshes beyond the lake. The girl has never been on a moonlit canoe trip and isn't certain what happens on such an outing but spends most of her afternoon imagining—in vivid detail—what types of things might happen.

So, when her parents tell her she needs to stay in the cabin to babysit her little brother while they go to an art show that evening, she flips and storms off. She eventually capitulates and agrees to stay home.

Arin almost laughed when the teenage character described the cabin walls closing in on her. Where she was a prisoner and her parents were villainous wardens forcing her to stay home. But the girl sees a sign hung in the kitchen that reads *Home is Where the Lake is,* so she leaves her brother with food and games and escapes her unbearable prison to meet her crush—consequences be damned. The young heroine was an inspiration.

Arin continued reading and picking at her dinner as the sun went down, then moved to the kitchen to clean up. As if she were expecting guests. She'd burn the place when she could, but she still lived there. For now.

As she put the cookware away, she held the bottle of vinegar for a moment. She looked over toward what she called the barely-living room. Toward the window and the fading dusk which somewhere held Melanie.

The wind picked up, whistling as it channeled through the labyrinth of skyscrapers.

She turned off the lights and stood at the window, gazing out from the darkness of her cell and observing the specs of light that filled her view. Little squares of life dotted the nearby towers as others enjoyed their evening. Or didn't enjoy their evening, as is their choice. She had that choice, too, she knew.

She placed a hand on the window and felt the cold of the blustery wind seep through. She pushed against it. Pounded around the edges. Scanned the corners and picked at the seal. Discretely. She didn't know how much the cameras could pick up in the dark.

Herself, though, she knew what her eyes could do. She twisted a strand of hair and looked back toward the kitchen.

ARIN WOKE TO THE SOUND of the lock releasing on the door. The living room door, her path out of this place. Without a clock, she didn't know how long she'd been asleep, but the cavity in her consciousness told her it hadn't been long enough. She shook herself awake and threw on clothes. She grabbed the paring knife she'd put behind her bedside lamp.

"I'm coming in," a voice snapped. "Get dressed."

Despite the paucity of words she'd heard him speak, she knew that voice well. Troy hustled into the room. She recoiled at his appearance. His face and hair were matted with blood. His clothes were filthy. He reeked of grime and sweat. He looked like he'd been hit by a train.

Arin took no delight in his condition. He looked exhausted and angry, and she didn't relish him taking that out on her. He threw an empty duffel bag her way.

"Clothes. Shoes. Grab them all. Hurry!"

She stumbled back into the bedroom as adrenaline pierced her sleep fog. She gathered what clothes she could. The rest were in the hamper. She came out to find Troy sitting on the couch and rubbing his arm. Oil smears and blood and raw scrapes—it all looked horrific. He held the dreaded ankle cuff in his other hand, extended in her direction.

His jacket lay on the book table next to the couch. Her mind fluttered when she looked at a bulge in the outer pocket. Something in there was warm. She knew how to read those signals now. It could be keys. She put everything on the hope that it wasn't.

"Put the knife down. Don't be stupid." He delivered his command with an exhausted resignation as if he were disappointed she'd attempted something so banal.

Arin looked down and realized the handle had shifted and was protruding from the bag's side pocket. She pulled it out and dropped it by the window. She demanded answers before she complied with anything else, and she knew the first question to ask. "Is she ok?"

Troy looked up in question, then at the window. After a flash of realization, he nodded. That told her he hadn't been watching the camera feeds. She needed every advantage, and that was a strong one.

"What did you do with her?" Arin snarled. She didn't expect an answer but needed time. She stood in front of him, duffel in hand. His only response was to hold up the cuff—unshackled and ready to strangle her ankle along with her chance at freedom.

She was awake now. Adrenaline and anger and more than a little wine coursed through her. He was injured. Depleted, sitting on the couch. She didn't care why. Decisions be damned—she needed to act.

Be the girl at the lake and make shit happen.

She threw the duffel bag in his face, then spun and mule-kicked him in the chest. Both he and the couch tipped backward, and he flailed his arms to brace for the fall. The back of his skull bounced on the floor with a thud, jolting his eyes wide.

She leaped over the couch and onto his chest. Like a long jump at regionals, and she stuck the landing. His yell fizzled into a pained gasp as breath vacated his body.

He was winded, hurt, but still lucid. He spun on the floor and slammed the door closed with one hand while he reached for her leg with the other. But she hadn't fled towards the door as he expected, and his grasp found open air.

How pedestrian did he think she was? She stood at the window, and he rolled to regain his breath. His face went blank as she kicked the pane. Once, twice, thrice. The window shivered at each rage-filled kick. But it held, intact.

"Crazy bitch, what are you...?" Troy groaned, attempting to rise and regain his balance.

Arin picked up the knife she had freely discarded a moment ago. Troy pulled a much more menacing knife from his belt. Arin ignored it and sliced the gasket around the window.

The rubber seal parted easily. That happens when the rubber is pre-cut, as she'd done earlier in the darkness. The versatile red wine vinegar she'd then poured down each slit was acidic enough to eat away at the gasket, giving her a head start in her urgent task.

She'd earlier seen—or perceived—which edge of the window was the warmest when she pounded it earlier. It vibrated and spoke to her in the language of heat patterns. She then knew which was the coldest—from heat loss—and thus which edge was least secure in the frame.

What she didn't know was that high-rise windows are framed to keep the glass in, so kicking outward would not work. With nothing to shatter it, she pried frantically with the knife. She found purchase under the edge she thought was poorly set, and it started to give.

Troy stood and blinked, his knife at his side. She glanced back and savored his confusion. She didn't need to accentuate the derangement in her eyes. That came naturally.

She saw his hesitation in coming near her. She held a knife and ensured he knew she would fight to an end. Next to a skyscraper window she was ripping loose.

"Stop!" Troy screamed again.

She got the knife up to the corner of the window and pried it inward. The weakened gasket yielded—just a little—and a gust of frigid air howled in. The sound filled the room. She pried further along the adjacent edge, and more of the window pulled inward. Cold wind whipped her clothes and hair and bit at her straining fingers. Troy moved toward her, shouting over the noise of the wind.

She flung the knife at him. He batted it aside—but it slowed him down as she turned back and ripped the rest of the window loose. The incoming wind assisted with the final pull as she peeled it out of the severed, acid-soaked seal. She spun and flung the large, undodgeable sheet of tempered glass directly at him.

With his knife in his good hand, he instinctually blocked with his injured arm. He caught a spinning corner and fell back with a pained shout. He cut his yell short when he looked at the wrist he'd used to block the glass. His eyes flashed back up to Arin, wide with fear.

Arin stood at the open window. The deafening wind whipped her hair sideways and pasted her clothing against her. With an outstretched arm, she held his jacket toward the newly vacant hole in the side of her cell. It flapped in the cold wind.

His expression told her that she had guessed right. His jacket pocket held the proximity device that controlled the cuff. The cuff that shocks and then incapacitates the wearer if they stray too far. The cuff she had deftly closed over Troy's injured wrist when she landed her long jump on his chest.

"NO!" He yelled and lunged at her.

She tossed the jacket out of the window and then hopped back. She saw his arm convulse as the jacket fell. He dove toward the open window frame, reaching with desperation. His face contorted with pain.

Arin held her breath. Her pulse was stories above. Her stomach stories below.

If the tranquilizer had done its thing—if he'd been honest about that part of his little toy—he should be entering dreamland by now. But she didn't know how long that would take. She didn't have long to wait.

She grabbed the lamp, ripped the shade off, and smashed the bulb against the wall. She braced herself, poised with her jagged little backup plan.

Troy ignored the improvised weapon. He looked down at the side of the building, and his eyes focused on something close.

The damned wind, which had helped her until then, must have pinned the jacket against the building. It was caught on another window frame or some other protrusion. Far enough down for a healthy shock but not enough to put him out.

How long would the battery hold?

He held his cuff-bound wrist as far and low out of the window as he could without falling. Every inch closer reduces the shock, she'd learned.

She could get closer and try to push him out. Shove the table, maybe. But she suspected he could sustain a quick bump in the bracelet juice to turn and grab her. If she wanted to jump from the window or kill herself in other creative ways, she could have done that anytime. Getting anywhere closer to him now would net her the same result.

The wind howled into the little apartment, creating a maddening vortex around them. Troy lay grim-faced and defeated, his arm hovering over fifty stories of nothing, twisting his head to stare at Arin.

"Tell me!" she yelled. "What do you need? You have my blood! My DNA! My phone tracked! Sick freak, you have my fucking underwear size!"

He shuddered as he bore the unending jolt of electricity from the cuff. The wind billowed his shirt and tore tears from his eyes. He moaned something that got lost in the wind.

She inched closer. Cautiously. "Speak up." Her voice had an edge sharper than Troy's tactical knife, which she recovered from the floor.

"They need you," he told her, his voice carrying over the wind. "The company. I was hired..." he grimaced, his voice breaking... "to bring you. That's all."

"Bullshit. What company?" Arin's face twisted with fury.

"They don't tell me. Part of the gig." He looked at Arin. He shifted his precarious position and squinted. Behind the pain, she saw a flash of questioning—*and understanding?*—in his eyes. "Who... who are you?" he asked.

She stared, incredulous. *Who was she? He knew every goddamned thing about her.* But there was no time. He was stalling for someone else to come. Or for the batteries in that thing to run dry. She had carved out this moment, though. She would own it.

"Where is she?"

"I don't know. She ran."

He was vulnerable. In dire pain. Lying prone and half of a roll from a final plummet. She believed him. "Who else is after me?"

"Right now, no one. You can walk out that door. I didn't get a chance to lock it. Tomorrow, though..." He let the sentence hang.

"You work for someone. Who do you report to?"

He convulsed and bit his lip, drawing blood. Veins throbbed in his face, and his eyes brightened to a pulsing red that flooded her vision. He wormed deeper into the window frame to lower his wrist a precious few inches. He hooked his boots against the wall and the overturned sofa to keep his vital hold inside the room. His desperate stance seemed to buy him relief from the shock of the cuff. His face relaxed when he answered her. "My mother."

"Robin. Why does she want me?"

He didn't answer but looked at her again. Studied her.

"I saw you and her blown up on a boat."

"That was..." He started, murmuring, losing his voice. "That was for you. To identify you. To know if you were real. You are, but they didn't tell me everything." A deeper pain welled from his eyes. "I've made a big mistake, Arin. I'm so sorry."

She jerked back—bewildered—as the wind snapped her hair across her face.

"What are you fucking saying?" she demanded, her voice cracking.

The wind shifted, and the tone of the incoming gusts changed pitch. Dane screamed—a feral animal howl—then went silent as his body convulsed. He clamped his eyes shut, and she saw blood roll down his chin from his bitten tongue.

Then a click. His eyes darted open for a second. He fixed them on his wrist, and Arin watched, transfixed, as they rolled back in his head.

His body went limp. The jacket—with the proximity device secure in the pocket—had blown free in the cold autumn wind. The tranquilizer needle had activated. And Troy's precarious grip on the floor of her elevated cell ceded to gravity. His unconscious body slipped out of the high-rise window.

Arin stared into the emptiness. Howling wind filled the vacant space.

She turned and threw the door open. The next door was unlocked as well. She expected to find a squad of armed mercenaries awaiting her, but they weren't in the hallway. Or the elevator. Or the parking lot.

Fear pricked the back of her neck. With each step, she imagined fingers gripping her hair and snapping it taut to flip her back to the concrete. Back to captivity. They didn't come, but they would if she slowed. She sprinted across the dark, empty lot and hurdled over the vehicle barrier. She awarded herself gold for the 50-meter dash and the clean hurdle. There weren't events for the rest of her showing that night.

The wind was softer and warmer at street level. She let her tears flow as she bolted into the night.

26

DANE DOWNED HIS drink and dropped cash on the bar, hefty tip included. The barkeep wished him well and to never see him again.

He made his way to a nearby bike shop before they locked up for the day. It was the regular tuning spot he'd used for years, and he caught his old courier friend Barry closing up. Barry had moved on from his messenger job to work at the shop.

"Dane, I heard you jetted away somewhere up north. Quiet farmland or something. A few cops came sniffing around. Told 'em you were out blowing goats." Barry tilted his head. "You look like unwiped ass."

"Rough day. I lost a girl. Two, actually."

"Wasn't too long ago you couldn't find a girl, my man, now you're losing multiples?" Barry flipped the door sign to Closed.

"Did my damnedest to get out of the city," Dane said. "And back here I fucking am. Long story, but I've got a cousin and her friend—mine, too, I guess—that are into some crazy shit."

Barry lifted his eyebrows.

"Not like that. I said she's a cousin. I think. But they're in trouble, and the friend is lost and probably still in shock. The other girl—my cousin—got taken by someone yesterday, and I think she's nearby. The guy who took her nearly got me, too. Ditched him underground a couple hours ago." He looked down at his dusty and torn clothes. "Barely."

"Fucksticks, what are you on?"

"Adrenaline and a few fingers of whisky. My new diet. But I need your help. Lost my phone. So did the girls, and I have no good way to find them. I do have a bad way, though. Only shot I can think of is to send their photos to the messenger groups. Probably won't get anywhere, but I'd kill myself if I didn't try. Not joking. Let me sit down and I'll blast the network."

Dane nudged Barry aside and took over the shop computer. He logged in and grabbed photos of both girls. Not hard to find as they both had an ample online presence. Dane himself had used his social networks for his messenger business and not much else. He'd planned to close them when he moved out of the city but hadn't gotten to it.

He dropped the photos into a few group chats with his former fellow couriers and added a note about his urgency to find them before they were hurt. For Melanie, he gave her last known location. For Arin, he shared a well-composed photo of her in minimal track gear. It would get attention. She might not even be in the city, but he had nothing else to go on.

"I need a place to crash," Dane told Barry.

"I heard you cleaned out the coffers at poker, but you're telling me you're broke—Hey, you got a response already."

They looked at the feed. Someone shared a screenshot of a police alert with Dane's face.

"Wanted in questioning for abduction and vehicular hit and run." Barry stepped back and raised his hands, palms outward.

"Yeah, I didn't fully think that through. She needed an out and she listened to my brilliant advice. So, again, I need a place to tuck in. Just for the night and I'll be gone. Hotels would flag me."

"You're not messing with me, right? You didn't kill someone?"

"Fairly sure I didn't."

"Admirable. And you didn't actually abduct this upstanding, attractive 20-something female?"

"I'm doing all I can to get her out of here. Safe."

Barry clucked his tongue. "I've got plans tonight that don't involve harboring a fugitive, but if you go upstairs, there's a loft under renovation that I happen to have a spare key for. And I'll keep checking the feed. Good luck, my man."

"One more thing, Barry. Let me buy a bike. And a lock." He looked at his wallet. "Either on card, which might flag and get cops back in here asking more questions...or on handshake credit. You know I'm good for it."

THE LOFT ABOVE THE SHOP was in rough shape, but it had a bedroom and a bathroom and was better than some other places Dane had in mind if Barry hadn't come through. He also brought him some pizza slices from a deli around the block. Barry was one of the few people he'd ever called a friend.

After eating and trying to rest, he descended to the shop to check his social feed once more. He had more messages and jokes about his digital wanted poster but no reported sightings of either Melanie or Arin. Nothing to ease his worry.

All of his life—at least in recent years—he'd worked to make his choices without emotion. Analyze the risk and reward and let that be his sole deciding factor. Feelings only muddle the picture and don't do shit else.

And they hurt. Repeatedly. There was no need for them. That's how he was able to leave the only city he'd known. He'd cast everything he had here, and had walked away—stumbled, really—to start again somewhere else. Staying would hurt. Leaving did hurt. But only as much as he let it. And he thought he was done letting things and people and places hurt him.

Then Arin showed up. And Melanie. They treated him like family, which was apparently the case, but that rarely meant much. He wasn't accustomed to the fast bond he developed with them. Sure, they were beautiful girls and easy to talk with—always an easy affection for him to throw effort at—but he'd never really cared for girls as he did for them. He hadn't had any flings that went longer than a month or two. Girls came and went, and sometimes came back again, but nothing lasted.

Was the difference that they asked for his help? People don't do that to people like him. What could he offer anyone? Nothing came for free. Everything was an exchange. A payment. A barter where a favor would be expected later.

But he helped them. He was set to flip his coaster in that bar and let good ol' chance make the call. Free of emotion and relinquished from that responsibility. He nearly did so, but he took control and set that coaster down.

And now he was in one hell of a mess. His mind full enough to evade sleep, despite bone-deep weariness. The sounds of the city assaulted him through the drafty windows. It hadn't taken long in the country to get used to the quiet.

The country up north where he still imagined he may have a life. Not likely a job anymore, but he could get another. Or talk his way back into the shop. And into Trish's life. He'd spent a couple of work shifts with her and was planning to ask her to show him some of her favorite trails, but that would need to wait. He didn't even know if she was single. Thoughts of her followed him to sleep.

He woke, showered, and put the same clothes back on. He cursed himself for not thinking to get another set. They were filthy and reeked of yesterday's fear. And the surveillance photos being distributed showed him wearing these very clothes. Brilliant. He went down to the shop before it opened and logged in to check his feed, expecting more jokes at his expense. He was happily mistaken.

Arin had been seen. She was in New York.

His long-shot post had worked and his extensive network of wheeled messengers had come through. He rubbed his eyes to wake himself as he read the message again.

A courier had delivered some early morning documents to a hotel in Midtown and had seen a lone girl on a lobby sofa. Distraught and scared. The biker knew he wasn't the type of guy who would ease the young woman's stress by approaching her or calling out her name, but he chanced it and took a sly photo to send to Dane.

It was her. And she was a dozen blocks away. He mounted his bike and sailed north.

27

ARIN DWELLED IN the silence and solitude of a hotel lobby corner. She sat for hours. It was the first open and safe-looking entrance she found after fleeing through the dark streets, far from the tower and her lofty cell.

The sun had yet to rise, and she had yet to settle herself enough to think. She mumbled something to the desk clerk about waiting for a friend whose plane was late. The middle-aged woman shrugged and went back to her tabloids.

She had watched a man—her captor—fall to his death from forty stories, maybe fifty. If he reached the sidewalk below alive, that is. That diabolical cuff may have done him in first.

Either way, she hadn't killed him. That's what she told herself as she huddled on the sofa.

She borrowed the hotel phone to call Melanie but got voicemail and didn't leave a message. She used a computer in the cramped business center but didn't know her social media passwords.

She had used the recommended random string of characters that no one would guess—or remember. They were all on her phone at the bottom of a cold creek two states away.

She searched for her own name. No missing person report. No APB. No news more recent than her last winning track meet a few years before.

What are friends for if they don't report you missing? She recalled the last text she had sent before she'd airplaned her phone. That may have complicated the process.

She had no phone, no wallet, no ID. If they found her and took her again, she'd be the unidentified body that washes up in the marshes. But that wasn't going to happen. Troy hadn't wanted to kill her, and it seemed his company or his god-forsaken mother or whomever else he was working for needed her alive.

Tossing their star agent out of a skyscraper might change that, though. She didn't want to find out.

She hadn't actually thrown him out of the window, she once again reminded herself. The camera feed inside the room should prove that. But she'd done enough to hurt him and to create conditions ripe for his death that she might as well have. Anyone without access to the cameras would jump directly to that conclusion. Police, say.

She replayed those last intense moments. He'd tried to tell her something. His demeanor changed right at the end before the jacket with the proximity device blew free, and the cuff severed any further communication.

He'd softened a little. He asked who she was like he didn't already know everything about her. Arin couldn't piece that together in any way that made sense.

She didn't feel sorry for him. All else on the level, she didn't want anyone to die. She'd relish the chance to demand answers from him through cell bars—a proper cell, not the luxury unit where she'd been held—but that chance was gone. And his last words were an *apology* to her. First impressions are lasting, but last impressions? They're carved in stone.

The lobby TV played the early morning local news with the sound off. There was a spot about the crash she'd seen from her window. She'd seen the aftermath, anyway. A car crash in Manhattan isn't typically newsworthy, so either it was a slow news day, or this crash was a little worse than the habitual bumps and scrapes.

She moved closer to read the closed captioning. A looped video showed Melanie's car, the ambulance, and cops keeping bystanders away from the scene. The driver had initially fled the scene, the captions said.

Arin held her a hand over her mouth as she read the next lines. The driver reported she had been carjacked and had attempted to fight back while driving. She rolled the car after several blocks of high-speed, erratic driving. The driver herself fled the scene to escape her assailant and then later reported to a police station. The man who had jumped into her passenger seat was still at large and presumed dangerous. Arin shrieked in the quiet lobby when they showed the man local residents should be on the lookout for.

It was Dane.

The receptionist looked over in alarm, but Arin waved her away. "Sorry, I thought it was someone I knew."

"Tragic days on those streets out there," the woman said from behind her desk. "I lock my doors and double-check every time."

"That's a good idea," Arin responded by rote. Her head swam as she tried to push through her weariness and make sense of what she saw.

The news gets things wrong all the time. Reporters make mistakes. Melanie would be the first to admit that. But accusing a kidnapper erroneously would be a big mistake. If police are looking for Dane, there must be some truth to the report. They make plenty of mistakes, too, but...she couldn't think.

The guy she had met a few days before—her cousin—was not the type portrayed with a headshot and a warning label on the morning news. He seemed genuine. He cared. Maybe a little hesitant to open up, but that was most guys.

Of course, he was why she and Melanie had that stupid argument. Arin wanted to push him to share more about his family—her family—but Melanie wanted to give him space. She was right, as usual. They'd shown up and unloaded a whole barrow of rot on someone trying to start a new life.

But carjacking a new acquaintance and coercing her into a near-fatal crash was one of the worst ways to downsize your life, so Arin was reasonably certain the news was wrong. She just couldn't piece together how.

She needed help. There were two phone numbers she had memorized. One was Melanie's, which went to voicemail on each of twelve attempts. She promised the annoyed receptionist that the next number was a different one and would go through. She hoped.

Her parents might not be awake yet. She wasn't even sure if they were home. And with Troy's efforts in tracking, abducting, and housing her, she had to assume his team had the means to track her parents as well. She couldn't say where she was and not expect someone to be listening in. The phone rang once, and she hung up. She returned to her secluded lobby seat.

A moment later, she stood to try the phone again, then swayed when she stood too quickly. She braced herself on the door frame until her vision settled, then looked up and saw Dane rush into the lobby.

Their eyes met, and they both froze.

He was filthy. He wore a tourist hat and cheap sunglasses. He started walking toward her, then stopped when she stepped back into a defensive posture. He held his hands open in the universal I-don't-have-a-weapon-and-I'm-not-going-to-hurt-you signal. She circled to position herself between him and the hotel entrance.

"Is everything all right, Miss?" asked the receptionist from across the room, her voice pitching higher. "Is this the friend you were waiting for?"

Most people would be in a poor state after a delayed plane flight, but none looked as bad as he did. The receptionist being suspicious here wouldn't hurt. Arin paused, and when the woman reached for the phone, she answered with an absolute untruth. "Yes. Everything's just fine."

Then, to Dane in a lower voice, "You have six seconds to convince me what I saw on the news isn't real."

He burned two of those seconds with a labored exhale. "Melanie gave that report that you saw on the news. I asked her to, and she listened."

"I can't take any more subtlety. Tell me what the fuck you're talking about and why you're both here in New York."

"That will take a lot longer than six seconds. What I need to know is if you trust me."

Arin hesitated.

"That's a yes or no question. And I can't stay here and wait for her to recognize me." He tilted his head at the receptionist behind him.

"Trust goes both ways. I need your unequivocal answers. And your history."

"You'll have it. Just not here."

"No, here. Now. Before I move. Tell me why you won't talk about your past. Your family. Why you're so hellbent on leaving this city."

"Pain," he stated. "It's all pain. Why keep it?"

She waited for more.

"A guy died under my feet when I was nine. I knew he was in front of the train my father was driving. Around the bend, in the dark. If he listened to me—trusted me—he wouldn't have gone to jail. I wouldn't have been alone.

Arin, I've never talked about that to anyone."

AFTER STOPPING AT A DELI for breakfast sandwiches and coffee, Arin grabbed Dane's arm as they passed a department store.

"I need new clothes," she stated.

He looked at her fresh leisure wear and then at his filthy, ripped clothing.

"Point made, so do you. Mine look clean, but I need them burned in Hades's fires, then I need the ashes mixed in Cerebus's food bowl for him to devour and shit out into the River Styx." She allowed a grim smile. "I'll explain later."

Dane was low on cash, so had to risk using his card. The police would have linked the surveillance footage to him by now, he explained. The news outlets had his photo so quickly because of his prior involvement with the law. Arin nodded as if such considerations were a routine part of her life now.

They were in the store just long enough to grab what they needed and toss their old clothes in the restroom trash, so using the card was reasonably safe.

She saw that Dane still had the map of the bike course in his old clothes and watched him tuck it into the pocket of his new shirt. *Leave no trace* was good advice anywhere.

She splashed water on her face in the restroom. The coffee was slow to do its thing. She demanded a lot from caffeine that morning.

28

ARIN TRUSTED DANE. She had to, but she needed a moment to back off the edge she'd been on for days now, body exhausted and mind reeling. She pulled him into a park and pointed to a bench. He looked around, then sat. She joined him, looking out across the quiet lawn of gnarled oaks.

Dane pulled a joint from his shirt pocket. He lit up, closed his eyes on a long inhale, and passed it over. Arin hadn't smoked anything for years. Didn't help track and field lungs, and she pictured her coach's face as she accepted it and took a deep pull.

"Storytime," she said, stifling a cough. "You first."

They recounted, in brief, their last couple of days. Following his tale, Arin appreciated that this guy was on her side. Melanie's side.

She shared a notable update about the man Dane had nicknamed *Limit*. "He's dead." She savored Dane's reaction. He'd nearly caught Dane, but she was the one who ended him.

Granted, he'd captured her first. Details.

Talking through the torment of her story eradicated any fleeting feelings of regret for Troy's death that she'd entertained. Job or not, misinformation or not, he did what he did, and she made him pay.

"Limit?" Arin questioned. "Why'd you call him that?"

"A thing I do. For poker, mostly, but any adversary I don't know needs a name. Puts them in context. I got close to reaching this guy's limit." He turned and looked her up and down. "And you're the one who did. I'm awestruck."

Arin settled her thoughts. Melanie and Dane hadn't come to save her. They would have driven right under her window, unnoticed, if Troy hadn't intervened. And she knew that if he'd been anywhere near full capacity, she never would have managed that escape.

"I might die today." Dane stated those words without inflection, looking ahead. He continued before Arin had a chance to respond. "It's something I say every morning. Puts things in perspective. Some days it's more likely than others. Hadn't gotten around to it today."

"*Memento Mori*," Arin responded, and received a questioning stare in return. "I know, it's a thing I do. But that's ancient wisdom you've tapped into. Speaking of, where's the nearest library? I have someone important to find."

DANE LOGGED IN TO CHECK his feeds again. Nothing from Melanie and nothing more from his network.

Over his shoulder, Arin read his query and the responses. That other biker at the hotel early in the morning would have sent her running. Good call on that guy's part, not trying to console her. She missed him taking the photo, though. She looked terrible—probably wasn't much better off now. At least she was out of her fashionable prison garb.

For Melanie's possible whereabouts, they had to list what they knew. She had no phone and probably no wallet. No way to rent a car. If she wanted to contact Warren, as Dane had asked her to, she might not have his number. That and his address would be in the depths of her hallowed notebook. Did she lose that, too? She wouldn't have grabbed it when scrambling from an overturned car with blood running down her face and a madman mere steps behind her. Dane had provided those details with remorse, and she assured him Melanie was tough. He said he knew.

Her notebook. She sat down at the next computer and began a search.

"What are you looking for?"

"She'd need her notebook. Did you see it? If it's still in the car, we need to go to the impound lot."

Dane said he knew where that was. Of course he did.

"But we can't just show up at an NYPD building, remember?"

"You can't," Arin replied.

"Don't you think they have your face connected to a guy who fell out of a skyscraper late last night? Street video of you running away? Fingerprints and DNA throughout the place?"

She looked at him. She hadn't even thought of that. She didn't have a criminal record. But a passport? Her prints were out there. She had to hope the databases weren't linked. Or that the scene hadn't been fully processed. The hope was shallow, but she had to risk it.

"We'll go. You stay back. I'll tell them I'm a concerned friend." True. "I'll say she asked me to get her belongings." Close enough to true.

"They won't go for it."

"We'll see." She checked her shirt buttons and her reflection in the nearby window. Even in her rough shape, she could probably emulate Melanie's tactics at the RV shop. Not her style of getting information, but she needed to pull all the stops. A few subway stops away, they strolled around the back of the police impound lot, doing their best impression of unhurried tourists. Melanie's car was there. Painful to see up close, but knowing she wasn't badly hurt eased the loss.

The car's condition earned the totaled status and then some. That twisted and shattered carcass housed thousands of miles of memories. It was the only car of Melanie's she'd known. But it was just a car, steel and plastic and glass, and they'll put thousands more miles on another one. Soon.

They circled toward the front, and Dane ducked into a pharmacy across the street where he could see the entrance through a window.

Arin approached and entered. The older woman at the counter was entirely uninterested in how many buttons on her shirt were undone. She gave her pitch, and the woman turned to her computer and scrolled for a moment.

"That vehicle is involved in an ongoing investigation, Dear. We can't give you access to it."

"Do you have an inventory of what was found? There's an important notebook."

"Everything is important. It's part of a possible crime scene."

This wasn't going the way she hoped. Dane was right. Again.

"If it's that important," the woman continued, "why didn't your friend, the driver, pick it up when she was here?"

SHE'S ALIVE. OF COURSE SHE was, but knowing someone spoke to her recently lifted more of a weight than Arin knew she was carrying.

"What would she have done next?" Dane asked as they walked away from the impound lot.

"She'd want answers, just like the rest of us. She didn't know I was here in the city, right? And she knows her story about you being a carjacker wouldn't hold up for long. Of the three of us, she's the only one capable of renting a car. Credit cards and licenses and not being wanted by the police for abduction and murder are all important parts of that process."

She stopped and grabbed Dane's arm. "No offense, but I bet she figured you could handle yourself, and she left as soon as possible. As far as she knows, I'm still in Massachusetts. Maybe limping back to my dorm after a boneheaded run across the state because I don't know how to face real problems and have never needed to, so I let others make my decisions for me. And my answer to that was to decide to run a ridiculous distance without telling anyone."

Dane raised an eyebrow.

She averted her eyes and allowed a smirk. "I've missed a couple of therapy appointments, and I'm exceedingly wiped out. Deal with it. Or I'll throw you out of a really high window."

He chuckled. She may have heard him laugh once or twice that night at the bike shop, but that would have been the only other time.

"I like you," he said, then clarified. "As a cousin. You'd be a trip across the Thanksgiving table. That's what your kind does, right? I've seen movies."

She looked at him. The dark circles under their eyes matched, at least. "Sure. That's what my kind does."

They kept walking. She'd fall asleep if they stopped again.

"Why wouldn't Melanie have checked in with my father?" Dane asked. "Before we split, I said to use him as a contact point. I think I said that, anyway. It was a quick parting."

"She remembered your suggestion about the carjacking. She damned sure didn't make that up on her own—false reporting must have scraped at her fibers like nothing else. But she did it. And she didn't want to bring anything else on you or your family. These assholes tracked our phones, right? Who's to say they're not listening in on all of our contacts? They were watching her, so they knew when she stopped at your father's place. Going back there again would put him in danger. That's not my girl. She cares." They crossed another street. "And I need her," she added.

They purchased a pair of prepaid phones from a bodega and Arin made calls. Difficult in an age where no one memorizes numbers and no one answers unknown callers. But they worked with the tools they had.

Arin called the university to get in contact with Ross. She left her new number with his RA and conveyed the urgency. She did the same for other mutual friends, some of whom she got through to. Those she spoke with hadn't seen Melanie in days. Arin thanked them. She didn't have the time to catch them up on a story they wouldn't believe anyway.

She again considered calling her parents. She would have if she knew they could get her out of this mess without putting themselves at risk, but neither part of that was certain. She convinced Dane of the same, especially since he and Melanie had stopped at his father's place the day before—presumably while being tracked.

"Our only lead on this whole mess is the old guy with the RV," she said. "And your father might have gotten somewhere with that. EZ-Pass scans at interstate exits, right? Is there a place to meet him discreetly? His home, maybe his work is being watched. We can't assume it's not."

Dane pulled out his wallet. "I have enough for bus fare across the river."

"Good enough. But first, I need to see something else."

ARIN'S THROAT CONSTRICTED AS SHE looked up at the skyscraper from behind the police barricade. Her cell—it damned sure was hers to claim with a possessive pronoun now—was easy to find.

Forty-seven stories up was a gaping void fluttering with yellow tape. Forms inside moved around the active crime scene. As they stood and watched, a piece of plywood tilted up from inside the room and closed the blemish on the otherwise immaculate building.

The base of the building was cordoned off. A large, red stain on the concrete spoke of finality, which was enough for her.

The body was gone, but investigators were still taking photos and measurements. She wondered where the jacket had landed. It was high-end performance wear, so it likely got snatched. Besides the proximity device, his phone was probably in there as well. There were a few filled pockets, but she hadn't had a spare second the night before to look.

They stood among other onlookers and weren't overly concerned about being spotted. Local news was perched at the other end of the block. She wondered if any of them had covered the crash the day before. Despite being only a block away, the two events would be wholly unrelated to even the best reporters.

"I knew this building when it was going up," Dane commented. "Delivered blueprints for the crew sometimes. Actually had a first date up there. Beer and takeout and a million-dollar view. Turned out to be a last date, too, but I didn't expect otherwise. Girl was down for slumming for a night with a guy with restricted access to a skyscraper under construction."

Arin looked at him and smiled. There was more to him than he let on. "Her loss. And I could have used those blueprints earlier."

They walked away from that scene and towards the other one. The car versus ambulance crash from the day before had been cleared up, and nothing remained to show how close Melanie had come to being killed.

Or captured. Or arrested. Or victimized by road rage or any number of other ways that could have ended. Dane, too. She felt a pang of shame for delaying his inclusion in her thoughts. He risked himself even now for her impromptu tour of the remnants of their recent handiwork.

Arin walked away, and Dane followed. Tour over. Time to find Melanie.

29

ARIN SAT WITH Dane at an outdoor cafe in the early twilight of a suburban New Jersey street. A Japanese maple in deep red foliage obscured them from view but allowed a sightline to the passing pedestrians.

Dane's credit access hadn't yet been severed. He hit an ATM before they fled the city and took the maximum cash advance allowed. Paper currency granted them the mobility and obscurity they needed. She'd grabbed a pair of cheap sunglasses from a street vendor to both hide her identity and cover her fatigue.

Arin picked at her salad and fought to keep her head off the table. Dane was surely just as tired, but he hid it better. They had coffee with dinner, unsure when their next shot at sleep would come.

On the bus ride and subsequent walk that afternoon, Dane recounted more of his childhood. Of his father and mother. He didn't blame Warren for his absence during his early life or for getting himself jailed and leaving his son to the whims of the foster system.

Dane wasn't one to bog down his present with regrets and anger, she noted. He didn't seem to worry about the future, either. She imagined he'd find kindred spirits in ancient philosophers. Seneca or Epictetus, perhaps. On a better day, she'd share some of that aged wisdom. Put what remained of her expensive studies to use, somehow.

Dane brightened when speaking about his father's current life. The felony of crushing a poor soul with a subway train while drinking whiskey with a splash of coffee limited his employment options, but Warren was apparently content with his desk job, his girlfriend and his dog.

And the quieter neighborhood where they sat, eating dinner and waiting. He was an uncle she had yet to meet, but his happiness later in life was a pleasing story to hear at the end of an exceedingly rough couple of days.

They ordered dessert and continued waiting as the sun went down. Dane looked at his watch for the third or fourth time, then perked up and nodded toward the sidewalk. Arin looked over and saw a tall, thin man walking a dog. He wore glasses and a puffy brown coat. The dog's coat was mottled grey. Mixed breed, friendly. Both looked content with their evening stroll.

Dane went to the patio fence and got his attention. Warren was startled to see his son but smiled and walked around to enter a side gate.

Arin petted the dog as he moved up and sniffed her. Warren followed a step behind and grabbed the empty chair at their table.

"You kids and your surprise visits," he said, and they both looked at him in question. "I mean your friend. She found me at a gas station during my lunch break. Apologized for following me, but she's all worried about phones or something—"

"You saw Mel? Spoke with her?" Arin cut in, leaning forward and propping her sunglasses on her head.

"Yes, I saw her, and you must be—" Warren froze as his eyes locked on hers. "My god, my Gina—." His voice broke, and he braced his hands on the table. He took a moment as his eyes grew misty. "I haven't seen that face in a long time. We met at your age. So beautiful. The old pictures don't capture it. Forgive me." He looked away and drew his arm across his eyes.

Arin put her hand over his. "I'm happy to meet you. I wish I did sooner. I wish I knew her." She glanced at Dane. What else could she say? She allowed as long a pause as she could bear before her impatience took charge. "What did Mel say? I need to find her."

"And she needed to find you. She said something about a chase and a crash, but she couldn't stay around and chat."

"And we need to be quick here, too," Arin replied. "The only thing we know is that these people are dangerous. And they're good at searching. I'm guessing dogs aren't allowed inside, but I'm getting nervous the longer we're out in public."

"I see. Fill me in later." He scratched his dog's head. "These people—what do they want?"

Dane spoke up. Arin was impressed with how well he processed the disparate facts he'd recently come to understand. There are more places than college to learn those skills.

"It has to do with us." He looked at Arin and then back at his father. "And mom. Something genetic we all share. Dad, we never really spoke about that night in the subway, but I did see there was someone around the bend of the tunnel. Think of my skills biking at night on the streets. Killing it at poker. That ability is what this is all about. It's what they're after. People who can see those things higher in the spectrum. She can, too," he pointed at Arin. "Maybe mom could, and her headaches were part of that."

Arin looked at him. They hadn't spoken of those connections before, but hearing them spoken aloud, she had no rebuttal. The table grew silent. She strained but held back from steering the conversation back to Melanie again.

"And the one guy who knew her," Dane continued, "who wrote Mom's obituary, he's bolted. Off hiding somewhere."

Warren snapped back to the present. "That's something I can help with. I worked a favor to get his plate checked. I gave the printout to your friend. Should have made another copy, I guess. I'm not good at this spy stuff. But she gave me a number to pass along. She lost her phone and got a burner." He took a slip of paper out of his pocket.

Arin snatched the paper and dialed, her goddamned thumbs unable to enter the numbers fast enough.

THEY FOUND A QUIET LOUNGE a few blocks away where a couch in a darkened corner beaconed. A few drinks later and they were both fighting needed sleep. Arin gave up. She turned her phone up and told Dane he had first watch. She curled into the corner and closed her eyes.

Melanie was on her way. They were safe, for now. The heavy pull of sleep overtook her.

30

DANE SHOOK ARIN awake when Melanie arrived. She shrieked as if he'd startled her from a nightmare, but her shock transformed into joy as she beheld Melanie, and the girls joined in a fierce embrace.

He took his cue to find another space and settled at the bar around the corner. The lounge was quiet and filled with dark nooks. Jazz from the golden age piped down from ceiling speakers, and soft conversations drifted around corners. He sampled their cocktail menu with caution—he was on the cusp of much-needed sleep himself. Plus, his cash reserves were just north of zero.

A growing tingling in his ankle caught his attention. He'd been favoring it throughout the day. He'd also been trying to ignore that fact. It was the same foot he'd nursed after his flight from the city the week prior, and he realized his latest escape must have aggravated whatever hadn't yet healed.

He pushed the concern aside and ordered another drink. He then hit up the ATM, as the hour was past midnight, and a new day meant another withdrawal would be available.

After waiting for what seemed a reasonable period, he rejoined the girls, and all three of them left in Melanie's rental car. He considered a joke about her recent driving demonstration, but a wiser angel convinced him to refrain.

"Swing by my father's place. I need to drop a note. Also, if you have cash, I owe him for dinner. Not sure when I'll be back to my apartment. I'm pretty much helpless right now." He wanted to square up and wasn't sure when he'd see his father again. He was in this with the girls. It was his family, his mother, who was somehow involved. If he couldn't find the answers and remove the threat to himself and his family, he didn't deserve to start over. Here or anywhere. Seeing this through was his ticket to the new life he foolishly thought he could poke into a map. Everything he knew told him it wouldn't be that easy, but he didn't listen. Didn't want to hear his old self anymore.

Melanie parked around the block, and Dane completed a hasty drop of a note with the cash in the apartment mail slot. The street was empty, so the risk of being spotted felt low enough. No one followed as they drove away. Even the late-night interstate seemed quiet.

They'd gotten out, all three of them. For now.

Their initial ambitions of driving through the night gave way to reality, and they found a hotel. Car parked in back, phones off, and the sleepy desk clerk didn't ask for their names. One room for him, and one for them. Off-the-grid travel would have to be their new normal.

Following overdue sleep, they found a greasy-spoon spot for breakfast. Dane watched Arin and Melanie drain cups of bad coffee while they filled in more details about their eventful time apart. Melanie scrawled in her notebook—she'd gotten that plus her hat and glasses from the impound lot—and he listened, adding details where needed.

He grabbed a newspaper from the next table while they waited for their order. Scanned the top, then flipped below the fold and froze. He cleared the sleep from his eyes and read again. Melanie saw his shock and halted her conversation.

"What is it?"

"Don't know, but I'm fairly certain it's not good." He spun the paper toward them and watched as they read it. Arin's hand went to her mouth. Melanie forced a slow inhale through her nose and grimaced. Dane held a *please wait* finger up to the approaching waitress.

Robin Carmine had been released following her arrest. Her lawyers challenged the evidence supporting her arrest warrant and got it overturned. The evidence Arin had provided. Against the woman whose son she had watched fall to his death—for which she would be blamed.

"Give me Linda's cell." Arin looked at Melanie, then at her notebook. Her call was picked up immediately.

"Linda, Arin here. Yes, Coppertree. Hello?" A pause and a stone-hard gaze at her phone. "Bitch hung up on me."

They finished their food, and Dane looked on sheepishly as Melanie paid the bill. Again. Even if he'd gotten around to opening a bank account before sailing back to the choppy streets he'd just fled, he had to assume the cops would be watching for more withdrawals. And opening a new account in a sleepy New England town with a sack full of sodden and blood-streaked cash would have put him on other lists.

He was beholden to another. Where he'd vowed never to be again.

"I KNOW MY CHARM IS difficult to remain in the vicinity of, but I really thought you'd both abandoned me. I called around, but no one knew where you were." Ross looked at Dane. "Thanks for rounding them up and bringing them home safe. These galavanters know the direction trouble lies, eh? Dane, was it?"

His sense of worth was already bruised, and letting himself get any more credit than due, especially at the expense of the two highly capable women at the table, would do little the next time he looked in a mirror.

"I was a convenient distraction, that's all." He tilted his head toward the pair of girls coming down the steps with a tray of coffee and warm pastries. "They did the work to get back here in one piece."

The four of them sat in a little-used study hall on the outskirts of campus. Ross was the only person with both the background and the trust they needed. Melanie called him and convinced him that meeting them here and now was more important than whatever else he'd planned for that morning. Four calls it took before he answered. Few answer an unknown number on the first call, and Ross affirmed that clearly when he answered the fourth. Until he heard Melanie's voice. He met them five minutes later, out of breath but sporting a glaring white smile.

The smile faded as their story unfolded. Dane didn't see Ross as someone he'd hang with outside of a situation like this, but he respected the girls and seemed bright enough to be helpful. If Melanie and Arin trusted him then he would, too. Not the type of guy who'd last a moment in a scrap, though. Or a chase. Or much of whatever else would come up if he hung around.

Not fair, he knew. It was judgemental of him to cast Ross aside. They needed all the help they could get, and options wilted by the hour. He listened to the conversation as the girls relayed their past few days. He watched Ross's face grow slack as the story unfolded. Pale, even. Chases, fights, kidnapping, dead bodies—these weren't real-life concepts for him. But to his credit, he cared, and he wanted to help. And anyone with access to cars and money and a face not currently on the news would be essential.

Dane wasn't sure how much longer Melanie would be straight with the law. They'd review street footage against her statement and shut her down, too. So Ross insisting he joins them on the hunt for the old doctor in his RV was an easy sell.

Convincing him to leave his phone at home and get a burner was not as easy, until they rehashed their recent highlights and showed a few scars. He held up the cheap phone they'd purchased for him and complained about a stint in the dark ages.

AN AFTERNOON OF ROUGH DRIVING on frost-heaved and poorly grated roads while looking for one RV among hundreds gave Dane a picture of a childhood he'd never known. He didn't feel like he missed out. The parks they visited blurred into one long, indistinct row. Sites crammed close with kids running around. Satellite dishes and plastic furniture. If that was camping, he didn't see the appeal.

Arin read during the drive, her button-nose deep in Melanie's journal. Her almond eyes flitted across the choppy shorthand as she flipped pages back and forth, squinting and nodding. Melanie drove, navigating rough roads and poor signage with skill. Ross talked. Dane tuned him out.

They found their target at the far end of the fourth park they visited, tucked into a secluded site with a single lawn chair in front of a well-used fire ring. No kids' toys, no satellite dish, no oversized cooler or radio. And no one home. Fresh tire tracks marred the grass near the camper. They decided to get food in town and come back at sunset.

They ordered burgers from the one place that seemed open in the sleepy town an hour from the nearest exit. They waited at an outdoor table across from a small grocery store. A laundromat and an auto shop and a few boarded-up storefronts completed the plaza.

If anyone had followed them here, it wouldn't matter if they waited inside or outside, so they used the opportunity to spread out and get fresh air after hours in the car.

Arin answered a call, her eyes widened, and she put it on speaker. *Linda,* she mouthed as she set the phone in the middle of the table.

"Arin, I want to apologize for cutting you off this morning. I needed to call back from another number, and this is the first chance I got. So I'm sure you saw the news...?" She trailed off, awaiting a response.

"About Robin? Yes, I saw that news."

"You're a bright girl, and so is Melanie. I figured you would connect those dots, despite our admonition against sharing any info about your testimony. The warrant was overturned. That happens, but in this case, with the high-profile subject, my team and I caught serious backlash. Nothing you did wrong, and I still thank you for that, but the nature of your testimony was too controversial for some. That's why it happened off-site, away from the courthouse. We push for justice, but sometimes the Lady bites back. I've been removed from the case and restricted from contacting those in it. That includes you, hence the need to watch my call log. I hope you can see that."

Dane pulled back as Arin emitted a shrieking laugh. "See that!? See what? How can you watch your call log when it's that far up your ass?—" She stopped as restaurant patrons at an adjacent table looked their way. She lowered her voice. "Let's try this, Linda. Do you know where Troy is?"

A brief silence from the other end, then Linda responded, with caution. "Troy who?"

"One more strike, Linda, and we're all fucking out. Don't bull-shit me."

217

"I heard he may have run into some trouble. What do you know about that? Nothing's on the news yet. Not with his name or face, at least."

"He may have *fallen* into some trouble, you mean. And there's no *may* about it. Tell me one thing, and I *may* trust you again. Why is Robin after me?"

The silence was longer this time. Arin checked her phone to see if she'd hung up again.

Melanie perked up and stabbed a finger in front of her, pointing across the parking lot. An elderly man in a heavy maroon coat and a knit red hat walked from the small grocer through the parking lot.

"That's him," Melanie whispered. "Marshall. Don't look—he spooks easy." She pulled up her coat collar and faced away from him. Melanie was the only one who'd met him, Dane recalled. The old doctor had high-tailed his life within a day, and Arin had shown up to a for-sale sign squeaking on a wind-blown chain. Dane had learned how hard it was to leave your old life. He might need tips from this guy.

"Arin, is that Melanie Hobbs with you? Who else is there?" Linda's voice broke in.

"Friends. People I can trust. And I can't include you in such a group unless you answer my question." As she waited, her eyes tracked the older guy across the parking lot and into his car.

"I'm not sure. Truthfully, I don't know. But we can figure it out together. I have resources—"

"But you don't anymore, do you? Can't call me on your own phone, don't know where I've been the last couple of days, and don't seem to know what these nefarious assholes have done? I've got to go, Linda. I've got more problems to solve. And I think you know which ones I've solved already. Call me again when the DOJ cares to help." She hung up. She closed her eyes and pulled a long inhale through her nose.

Dane gave her a smirk and a slight nod. Was that stemming from family pride? He couldn't remember what that felt like.

The man Melanie had identified as Marshall drove toward the RV park. They knew where he was headed, so they took their time to finish the mediocre burgers and domestic beers.

Marshall would tell him about Gina tonight. Dane would demand that of him in whatever way he needed to. Age was rarely relevant in fights. He'd twist the neck of an old man if that's what got them answers—and perhaps a path out. A path back to his new hometown in time for the bike race. He'd churned out a lot of work and wanted to see the event through. If he still had a job.

They headed for the campsite, primed to wring obstinate truth out of an old man.

31

D **USK CAME QUICKLY.** Arin watched the sun wink away behind racing clouds. She pulled her jacket tight as she walked with what had become her crack investigation and evasion team—Melanie, Dane, and Ross. She'd buy them all custom team shirts if they made it through.

When they made it through, unscathed and with justice duly served, to whatever was at the other end. A prospect far from certain as they walked down the rutted dirt road past families of campers and tents. To any who bothered to look their way, they'd look like college kids out for a night free from supervision.

They'd parked around the corner from Marshall's site. Clanking up in a car in the thin night air would give him too much warning for him to—flee again? Grab a weapon? Call someone?

They didn't know and didn't want to find out, so the venerable tactic of surprise it would be. She saw firelight flicker behind the camper. Noticed it through the trees before they turned the corner, and she assumed Dane did as well. They had discussed their increased ability to hone in on those formerly subconscious signals—their sight at the heart of their troubles—now that they understood what to look for.

The old man sat on a lone plastic chair, leaning forward and fanning a nascent flame with a flattened cracker box in one hand and holding an open beer in the other. He didn't look up at the crunch of their footsteps as they neared him, but he did when they stopped. Foot traffic by his site was common. People stopping, unexpected.

He tilted his head, squinting past the low flame into the fading light behind it. His face looked withered with age, but underneath his wrinkled eyelids sat dark, intelligent eyes. He leaned around the firepit for a clearer view of his visitors.

"Can I help you?" He asked with a tone suggesting he didn't intend to help anyone.

"Dr. Brock," said Melanie as she stepped forward. Arin watched his face descend from mild annoyance to anger. Hostility, even.

"Christ!" he snarled. "You again! Can't leave an old man to himself, can you, kids? Respect? Privacy? All gone to the birds." His knuckles went white around his bottle. He mumbled, "Need another good war to bring some discipline to your generation."

Arin didn't hesitate to take control. She eased forward into the growing firelight, waving down Melanie and anyone else who had a response forming.

"Dr. Brock, my name is Arin Coppertree. This," and she turned and nodded, "is Dane Hardy. His mother was Gina Rosewood. You knew her. You wrote her obituary." She knelt down to his level. Crossed her arms on one knee, hands open. A non-threatening pose like she'd use with a frightened animal. The others remained behind at the edge of the firelight. His sneer eased. A little.

"I don't know who you are, but I want to," Arin continued in a low voice. She was desperate to wring some answers out of him, but he wasn't the type to be intimidated. She had no threats or bribes to use, only kindness and an appeal to decency.

"There's something you know that would help us. We're facing threats we don't understand, only that it's because of our family. As serious as it gets. Endgame trouble. Dane and I only met a few days ago but have been through some real shit since then—we barely scraped out of it. And the only person who might have some answers is you. You made yourself very difficult to find, which has got to mean we're right."

She watched his gaze bore through the flames in front of him. Jaw grim. Purposefully avoiding her eyes. She glanced back at Melanie. The rest of the group moved forward. The fire was taking off, and Arin's soft voice was lost in the snaps of dry hickory. She needed to remain cordial but also needed a barbed question to get his attention. She'd been gleaning some of Melanie's interview strategies over recent weeks. She sharpened her tone.

"Did you know Gina was there that night? The night of the storm?"

The question broke through his obstinance, and he snapped his gaze at her. He opened his mouth, clearly surprised, but instead of questioning how they knew about him being at the hospital that night, his only response was to lower his eyes again.

Arin let the question linger. The others inched a little closer, and the rising flickers of the fire lit them up against the dark sky. She held up a discrete hand to keep them back, and quiet.

The old man finally spoke. His voice was soft, resigned. Hollow—a tone of surrender. "I didn't know she was there. That night. And that's something I can never fix." He looked at each of them in turn. She saw his chest catch mid-breath when he looked at her and then at Dane. He lowered his eyes and covered them with his palms. He sat with his elbows on his knees, swaddled in his thick coat, face concealed.

A long moment passed. When he looked up, his eyes were misty. Red, even in the firelight.

"There's some stumps," he said, waving a hand toward the treeline. He stood up and went inside his camper, drawing a sleeve across his eyes.

Melanie was the first to realize what he meant. He only had one chair by the fire, so if they wanted to sit, they'd need to roll over some cut stumps from the woods. They'd been invited to join his fire.

He came out of the RV with a bottle of something amber-colored and a stack of clear plastic cups. "You're all quite young, but someday you'll want some part of your past to stay there. Float back and away forever. And sometimes it will, for a while."

Arin looked at Dane, who may not have realized he was nodding in agreement.

Marshall passed the stack of cups around, and they each took one. The bottle followed. A single malt whisky, Arin noted. No ice on offer. Whatever was coming would burn, she knew. Might as well have a well-paired drink.

"But it all comes back. I'm old, thought I might have made it to the end, and the world could keep moving on, as it does."

He took a long, low pull at his cup. "But you all show up, and here we are."

Arin looked at Dane again. He'd made clear his desire to begin his life anew, which Melanie recognized and Arin wanted to ignore. That's what their fight was about the morning she was abducted. She had embarrassing anecdotes and close calls throughout her youth, but nothing she needed to jettison to move forward with life. Dane did. This old doctor, Marshall, did. Maybe Melanie, maybe even Ross, but she couldn't relate. She grew up with maids, not with skeletons in closets.

They watched from the rough perches of their makeshift chairs as Marshall added more split wood to the fire. It was dry and it caught quickly. His movements, however, were slow. Age was part of the reason, but he'd refused to face his story for days—decades, maybe?—and didn't know how to start. He did, eventually, with an answer to Arin's question.

"I was there that night. The night of the storm where your mother died." He said that while looking at Dane. "That was long ago. I don't know how you kids found that out—doesn't matter. She was right there, and I didn't even know." His voice caught. He coughed and again pulled deep from his cup. "Didn't know until it was too late. She was gone by then."

"Was she your patient?" Dane asked.

"Patient? No, she wasn't. She didn't know me. I didn't know her either. Only met her once."

"So why did you write her obituary?" This was Melanie, with her notebook open, shorthanding in darkness.

Arin watched Melanie's journalist mode click on despite a promise to keep to the background. She was good at what she did and wouldn't push the old man more than needed. He couldn't run this time, but he could shut down. He seemed on the verge of doing just that. It would be a delicate dance to keep him talking.

"Doesn't everyone deserve an obituary?"

"There was another man who died that night, too. Fell down a ravine. He didn't get one," Melanie responded.

"It's a shame. I didn't know him."

"But you did know Gina. Who was she to you?" Dane asked. "Hey. I can take it, whatever it is. I've seen a lot. My family was broken. I want to know who my mom was. Why she suffered from headaches that drove her mad. Anything about her. I was a kid when she went away. Still a kid when she died."

"If I could tell you, I would. But I don't—"

"Stop with the horseshit!" Dane cut in, standing and towering over him.

Arin winced. They'd discussed keeping calm in hopes of coaxing out what the old doctor knew. They were already invading his space—uninvited and unwanted—and anger would clam him up and end their investigation.

"What aren't you telling us?" continued Dane, standing up and raising both his posture and his voice. "We were nearly killed, and we don't have time for whatever game you're on. How did you know my mother? I'm halfway to assuming you killed her yourself. Your truck was on the property. Storm at night, power out, house full of mental patients. It was chaos. I'm not good with the law right now, but I'll go to them for this. You've got about six seconds to convince me you didn't kill her that night, or I'll take you in myself. The woods are deep out here, but I know how prisons are, and I wouldn't want to do you the favor of denying you that experience."

Arin reached out to calm Dane down but retracted. She'd hadn't seen him angry like that. He needed to vent, but she wished it wasn't on the one guy they needed to keep in a cooperative mood. And accusing him of murder wasn't a thought anyone had said aloud.

At least Dane brought them to the edge. The old doctor would talk, or he wouldn't. No more dance.

Marshall took Dane's outburst—and his accusation—with little response. The echoes of Dane's shouting faded, and Marshall motioned for him to sit.

He handed him the bottle for a refill. The fire snapped in the thin night air. Voices from other sites echoed up and down the road. Children shouting and adults laughing. Headlights from a passing car lit their circle, then faded again. They sipped their drinks as the old doctor cleared his throat.

"I didn't kill her. I didn't even see her that night. Her funeral was over by the time I knew she was gone, so I didn't even say goodbye. I had to ask around to learn enough about her to write her obituary." He paused for another sip. "I saw her when she was an infant, and never again. If I'd known she was there—oh, merciful God, if I'd just stayed home—it might have been different. I didn't kill her, but I can't face myself and say I didn't have a hand in that terrible night.

"I worked in that hospital a long time ago. Late sixties. I hadn't been back there since, but I needed to get some records from my time there. They were still in the archives, as far as I knew. I didn't have access anymore, and that type of request would raise too many questions, and those questions wouldn't help anyone. So I needed a different plan.

"I read that the place had gotten funding for a security upgrade, which would make getting in much harder. One of the problems the upgrade would have fixed was the magnetic door locks. When power is lost, they release. We'd known that forever, but it never got fixed. So I waited for a storm. A nor'easter came a few weeks later, and I drove up. Parked down the road and crept up in the rain and wind. Hell of a storm. I can't hear much these days but I can still hear that wind whining in the trees. I tripped the main breaker outside and gave the place another good half hour to get whipped up into chaos, then opened a side door and went down to the archives. Nobody saw me."

Arin broke her rapt attention from his story and glanced at Melanie, who was still taking notes. She'd mentioned something about a security upgrade earlier. Back during the quaint school-research-project phase of this ungodly nightmare.

"After that," Marshall continued, his voice breaking again, "I left. Soaking wet. Lightning strikes outlined that huge old goddamned fortress like God above was trying to bring it to life. I let Him keep trying, and I drove off. I didn't know anyone got hurt until later."

"All for some old files?" Dane questioned, the edge returning to his voice. "My mother died in the chaos you caused so you could walk out with some old papers?"

Marshall choked back a sob. "Yes. Jesus, yes. It's a pain I'll never lose. And if my actions that night could get any worse... I didn't even get the papers. I knew where they were locked away. The cabinet was still there, still locked, buried behind decades of boxes. Files were still in there from the same time, but the ones I went for were gone. Someone else had gotten there before me."

Night had fully descended, and the cracking fire danced stark shadows on each face leaning into the story. The old doctor drained two fingers of his drink and passed the bottle around again. Each took a needed refill.

"So those files, they were about Gina?" asked Arin.

"Maybe she had a mention or two, but not by name. They were mostly about a girl named Carmen. A Navy nurse. A stunning young woman."

His eyes softened, and the fire absorbed his memories. He continued after a quiet moment.

"I hope your stools aren't too uncomfortable. Carmen's story, though, there's not much comfort there."

32

CARMEN REDWOOD AND a pair of friends from the Navy Nurse Corps pranced into the luminescent dance hall. They giggled from the drinks, the warm night air, and the unparalleled joy of safe, solid ground after gruesome months of hell on a hospital ship. Their fleet had docked, their tour was over, and the night was theirs.

It's like being reborn. The freedom and the music and the boys. Until the next tour—but that wasn't worth a thought now. The only duty left was to celebrate, and she would fulfill those orders with abandon.

The trio quickly found eager dance partners. They danced with fellow sailors but also with some locals who tracked port calls and knew when to show up at the clubs near the base. The civilians were mostly girls chasing hungry Sailors, but there were a few civilian guys who knew nurses, just as hungry, would be among the returning heroes.

There were new songs and bands out by then, but their dance moves hadn't aged much, and they were eager to spin holes into the polished wooden floor. Carmen shared several dances with a young man who caught her eye. Or maybe she caught his. She couldn't remember, and it didn't matter. A civilian, which was just as well as she'd been surrounded by sailors and Marines for months. Her shipmates were good people, mostly, but she didn't come here to see those same faces yet again, and she had to be careful with bothersome fraternization regulations.

Will, her dance partner, had some job in town, but she didn't catch the details. Smooth talker, good looker, great dancer—all a girl needed. He led her through a few newer dances that had become popular since she'd been underway. She was happy to learn everything he taught her.

They laughed and drank and ran the clock into the small hours before they left. Her friends went on with a group from their boat, and she trailed off with Will. They walked through the warm summer night and talked. He did something with supplies for the war, so he was interested in the ships and the personnel she had seen. Not the most romantic of topics, but she shared what she knew and steered the conversation back to more pleasant pastures.

They walked a few miles into town until they reached his home on a quiet street. She blushed as they stood at his door. She was supposed to be brave and mature after the horrible experience of her tour, but this was a different battle. The euphoria of being back on home ground won the night. He offered his hand, and she took it. She went inside.

SHE MET HIM A FEW times over the following days. They took bike rides, and she rode in his fast car with the top down. He wasn't interested in meeting her friends, she realized, but she was content to keep him to herself. She'd never had any problem finding dates, and she'd been on enough to know when something was serious and when it was... well... just for some quick fun. This seemed to be the latter, and she was resetting herself from the tour and didn't want to deal with emotions. They complicated things, and she didn't have the energy for that. She'd be leaving for home at the end of the week, too, and Will didn't seem interested in her family, either.

Fine. He was fine. All was fine.

The summer wind blew her auburn hair back as they cruised down a long country road out of town. Sunglasses covered her green, almond-shaped eyes. Her sundress flapped dangerously open in the wind, and he looked over with a grin.

"I'd think you could heal those troops with just a smile."

"Sometimes, maybe. I do what I can."

They pulled down around a bend on a quiet farm road and shared lunch and a few beers. He asked more about the ships and the number of troops she had seen.

"I'm not all that eager to keep talking about the war. Surely there's something more fun to discuss?"

"It's my job, Carmen. I can't help it, I guess. But sure, let's talk about you. Or let's not talk." The beers were cold and the sun was pleasant and there wasn't another soul in sight. Her sundress came off and they did a lot of not talking before heading back to town. They promised to meet again the next day.

Carmen went back that night to her barracks on base. She would take leave to travel home soon but wanted to enjoy a few more days of revelry with the friends she had made and laughed and cried with during her deployment.

It takes time to wash away all of the blood and horror and death she saw as their ship floated around the South China Sea. She helped a lot of boys, but there were too many that she couldn't. She saw some of them moving around the base and getting accustomed to their new prosthetics. Some didn't go to the clubs or do much of anything, but rather sat around with downcast eyes. She didn't know how to help those kinds of wounds, but she tried with a smile and a friendly greeting where she could.

A boy named Tommy—or Corporal Mullins, but she and her fellow nurses usually got away with first names after a fashion—had been one of her patients. He was quiet, but she got him to talk about classical books and art and other topics that weren't common subjects along the quarterdecks and mess halls that had made up their little floating town. He was worried, it seemed, but Carmen couldn't get much from him. Whatever was gnawing at him was different than the fear, or indifference, or facades of bravado that most of the others showed. He didn't seem to have a girl back home, and he didn't talk about dreams for life after the war.

She considered him a friend and wanted to heal him if she could, but he didn't make it easy.

She saw him walking back from mess the next morning. She turned toward him to see if he might want to walk around town with her. There was a bookshop she'd wanted to peruse, which would be a sensible morning activity to balance out the excesses of her recent nights. Perhaps he would join her. She outranked him and couldn't be more than a friend to him, but she cared, and a friend was what he needed.

Carmen didn't get a chance to ask him about the bookshop. As she approached, two Military Police sergeants stepped in front of Tommy and blocked her view. She hurried toward him but was ordered back by the officers.

She saw Tommy's shoulders slump even more than usual. His eyes met hers as one of the officers cuffed him and led him away. The shame at that moment, when he saw her, was the most profound expression she'd ever seen on him. She stood in shock, helpless, as he was led away. The military is exceedingly tight on sharing information, but she hoped to learn what had happened to her friend.

The rest of her day was marred by thoughts of Tommy. She told Will she wasn't feeling well. That was true. She told him she'd like to meet him again the next day. That was also true. The usual gossips around base didn't know why Tommy had been taken or even where to. The drunks and the brawlers ended up in the base lockup or local jails in town but were back in the barracks the next day. That wasn't him, though, and no one saw him return. She wished him well and hoped she'd get a chance to talk to him again.

She met Will at the movies the next night and went home with him afterward. Enjoyable, but it needed to end. She'd been back on home soil for a few days now, and the carefree bliss of freedom from the boat and the war was wearing off. The next part of her life was waiting, and it didn't include him. She'd tell him that she was headed home for leave and then was being reassigned and wouldn't see him again. That was true. He wasn't the kind of guy who thinks men alone should make those decisions. She hoped that was true.

SHE STOPPED BY HIS PLACE in town after lunch the next day. She wanted to tell him in person, so she left a note saying they needed to talk. That would be a fair warning if he were bright enough to glean the subtext. As she turned to leave, one of the MPs that had taken Tommy walked toward her.

"That apartment is vacant as of today. Did you know the occupant?"

"Will? What happened?"

The Sergeant checked a notebook. "Ma'am, are you Lieutenant Redwood?"

She was in civilian clothes. How did he know her?

"I am. What happened to Will?"

"That's not his name." He looked around. The street was quiet. "Lieutenant, can you come with me?" He had parked his vehicle down the block. They entered and drove off. He wouldn't answer any more questions.

Carmen was led into a low brick building near the perimeter of the base. She sat down at a wooden table in a windowless room. Her pulse quickened. Had she done something wrong? She couldn't imagine what.

She was a nurse, a damned fine one at that, so why was she being treated like this? The MP left and locked the door behind him. The quiet moments that followed stretched into an hour, more. There wasn't a clock in the room. By her hunger, it was well past lunchtime. She had planned to get a sandwhich in town but never got the chance.

A knock, then an Army Major entered, followed by another gentleman in a suit. Both wore glasses and had the look of those who spent most of their time at desks. The suit opened a folder and showed her a photo of Will.

"Do you know this individual?" The suit had a thin face and small eyes that bored into her.

She hesitated as her mind raced, but delaying wouldn't help her. "Yes."

"What was the nature of your relationship?"

She wouldn't have called it anything close to a relationship. "I met him dancing. Then later for a drive. We saw a movie." She sighed. "Look, I left a note on his door that I wanted to talk. It's probably still there. I'm sure you gentlemen can read between the lines, but I was moving on. Leave and then reassignment, and he won't be part of any of it."

"Did you spend nights with him? At his place?"

That question didn't justify an answer. "What's this about? Where is he?"

"The better question would be, who is he?" said the Major. She questioned him with a look.

"Lieutenant, did you discuss military matters with this dancing and driving and movie-going partner of yours?" The man in the suit asked this.

Her stomach dropped, and her mouth went dry. She knew what this was about. She couldn't answer.

"Did you," he continued, "discuss specifics about troop sizes and ship deployment in the South China Sea?"

"I barely even know any of that," she blurted. "He said he was a supply contractor and wanted to know how things looked on the other end." She buried her face in her hands, but she wouldn't cry. She'd done her crying over there.

Carmen looked up again. "Who was he, really?"

"Your young companion is a foreign agent. I'll admit he walked and talked the part quite well. That's over now. We have him. And his notes."

Carmen closed her eyes, and her breath went choppy.

"I assume you're familiar with the Espionage Act of 1917 and its more recent revisions and court rulings." The Major clipped his words, holding his lips tight after each one. "If you're not, you soon will be. Factors like intent are no longer relevant, so whatever you're thinking, it won't work."

She stared into the wall in front of her. She worked to settle her breath.

The suit picked up where the Major left off. "Now, Lieutenant Redwood, your infractions are not to the level of the Rosenbergs but will nonetheless be taken seriously. Do you have any mitigating information to provide at this point? You have the right to retain legal counsel, of course, but a judge sympathetic to the blatant disclosure of classified information will be quite rare."

She didn't answer. She continued to stare at the wall. If she'd just tripped the bastard on the dance floor, she would have been done with him right there. Then she'd be packing for home and planning a road trip across this great land she'd done her part to defend. Now she was facing the brig.

The Major and the thin man in the suit looked at each other. The latter nodded, and the former grimaced before standing up. He shed a final look of contempt on Carmen and left the room. The door swung closed as the snap of his footsteps echoed down the hallway. The suit turned back to face her. He waited until she met his gaze.

"Lieutenant, I understand you are scared right now. Worried, angry, feeling betrayed. Perhaps hopeless."

She didn't contest.

"And you should be. If facing an espionage trial were your only option."

She widened her eyes. Just a little."What do you mean?"

"You caused damage to our country with your reckless disclosure. There may be a way you can right that balance. I work with a group that's exploring ways to help our ground troops. Save lives. End battles more quickly."

"And how in God's name would I help with that?" She was beyond protocol befitting her rank.

"Medically," he replied.

She tilted her head, but he didn't seem willing to elaborate.

"What do I need to do?"

"Work with us. And show a level of discretion much higher than you've shown so far. Friends, family, boys on the dance floor—nobody will know what you're working on."

"How long?"

"Until we're done. You need to decide now. You help us and right your wrong. Or I'll call the Major back in, and you'll face justice like anyone else would."

She didn't have a real choice. She held back tears as she nodded.

33

CARMEN LEFT THE base that evening. The thin man in the suit allowed her the gracious accommodation of writing a letter to her friends and parents, in which she could mention a special project but couldn't give any other details. The brevity wasn't a problem, as she had no other details to convey. He read through each one before sealing and stamping them. Her clothing and personal items would be gathered from her dorm, he told her.

She'd seen sailors and Marines go to the brig. They had ample time to say goodbye and tend to their affairs, and even to throw a party if they wished. They had a chance for a last meal at a restaurant, a last round at the bar, a last roll in the hay. She was given a cold sandwich and an apple for dinner. She'd need to be convinced that her choice was the better one.

A van arrived outside the building where she'd been held that day. Another man, also in a suit, drove her away. She shared the van with a young man in a crew cut who looked more scared than she was. He'd been picked up somewhere else, it seemed. She waited for him to start a conversation or even introduce himself, but he didn't.

They drove north as the sun set. Night had long fallen when the van slowed and a third passenger climbed in. Another guy in his twenties, also with a standard military crew cut.

They drove through the night, and Carmen tried to keep track of road signs but gave up. They were headed northeast, and she wasn't familiar with any of it. The two boys offered her the bench seat in the back of the van so she could get some sleep.

She woke as they left paved roads and rocked over dirt ones. She found a bag with a cold hamburger waiting for her, and ate it. She asked where they were, but got only sleepy shrugs in response.

They drove among steep, forested hills. She didn't see any signs. They climbed a long, winding road and reached a clearing near the top. A large, ornate building filled the space. Carefully kept terraced lawns and shrubs stretched out from all sides to the forest. It looked like a college campus or maybe like one of the nicer hospitals she'd seen, and studied in. Much nicer than most. Mental institutions, for some reason she didn't know, were opulent. This looked like one of them.

Mental issues were not her specialty—she'd received minimal training at best—but her experience working with shell-shocked troops had to be worth something. Despite the secrecy around her new assignment, she was eager to start helping where she could.

The place was gorgeous. A spacious entrance hall exhibited marble floors, chandeliers and paintings. They were led up a wide, curved stairway and into a wing on the third floor. The room they entered looked like a classroom, except for the plush chairs and ornate desks. A table on the side was neatly arranged with crackers and fruit and coffee. There were a few dozen other young people there. Some sitting, some picking over the food. All in military cuts except for one other woman who sat near the back, sipping water. One man stood and stared out of the large windows, and she recognized him. Tommy, the sailor who had been taken by the MPs the day before. She rushed over and grabbed his shoulder.

He turned, startled, then stepped back. "Lieutenant Redwood! Why are you here?"

"I'm not certain. Some type of project. You?"

"Same. That's all they told me."

"Can I ask... were you in trouble for something?"

His eyes lowered, and he folded inward. "Doesn't matter now. I came on some antiques over there. Valuable stuff. I brought them back, but they found them. Stupid. But they gave me this option. Can't say if I made the right choice."

"Same here." His eyes lifted back to hers. "Yes, I did something stupid as well. As did, I assume, everyone else here."

The door to the classroom—if that's what it was—opened, and an older man entered. He had long hair, glasses, and a paunch that hung over his belt. Not military, at least not anytime recently.

"Folks, ladies and gentlemen, please grab some food if you would like and find a seat. I know you didn't have much choice in coming here, but I thank you nonetheless." His demeanor was serious, but he radiated enthusiasm as he looked around the room. Carmen took a seat near the front, and the rest of the group also settled in.

"My name is Doctor Edwin. You can call me Rick. You're all coming from the service, but while you're here, first names will suffice. Rank isn't important, either—we're all in this together." He let that settle as he met each one of their eyes.

"Why the hell are we here?" someone behind her piped up.

"I will explain in due time, Charles. Yes, I know each one of you. I

239

had the chance to select candidates for our training program from a group of military members who would otherwise be facing unpleasant years in military prison. I hope you consider yourselves lucky. I do."

He leaned back on a desk. "You've all been spared the brig. And you now have a chance to make amends for your mistakes. Help your country. Help your brothers and sisters who are still out there. I don't know how long this will take, and this is a highly experimental program, but I'm confident we'll succeed.

"You're all here of your own free will. That means you can leave anytime." He pointed toward the door. "If you do, though, it'll be to wherever the Uniform Code of Military Justice deems you should be sent. And as this program is classified, you won't speak of it outside these walls. To anyone. Even when the judge asks why you missed your trial dates. You'll be on your own. I hope you all understand that."

The room had been silent, but after that statement, the low noises of chairs shifting and throats clearing ceased.

"So, before I continue," he said as he stood up again and motioned toward the door, "I'll give each of you the opportunity to leave."

One man near the back stood up and walked to the door. "I'll take my chances in the brig. Good luck, cats." He walked out the door. The doctor crossed his arms but remained silent. Nobody else stood up.

"We've got a great group here. We're going to do good things. You all have nicely accommodated private rooms, to which my assistant here will direct you. Settle in, and we'll get lunch delivered shortly. After that, we'll meet back here, and I'll explain Project Cardinal."

A younger man entered, holding a clipboard. He looked uncertain. Nervous, even. Kind eyes, Carmen noted, and even his forced smile wasn't half bad.

"Hello, I'm Dr. Brock," the assistant stated, attempting to show confidence.

He was young for a doctor, and his voice shook as he addressed the room. "But call me Marshall. I'll get you all to your rooms if you would kindly follow me."

CARMEN'S ACCOMMODATIONS WERE INDEED PLEASANT. Spacious, comfortable, and immaculate with an en-suite bathroom and a deep closet. A well-stocked bookshelf and a writing desk framed a window that looked out over the lawns and toward the forested hills beyond. A room designed for lasting comfort in a place she hoped not to remain for long wasn't encouraging, but after months at sea and a thought toward the alternative of a brig cell, she didn't complain.

Following time to relax in her room, she was led into a dining hall further down the wing. A long, stout table and plush chairs filled the room, and a row of serving trays covered the far wall. Wide windows displayed a view of the lawns on the other side of the building, including the winding entrance road and well-tended flower gardens.

She and her fellow—guests, would that be right?—filled their plates. The food selection was diverse and fresh. She chose a garden salad and roasted chicken and a glass of iced tea from among the many options. The food was delicious, and she'd been back on land long enough to raise her standards.

Some of the guests attempted half-hearted joking, but the meal was mostly silent. After lunch, they were directed back into what she called the classroom. Rick, Marshall, and another woman who introduced herself as Joanne stood in the front. Carmen felt a flutter of worry when the woman noted she was a nurse.

What did they need her for, then? It was a training program, though, and any place like this needs more nurses. But that woman was standing in front, and her ass was the one in the chair. She'd find out soon enough, it seemed. After everyone settled in, Rick addressed the room.

"I thank you all again for your agreement to participate in what promises to be a critical program for our country. I trust you found your rooms and dining options to your liking. If you have any requests on either front, don't hesitate to ask, and we'll do our best to accommodate. There's a game room and a reading room down the hall, and we'll arrange for hikes and outdoor games when the weather accommodates.

"As the program is classified, we're limiting our wing and any interactions to as few people as possible. Those of us in this room are the extent of the program. Meals and supplies will be left at the entrance, and we'll take it from there. You'll all help with that when needed. You'll also bear responsibility for cleaning and restocking your rooms. We'll review other details such as laundry, exercise, and any current medical requirements later."

Carmen and the rest of the program participants remained silent. Despite their lavish surroundings, it felt closer to prison than to a new training division. The guy who left the first day, or anyone who had opted for the brig when first given the choice, might be the bright ones. Walk with the devil you know.

"You are all members of our nation's defense forces," Rick continued. "Either directly or in support, but it's all the same mission. Building the strongest and smartest fighters we can to defend our people and our way of life. You all took the oath, then betrayed it, but this is your chance to rectify your grave mistakes." He took the time to look at each one of them.

"America is sending her boys into new battlefields. From the streets of Paris to the caves of the Pacific islands. The forests of Korea and now the jungles of Vietnam. What's the pattern? Close combat. The enemy isn't across a sprawling battlefield waving flags by the dawn's early light anymore. They're in your face. Beside the window. Behind a tree or lying in the bushes. Night and day. Rain and Snow. Anytime, any weather. We can't see them. And we're getting cut bloody at every turn."

Low murmurs from some of the veterans around the room acknowledged that stark reality. Carmen had gotten her hands deep in too many young men who hadn't known how close the enemy was until it was too late.

Rick continued. "Our night vision technology is improving, but it's still not practical. Too much gear. Unreliable. Easy to defeat and injure the wearer with flares or muzzle flashes. Even a damn flashlight will blind you when you're wearing it, and then the fight is half over. So we need something better. And when we humans can't find the right answer, we look to nature. To animals."

He unrolled and taped a large poster on the wall.

"I think we've all been to kindergarten," someone behind her shouted out, hoping for a laugh. "I know what a damn frog looks like. Know what them bastards taste like, too." A few nervous chuckles started, then died out. Rick and the younger guy—Marshall, was it?—ignored him. When the poster taping was done, five animals looked out over them.

Marshall stood up, apparently getting the cue to take over. He was nervous. He looked a few years older than most of the troops there, but that was only counting the years he'd lived. The veteran's experiences gave them age and an edge, and the young doctor struggled to address them.

He turned to the board as he pointed out the posters. "Bullfrogs, vampire bats, goldfish, mosquitos, and salmon. These animals and many others can see things we don't. Light that the human eye can't perceive. We don't have the right enzymes and receptors, but they do." His speech sped up, as if getting his words out and sitting back down were his only goal. "The visible light we see is only a tiny slice in the middle of the electromagnetic spectrum. The whole range spans wavelengths from gamma to radio waves—"

"Christ on the shitter, you're killing us here, Doc!" The same guy yelled out. "Tell us why the hell we're here and get on with it. I've got tickets to the bowl game next week and I'll be damned if I miss it while you prattle on about bats and radios."

Rick stayed back, leaving Marshall to field the question. Carmen had seen that same behavior with senior nurses training new graduates. Books only go so far, and you can't have a green nurse at the beds or a green grunt in the field. And they don't stay green for long out there. Facing down battle-weary troops in a classroom was as much pressure as a young doctor could get in the hills of western Massachusettes.

Marshall turned from the board and faced them. He looked at Carmen, and she softened her eyes. Following a deep inhale, he swiveled his gaze to the heckler. "I'll prattle on about bats and radio waves and whatever else I want to. You can ignore me or talk over me. It won't matter. But when we start the training and testing you'll be doing here, it might help to know what's happening. Or we can just poke you with needles and have you point at pictures like monkeys. You made the first choice to come here and help your brothers in arms. To serve our country. How much you want to understand is your next choice."

Rick stepped in. "That's right. This young doctor has the bright mind we need here. And for those who may have missed some of his implications, I'll make it clear. We're going to do our goddamned best to give you sight that no human has had before. And none of you are leaving here until we do."

34

ANY NOTION CARMEN and her fellow subjects had that their unique training program was based on elite selection or a fortunate privilege faded with the colors on the leaves outside their window. They were medical test subjects.

The two doctors and the nurse began with a barrage of tests far more thorough than any basic training or pre-deployment physicals. They tested everything. Took samples from everywhere. As indicated, though, their focus was on eyesight. Vision and perception tests across the spectrum. Notes about all manner of lights and shapes and movements went into their growing collections of charts.

After the baseline tests came the trials. Being a nurse, Carmen was more familiar with some of the medication and equipment, but even she lost track of the names and types of everything thrown at her. Injections and pills. Curated diets. Long sessions of exposure to specifically tuned lighting. Or to no lighting at all in the darkroom set up near the end of the hallway. All of it was recorded in their charts.

Games, too, seemed to be part of the tests. Dr. Brock spent hours playing card games and board games with Carmen, which she looked forward to. He would bring snacks and wine and beer, too. Those days were treats. The time he'd spend with her, she realized, had to be much more than he spent with anyone else. There just aren't that many hours in a day. She didn't complain.

But as long as she stayed there—still an apparent choice—Carmen had no rights. She took the oath of service when she joined the military, understanding she'd lose rights she'd enjoyed as a citizen, whether or not she appreciated them at the time. But this was beyond any expectations. Even prisoners had rights around bodily autonomy that the subjects of Project Cardinal did not.

Fellow subjects expressed regret at not choosing the brig. They could still leave, they knew. But the longer they remained, the more serious their pending charges would be. Failure to appear for their appointed trial became desertion—the most serious of offenses in any military. Not only lifelong sentences and possible execution but the oppressive weight of shame that burdens not just the bearer but their family and friends as well. Rick made that clear. He freely shared examples of others who had broken their oaths and detailed how their families had suffered.

Still, some left. Shortly after, Carmen would find local newspaper articles left around the meal room, helpfully opened to articles about the fates of those same former subjects.

WEEKS PASSED, THEN MONTHS. WINTER came and roared and eventually faded to a chilly spring. They went through more tests and received more medication and supplements.

The doctors hadn't been clear about the duration of the program other than Rick's admonition that they would see it out. Carmen hadn't thought it would stretch into new seasons, though, and not into the new year.

No changes or improvements in their vision were apparent. Rick, Marshall, and Joanne, the program's nurse, didn't show discouragement at the lack of progress. Carmen got the impression they expected the program to extend even longer.

The repetition bogged down morale as much as anything. Between appointments for testing and receiving medications and other treatments, they'd have days with no agenda. Free to read or exercise or play games, but only on their secluded wing. Sometimes in small groups around the grounds and along the steep forested trails outside, but in those cases, they were indistinguishable from the certified mental patients in the other wings. The contrast between the two groups blurred as the year churned on.

Marshall was as friendly to Carmen as he could be within the confines of the program. They'd play games and take walks outside. He was gentle and seemed sympathetic to their plight. Maybe with hers more than the others, or maybe that was her imagination. None of the testing or treatment was pleasant, but the days he administered them were her better days. She wondered if he knew what he was getting into when he started here. She wanted to believe he didn't. Like herself.

After a year, only half of the subjects remained. Fourteen subjects and three administrators. The sailor she'd known on the outside, Tommy, had left. He'd begun getting incapacitating headaches to the point that he couldn't sleep or eat. He was removed from the program, along with a few others who showed new medical issues that kept them from continuing. Carmen didn't know what their fate was, but they didn't quit on their own. She hoped Tommy was well and recovering somewhere. They'd become friends. Talked about books and art and music.

She was the only woman left in the program after the first year. That first year, where there was no progress at all to show. By that time, the doctors were hoping for tangible results, and their frustration began to show. Carmen and her fellow subjects should be able to notice wavelengths above 700 nanometers, they said. All those animals could, and they were being treated with the same enzymes that should augment the red-seeing cones in their eyes.

Carmen knew that the program was a stab in the dark, so to speak, but Rick and Marshall wouldn't admit that.

Testing became less frequent, but the treatments were increased. She recognized the name of a new medication they'd introduced to the routine. Lysergic Acid Diethylamide. She'd seen it on the outside, both in military units and on civilian streets. She'd never tried it, but if there's a way to get someone to see something they couldn't before, LSD would be it. It seemed like the doctors were grasping for ways to write something other than "no noticeable change" in their omnipresent notes.

She hated the loss of control from the drug, but it was a break from the stasis of what her life had become. She could dream a little bigger and smile a little wider. Until it wore off, and she found herself grounded again in the big stone building on top of the isolated mountain.

They tested both during and after those treatments. She couldn't imagine what useful information the doctors would get while their subjects were high, but they took notes nonetheless.

Carmen grew to appreciate those treatments and even to look forward to them. And the doctors seemed to be noticing more changes. Maybe not what they hoped for, and not effects centered around the program's goals, but changes were changes.

She didn't know what else they were giving them or in what doses. It seemed to be a variety of chemical compounds, but the treatment approach was well beyond her expertise.

What she did know was that she had become addicted. She, along with some others who remained in the program, would get headaches or other adverse symptoms between treatments. And they'd ease after the next session. For a while.

She knew now that leaving wasn't an option. They all knew that, the dozen or so who remained. Serious state charges awaited them on the outside, and now a need for substances would drive them down paths that wouldn't end well.

Carmen was comfortable there, in that opulent prison. She could read and play games and take walks. She ate well and made friends and listened to records. Compared to life underway on the hospital ship, days here were better.

She kept in mind the goal of Project Cardinal. If a breakthrough happened and a way of augmenting eyesight for the troops was possible, it would do wonders for America's success in this and future wars. She tried not to think much beyond that. To enjoy what she could and bear the rest. She'd made a mistake and was serving her sentence in a way that might not be the absolute worst option. She supposed that she would never know what the worst option was.

Another year passed. More subjects—or patients or students or prisoners or whatever they were—had left. Some by choice to face a legal reckoning at the whims of a country torn by war, and some from personal medical conditions.

Carmen's headaches had gotten worse but were usually manageable. They'd given her enough substances of all types that a few more to control her headaches wouldn't make a difference.

She'd grown closer to Marshall during that time. He confided in her that he had also done something wrong and been forced into this program, but on the other side. What a civilian doctor could do to be forced to administer something like this she couldn't imagine, but he didn't elaborate and she didn't press.

She respected him, but more than that. He could be charming at times. Soft brown hair and the easy smile of a civilian who'd never seen combat. She found him endearing and softer than the veterans she'd been around.

Rick, the lead doctor, left for a week the following spring. Project Cardinal had been running for over two years, and only Carmen and five others remained. That night was warm, and the windows were open to allow the fresh spring breeze to clear stagnant memories of winter from the old stone walls. The evening grew late, and Joanne, the nurse, had retired to her room.

Carmen's windows were open, and she saw light reflected against the trees from another open window a few rooms down. That would be the office. Marshall was still awake, processing notes or simply reading, perhaps. She left her room and slinked in her sleeping gown down the old hall. Without knocking, she entered the room and nudged the door shut behind her.

"Carmen," Marshall said, looking up from his work. "Headaches again?"

"No, Marshall." She walked closer, keeping her voice low and her eyes on his. "I haven't had a headache for days. I'm feeling just wonderful, in fact."

She walked up to the desk, her slender fingers picking at the buttons on the front of her gown. "Must be this lovely spring breeze and the new flowers in the air... I saw the light from your office..."

She reached the lowest button, and her gown fell loose. A gust from the window blew it open, pulling it from her shoulders to the floor. She wore nothing underneath.

Marshall put his pen down as Carmen walked around his desk.

She spun his chair and moved in without another word. She lowered herself, straddling him in his chair, and brought her mouth to his. He answered as he wrapped his arms around her back. The breeze combed her hair to the side and pulled eager goosebumps from every inch of her bare skin. She arched in closer, leaving just enough gap to work his shirt buttons loose.

His notes spilled onto the floor, and the two of them soon followed.

CARMEN AND MARSHALL CREATED OPPORTUNITIES to meet during spring and summer. Planned rendezvous in the forested trails and purposefully timed appointments in her room. Carmen didn't know if any of her treatments affected her libido, but they certainly didn't hurt. Her bearable existence in those old stone walls became enjoyable, at least on occasion.

With only six patients remaining in the program, Joanne was rarely present, and Rick only appeared a few days each week. Marshall seemed to be the only one restricted from leaving. Like the rest of them. She didn't ask. She couldn't lose what she had built.

It was a late summer day when Marshall called her to his office to deliver her latest examination results. There was no change in the vision tests—the program's sole purpose—but he had other news to deliver.

Carmen was pregnant.

35

ARIN LISTENED TO Marshall's story, enraptured and appalled. A young nurse forced into a years-long lab experiment—ethics be damned. To arrest her running thoughts, she stood to feed the dwindling fire. She needed to burn something. She already knew how the story ended, but wasn't ready to face it.

"Of course, she couldn't raise the baby there," Marshall continued as flames peeled back the bark on the freshly added firewood. "And she couldn't leave by that point, even if she wanted to. We were all in too deep by then, searching for a miracle but knowing we'd all be prosecuted if the program became public. The child, though, the poor little girl—she was innocent. As all children are. Her fate would be better if loving and unassuming parents raised her. Elsewhere. So, we found a local orphanage, and I drove the baby there myself. Left her there, anonymously."

Dane pulled a joint from his chest pocket and leaned forward to light it on the open flames. Arin watched him nearly singe his eyebrows, but he didn't seem to care. Following a deep pull, he exhaled and looked at Marshall. "My mother."

The old doctor looked up, his eyes misty. "We needed a name that wouldn't link the little girl to Carmen. Or to me. So Redwood became Rosewood. And Carmen chose the name, Gina. Yes, that was your mother I left in the soft arms of a caretaker at the orphanage. I couldn't bring myself to visit her again. I told myself that the risk was too much, but I know now that it wasn't the risk of the program's fate, or even mine or Carmen's, but the risk of attachment kept me away. And the shame. I shared news of the child with Carmen when she asked, but it wasn't real. I made it up. I drove by a few years later and watched children playing outside, but I didn't know who she was or if she was even still there."

The snapping fire cast shadows on each face. Arin watched Dane as he followed the sparks upward until they disappeared against the backdrop of the stars. His joint followed the whisky bottle around the fire, and even the two medical professionals in attendance partook.

"The next time I saw Gina's face," Marshall coughed, then continued, "was a lifetime later on the back pages of a local paper. She was gone, the funeral was done, and I knew I could never forgive myself. I'd opened a family practice but couldn't carry on anymore. Not as a physician. Not as anything. I retired and bought that house. I had no family, and never would. Judge me as you wish. I certainly have."

He refilled his cup and then looked at Arin. "I went back to that orphanage one more time."

"To leave my father."

"Yes. Randall Coppertree. Another child. Another name that wasn't Redwood but was close enough to honor where he came from. That's what I told myself. It was a few years later, and Carmen was one of the only remaining subjects in Project Cardinal."

"And you never visited him."

"No. I buried myself in research. Progress was fleeting where it existed at all. We knew it would take time, but the lack of repeatable results after years of trials was disheartening. Government support would be cut, so Rick consulted with a private medical company to secure additional funding. We'd all put so much into it by then, and more boys were dying in jungles and swamps every day."

"You put time and knowledge and work in," Melanie said through a sharp grimace. "But the patients put their health and sanity on the line, doctor. It's hard to sit here and listen to you explain away your actions in the name of national security. That's been tried before. Where were the ethics? What kind of human forces other humans to be lab rats?"

He stared into the flames as her barbed words cut the night air. "That type of thing, ethics and all, didn't come up much. Listen. I'm old and don't have much longer here. I intended to take my shame with me. The horrible things we did. I did. To her. But you showed up and didn't let me. So here were are."

Silence built until Ross broke it with some questions about the medical trials. Arin tried to follow, but her mind swirled. Her family history was laid bare. She felt pain for someone she didn't know existed until that night.

Ross's raised voice brought her back to the fire circle. He'd pressed into an area that Marshall was even more reluctant to reveal. "So those all could be side effects of your kitchen-sink approach. Throw everything you have at the subjects and see what sticks. And keep at it? The headaches and sicknesses among the group, and you just kept going." He let out a low exhale. "Sixties were a wild time, eh, doctor?"

"I did leave. Eventually. The program died down, at least I thought it did, with no proven success. Carmen, that beautiful young nurse, was the only one still there. Others left to face trial, some ran off. A few lost it, really went loony, and simply got moved to one of the other wings of that same hospital. We were ok with that, as no one would believe their story if they tried to tell it."

"Carmen." Arin started. "After you left, what happened to her?"

"All I know is that she got sick and died a few years later. I left one night and never saw her again. Like the two children at the orphanage, I couldn't face going back. I wanted a new life. To be a doctor who hadn't been part of that. One who could help people.

"I went to get the records that night Gina died, decades after the program was mothballed. I told myself it was to erase that past. All traces of it. I'd get the files and burn them." He tossed another log on the fire. "But I know I would have looked at her notes first."

"So, who took them?" Melanie asked.

"Who knows? The government. The company that sponsored the program. Maybe the janitor was told to clean out musty old boxes. But things like this don't just go away, do they? They can't be burned and buried."

Ross spoke again. "Your program. Project Cardinal. You called it a failure, but you now realize it worked, right? Arin and Dane show that it must have, at some level. You didn't have the tools or the knowledge to see it back then, to test properly, but it was successful. The epigenetic changes you deliberately effected onto Carmen, and maybe some others, were passed down through the generations. The theory is called epigenetic inheritance. Truly remarkable, even if it was just random chance on the part of your appaling trials. There's almost no reason it should have caused anything but sickness and suffering. Almost. But the human body is more complex than any of us know, and your moral fucking quagmire churned out something amazing."

Ross looked around the group and then back into the flames. "From my modern vantage point, sitting here tonight, you ran a bleak and soulless program. A rose-tinted hell for everyone involved and a disparagement to the medical and scientific community. Jesus, I can't even picture the path to something like that happening today. Not in America, anyway. Ends don't justify the means, but still, you broke into a new realm of medical possibility. Astounding."

Arin watched Ross as he went on, transitioning from disgust to awe and back again. Her own revulsion at what she'd just learned about her family history tore at her. She felt hollow. Betrayed by what had been kept from her and sorrow for what had happened to Carmen, a grandmother she never knew. A woman who risked her life to serve her country, and was then forced into a desperate experiment run by that same country.

Did Carmen love him, this young doctor who drove her through years-long imprisonment and forced medical trials? Was it Stockholm Syndrome that drove her to him? The old man was remorseful, but she felt no sympathy for him. The man who told Carmen's story on the other side of the flames was not her grandfather. She refused to give him that title. He'd earned no such place in her life.

The night grew colder, the questions died out, and they left Marshall to his fire and his drink. He'd unloaded his story on them. Left it putrid and lingering for them to process. There were no thanks given. No handshakes or hugs. Arin saw Dane give him a slight nod, but it was perfunctory at best. Not a gesture given to a beloved grandfather.

They walked back toward the car. Ross nearly stumbled on the rutted dirt road, the looming trees between sites blocking the thin moonlight. Arin saw he'd been thumbing and swiping at his phone, an activity not used on prepaid units. She grabbed his arm as he recovered from the stumble.

"Thanks, I didn't have time to get my hiking boots for a trek like this. I mean time to buy some. Not the type of footwear I keep around these days." Ross turned his head back to the glowing screen.

"Ross?" Arin's tone was sharp enough that the others stopped walking and faced her. "Tell me that isn't the phone you said you'd left at home."

"It's ok, it's on airplane mode. I'm taking some quick notes while they're fresh to research later. What that old guy did with his program? I'll have a dissertation that'll rock the medical world."

Melanie snapped toward him and grabbed his shoulders. "How did you not understand us?" She seethed. "You do remember the shit we've been through, right? Did you take notes then, or did you forget? Turn that off, or I'll crush it and throw it in the woods. Right goddamned now!"

He powered it down and tucked it away.

"And when we get to town," Melanie continued, "leave it outside by the table where we ate. Call the restaurant later, and they'll hold it or mail it or whatever. I don't care what you do, but it's not going in my car again."

The phone didn't make it to the restaurant, and none of them made it back to Melanie's rental car. Around the next bend on the dark road, three men clad in black tactical gear, brandishing flashlights and pistols, eased from shadowed trees and surrounded them. They were joined by a woman in a dark parka and a darker expression.

Arin recognized the former congresswoman. "Hello, Robin," she said.

36

"SECURE THEM. TIGHTLY." Robin barked orders at the three armed guards who proceeded her out of the cover of the trees on the side of the secluded campground road. "Starting with that one."

Arin's stomach flipped as the woman locked her down with a piercing gaze. Plastic cuffs pinched her wrists before she could react. She saw Dane tense and she sent a frantic head shake his way. *Don't do something stupid.*

Their captors were armed and had caught them unaware. Exhausted. Still processing the revelations about her and Dane's family, all on the far side of shared whisky and weed and in no shape to resist. They were each bound and led back down the road toward the campsite they had just left.

Arin glanced Melanie's way but was jerked forward by the thug assigned to her. The other two men walked Dane and Melanie forward. Robin—the woman Melanie had identified in the dark—walked

Ross forward. She was older and assigned herself to manage the tall, skinny guy she assumed would put up the least resistance. Arin wondered if Ross realized that.

No cars passed, and no sites within shouting range indicated anyone was still awake. Crying for help would get them nothing but shot.

The abduction—Arin's second such event in the last few days—took all of a few frantic breaths. She had time to comply and nothing else. A last wind of energy had hit her as the guards jumped into view, but she had no reasonable path to direct it.

The four captors and their equal number of scared, tired, angry, and confused captives approached the waning firelight of Marshall's campsite. Marshall sat there yet, hunched and head lowered, empty bottle in hand. If he heard them approach, he didn't acknowledge it.

"Doctor Brock." Robin's voice cut through the flames.

He looked up, startled, nearly dropping the bottle. Arin saw his red eyes as he wiped tears away, trying to focus and make sense of the group before him.

Robin continued before he had a chance to respond. "It's quite a surprise to me seeing you here. I was led to believe you had long since retired and would be of no use to our continued efforts. Yet here I find you working with this precious group. How curious."

"Who are you? Let them go!" He yelled, standing up and gripping the bottle by the neck.

"I work for the outfit that supported your program all those years ago." She waved a dismissive hand. "You gave up, they didn't, but that doesn't matter now. What does matter is that I need a way to transport a group of four difficult people, and you happen to have just the ride." She nodded towards his new RV.

"What the hell do you want with them?" Marshall demanded.

Arin read genuine confusion in his tone, stacked on sorrow. And on pain. Whatever he'd been part of back then, he thought it was done, and only atonement remained. His past had roared back in a way he couldn't control or even understand. A familiar feeling.

"Let them go, damn you!" he shouted, his weathered voice cracking.

"You're of no help to us anymore," Robin stated. "Give us the keys to the camper, and we'll be on our way. I trust you know to remain silent."

Arin watched the old man heave out deep breaths, clenching the bottle and looking at her. And at Dane.

His face softened. In those concerned eyes, she could see him as a father. As a grandfather. With resolve, he stood as tall as his long years allowed. With a wince and an audible grunt, he stepped into a forward lunge and flung the heavy glass bottle at the guard holding Arin. In nearly the same motion, he stooped to barehand a burning log from the firepit and flicked it at the guard near Dane.

All three guards raised their pistols to fire at their elderly assailant. Arin, Melanie, and Dane instinctively drove themselves into them as they fired, sending the shots wild.

Most of them.

Marshall crumpled as one of the rounds struck his chest. He fell forward into the edge of the firepit and rolled away, his shirt sleeve alight. A dark stain spread from his torso and contrasted with the light brown of the dead grass beneath him. He moaned and rolled further from the fire.

The captives fought. Arin got in a powerful stomp to her guard's head before he had a chance to recover from her shouldering. She saw Dane kick his guard down as Melanie ran for the trees. Arin couldn't see Ross but heard Robin shriek and fall as well.

"Them!" Robin yelled from the ground, pointing at Arin and Dane. "Fuck the others—get those two!"

More shots sounded. Arin saw Melanie stumble as she broke into the tree line. She tried to run after her but was ripped to the ground as a guard grabbed her by her bound wrists. The cuffs bit deep into her skin.

A guard struck Dane in the back of his head with the butt of a gun. He dropped to his knees and braced himself with his bound hands. Ross ran and tripped on a shadowed rut in the road. With his hands also bound, he face-planted into the unforgiving hardpack.

Arin's vision blurred as she yelled into the dark forest after Melanie, her body pinned to the ground, her head twisted to see but fire-blinded to everything behind the flames. The guard holding her down panned his flashlight along the ground with his other hand. He'd lost his pistol. Arin caught movement and looked to the other side of the fire.

Marshall had recovered himself and the stray firearm and pointed it at the nearest guard, the one holding Dane. Sticky darkness covered his shirt and angry blisters reared up along his fingers where he'd grabbed the burning log.

Marshall wrested a moment of tranquility from the chaos and looked back at her. Arin held his gaze for the length of a stolen breath, and she saw compassion in the folds of his aged and worry-strewn face.

A smile. A memory.

An acceptance and resignation, all in one final sight.

He turned back toward the guard holding Dane and fired. The thug jerked up and twisted away. The other guard, who had lost Melanie earlier, snapped towards Marshall and sent three rounds home.

Arin watched her grandfather fall with a groan and lay still.

She tried to stand but was thrown back to the ground. Her head hit a rock at the edge of the fire ring. Her last thought was a vain hope that her hair didn't splay too close to the hungry flames. As her vision tunneled away, she saw Dane fall with another blow to the back of his head.

A ROUGH JOSTLE, AND ARIN woke to find herself bound tight on a carpeted floor. A loud, shaking, rumbling floor. Her head pounded. She waited for her vision to return, but it didn't and she realized she was blindfolded. She then realized she was taking the promised RV ride.

She reached out with her feet and connected with another body. No response. Tried to maneuver further but her ropes hit a limit. Whispered but received no reply.

She drew her focus inward. Her breathing eased and the pounding in her head subsided enough to allow sleep.

SHE NEXT WOKE TO A cold, hard floor pressing her upward. The floor was stone and unyielding. Her eyes remained covered and her wrists were still bound. With consciousness came an involuntary moan that echoed and told her she was somewhere big and unadorned. She heard nothing other than the sharp echo of her moan.

Her inner focus returned to Melanie. Arin had last seen her stumble in the woods. God, she hoped it was only a stumble.

"Hello?" she ventured a soft call into the cavernous room. No response came, other than the fading echo of her call. Cold drafts pitched an eerie note in the distance before encroaching to cross her face and raise goosebumps on her arms.

She smelled a must she recalled but couldn't place. Old stone and encroaching earth. *Why was that familiar?*

She scooted herself to her knees and then to standing. Blind and bound, she stood, listening. Her head rang with a thudding torment and she swayed to keep her balance. Tried walking but stood on something soft. Nudged it with her foot, and it stirred. Someone's leg. She tapped harder and got a low groan in response.

"Holy hell, my head hurts. What fucknut tied me up?" That was Dane.

She shuffled around until she ran into two more bodies. No response from either of them, but she smelled the lingering trace of a familiar lilac shampoo cutting through the odor of campfire smoke and sweat and raw dirt.

Melanie was there. Breathing. Arin felt hot tears swell under her blindfold.

"Wake the others up," commanded a distant voice.

Arin worked to clear her mind and placed the speaker as Robin. The woman who ordered her to be abducted and imprisoned. The woman who captured and dragged them to wherever she stood now. The woman whose security team killed her newly acquainted grandfather and nearly killed Melanie.

Arin had killed Robin's son, though. Perhaps her displeasure about that still lingered, a full two days later. Maybe it had been less. The hour felt early, but she didn't know the time, and didn't have free eyes to look at her watch.

"Secure them all there. Particularly that one." She didn't need to see to know Robin was pointing at her. Malice barbed the woman's words.

The sting of that voice drilled through her pounding head and honed her resolve to end this. To somehow get herself and Melanie and the others out of there. Whatever Robin needed, she wasn't going to get it.

Heavy steps thudded her way. A meaty hand grabbed her arm and pulled her back against a wall. She heard the others being dragged. Another moan, followed by a whimper. That would be Ross.

He didn't earn this. They'd pulled him along on their trip to find Marshall. He was fascinated by the groundbreaking biology she and

Dane exhibited and was invested in hearing from a reclusive doctor who might have answers. He also had a distinct lack of interest by law enforcement, which was an advantage among their group. Arin had explained the peril before he jumped in the car with them the morning before, but she sent a mental note of apology toward the sound of his whimpering.

But it was his cell phone that got them tracked and caught. They'd been careful since leaving New York, but Robin and her group must have had Ross higher on their radar than they thought. She had contacted him with a job offer after he sent out his fMRI notes and had apparently kept close tabs. Troy had likely tagged Ross's phone along with hers and Melanie's. Arin was tempted to rescind the apology she'd just sent.

She snapped her thoughts back to the room as a familiar weight constricted around her ankle. She heard three more sets of clicks along the wall. They must have a boxful of those heinous proximity cuffs. She didn't anticipate this one coming off anytime soon.

"Pull their blinds."

Arin blinked as light flooded in, augmenting her pounding head and fatigued body with yet another sensory overload. Early morning sunlight pierced through vacant windowpanes and broken stone. She looked left and saw the others lined up along the wall beside her. Dane straightened his back from a dazed slouch and moved to stand up. The nearest guard shoved him back down. Ross was curled, nearly in a fetal position, and writhed slowly upward to brace himself on one shoulder.

And Melanie. Melanie lay at the end of the line, facing away, unmoving. Arin held her breath until she saw a slight wrinkle in her shirt come and go. She was breathing. Arin allowed herself to do the same.

Until she saw a dark stain on the side of her shirt. It could have been from a stick as she fell in the dark woods. Or it could be someone else's blood. But Arin knew it wasn't. She'd been shot.

Every one of these vile motherfuckers would answer for that.

She drew her head through the mire of partial consciousness to access the room. Huge, cavernous. Her eyes adjusted to the light and saw the remaining pair of armed guards pulling blinds from the rest of the bound and helpless group. Robin stood several paces away, arms crossed, face grim, eyes boring into hers. Arin held her stare, willing the hammers in her skull to burst free and crush the woman to sinewy bits.

The rest of the room came into focus. Low parapets ran lengthwise along the walls, and a grand staircase filled the far side of the hall. With restored clarity came memory and a realization of why the earthy must of the place smelled familiar. Why the eerie singing of cold wind above chilled her. She'd been here recently, and now, knowing the history of the cursed place, the weight of the old stone walls oppressed.

Deep in forested hills, miles from anywhere, Arin watched Robin stride across the graffitied and burn-marked floor of the derelict former hospital to address her captives.

37

"THOSE ANKLE CUFFS** will keep you in place. I'd advise you not to test them. I'd explain how they work, but I'd honestly rather see you learn for yourselves." Robin's words were clipped sharp, piercing the room. She wore oversized designer sunglasses, but Dane was sure her eyes matched her words. She stood between the two remaining guards, the three of them facing the group of bound captives.

Dane looked down at the plastic cuff pinching his right ankle. The ankle he'd injured during his escape from the city and had ripped open anew at some point the night before. He recalled stomping on one of the guards, and guessed that he'd rolled it in the process of trying to save his life. And his family.

Tilting his head, pain flared from somewhere on the back of his skull. He couldn't remember what had put him out at the campsite, but he guessed that jackhammer headache was related.

The woman stomped out half the distance towards Arin before halting, catching her breath and gathering her words. "*She,*" Robin sneered at Arin, "can explain all about the cuffs if you need to know. In short, you'll want to keep your asses right where they are."

Dane looked at the cuff around his ankle. It was warm, not just by contact but by his sight. By the enhanced sense he'd come to understand. He looked at the other three around other ankles, and they were all active, too.

But not equally. The difference in heat emitted from each had to mean something. Arin had explained how they worked earlier. Where was the transponder? He whispered to Ross, who was starting to stir. His question about that heat difference got through, and Ross returned a nod.

From the side, he watched Robin bear down on Arin with the ferocity reserved for a mother who had yet to bury her son. A grown son who had taken many other sons from their own mothers during his life, but that calculation didn't exist for this woman at that moment.

"All you needed to do was to comply," she lowered her tone and added a menacing grit to her words. "To sit there and let the doctor take samples, and you'd be on your way." Robin's voice prickled with enmity as she stared down at Arin, arms crossed and teeth clicking. "Back to coffee shops and jogs along the river and a comfortable life of contributing nothing."

She turned toward Dane, and even through her glasses, he felt the ice of her gaze compound the throbbing engulfing his head. She pointed, and a slit opened to emit froth from between her clenched teeth.

"And you! You who showed up out of nowhere and scattered everything to hell. My son, my dear Troy, do you know what his last words to me were? He called and said he'd spent a horrendous afternoon with you in New York. But he didn't want to kill you. He said we needed to add you to the line. Behind her," she snarled as she flicked her head back toward Arin. "You have what we need, and he saw that.

267

And then he died. I would have brought you in with only his suggestion, but now, know that I'll be wringing the fucking essence out of his
last request. And out of you!"

Dane had no idea what she meant but began to respond. Arin called
out before he could.

"Stop! She needs help."

Dane followed Arin's gaze toward Melanie. "Your thugs shot her.
She needs medical attention."

Arin's tone was more reserved than his ever could have been. His
habitual efforts to keep his reactions emotionless failed. He knew
Arin was holding back for the sake of Melanie. He didn't know anyone
who cared for anyone like that.

"That depends on you, dear," Robin responded with a false tone
of compassion. "I'll happily send her off to get the care she needs.
More than she deserves, but I'll make that call. It's up to you. I don't
need her. And to be clear, I don't need him, either. Kid, the job offer is
rescinded."

She nodded in Ross's direction and then to her left. The guard raised
his pistol and fired at the semi-conscious and semi-sitting medical
student. Dane watched the bullet strike his upper arm and spin him
to the ground. Ross yelped and curled up with an agonized moan.

"You ruthless bitch!" Arin lashed, her composure shattered. "What
the fuck do you need? Abducted us at the cost of a tired old man's life.
Me, for the second time because the first didn't end so well, did it?
Forcing a wounded, innocent girl to suffer. Now shooting a helpless
student who wasn't even a threat?"

"To demonstrate our resolve and to convince you two to comply. A
simple decision, really."

Arin inhaled through her nose, keeping her gaze locked on Robin's.
Her mind raced. *"Simple.* It means from one part, the word you used.
A medicinal ingredient from one plant. Uncompounded. Unmixed.

Pure." Arin straightened her back against the wall. "What is the one *simple* thing you need? The pure force that drives you to be the unrelenting demon beyond your own control? Are you doing this for money? To sell our DNA to the highest bidder? Or does this get you out of jail after you sold your ass to the wrong people, and they promised a new life somewhere overseas? The country that voted you out of office is only worth what you can loot from it?"

Dane watched with growing pride. He hadn't seen this Arin in the girl he'd come to know over the last few days, but he knew that fire was in her. He recognized it. It felt good to call her family.

He had nothing to add, so remained quiet. He was back in survival mode—what he called *fight or bike*—yet again. Whatever she was going on about, it didn't matter. He needed an opportunity, and his deeply aching foot might just give him one.

The two guards stood a few paces away, pistols in hand. Clean-shaven, fit. These weren't rent-a-cops. They were mercenaries. Marshall, the grandfather he met and lost within a few hours, had taken out one of them at the campsite. The two mercs left were wary but counted on the cuffs to keep their charges in place. They listened and exchanged a glance or two. They were hired muscle who didn't know what they were here for, only that they were getting paid.

They needed names. The guy nearest the windows had a burn wound on his forehead, likely from the log Marshall threw, Dane assumed. The other one had that haircut that gave Marines their nickname, Jarhead. They'd be *Char* and *Jar*. Both were formidable. He'd have one chance, but didn't know which would be the ideal target.

His head throbbed as he gauged the distance to each guard. Their size and their stance. Their focus. He had to pick one, but with the chips on this table, he couldn't leave that to chance. He inched forward, arranging his feet under him in a show of discomfort. Char didn't notice. Jar looked his way.

Char—the less attentive one and the one who shot Ross—would be his target. And he watched Jar as Robin spoke. Dane could read a poker bluff, and that guy was holding back to keep his face neutral. The heat rising in his cheeks said he wasn't happy with this job. Dane focused back on Robin and awaited his chance.

"Dear, your *simple* thoughts don't matter." Robin adopted a softer voice as she leaned into Arin. Almost matronly, but the vitriol still held. "What matters is what you've been seeded with. Both of you. How fortunate that you'll be helping to end wars quicker. That old man may have told you what the program all those years ago was about. He left, the patients left or died out, but the company that invested so much never gave up. Not to this day. They knew the fruits of their labor would blossom.

"Think about it—you're a bright girl from a prestigious graduate school," Robin continued. "Squads of soldiers who can see the heat of the enemy around corners and through vegetation. Day and night, without unreliable and easily beatable night vision gear. Urban and jungle battlefields would be our domain. Fights would end quickly, in our favor, and lives would be saved. Wars would be shorter. It's not just possible. It's reality. And you will be a part of it."

At this, Robin eased lower, bringing herself level with Arin. She pulled her glasses to the top of her head, locking eyes with her. "Did you see the pumpkins growing outside in the old garden when you came here earlier? Such a lovely time of year."

She pointed toward Arin's belly with a thin finger. Dane could barely hear the following words she spoke. They were wiry but piercing. They broke Arin's form. She blanched and wrapped her arms tight around herself at Robin's next words.

"Harvest time."

38

ARIN SHATTERED. HER breath vacated her lungs.

Harvest?—she couldn't mean—

But that's what she meant. To take everything. Robin and her company could breed an army in a lab, and they had what they needed within her body.

Bile rose and she vomited. Uncontrolled but to the front, directly at Robin. The woman stumbled backward and fell while trying to get away.

A shot rang out and echoed around the stone-encased room. Then another. Through watery eyes, Arin saw a struggle at her side.

Where Dane had been.

No time to assess. She lunged forward and with bound hands, she grabbed Robin. Dragged her back. The shock of the cuff bit at her ankle until she returned closer to the wall. She slammed a knee into the older woman's chest. The vile wretched-up pizza and alcohol from the night before splattered across them both.

Next step. Arin retrieved a shard of stone that she'd worked free from the wall a moment before. She held it to the older woman's throat, drawing blood, which mixed with the vomit covering them both. She looked up.

Dane had pinned one of the guards, but the gun skittered away on the floor. He was away from the wall, much farther than she'd gone to grab Robin, but he still stood.

Did his ankle cuff fail? She saw him shift his balance from his bad foot and realized it must be numb. The shock would be diminished through the damaged flesh. Undoubtedly painful, but he bore it. She realized that his hands were free. He'd somehow broken the plastic zip-ties on his wrists.

"Stop!" Robin screamed, and Arin felt the tendons in her neck bulge into the keen edge of the rock she held. "Don't shoot him! Kill them, and we're all dead. The company won't allow another failure, do you understand?" She emitted a low snarl at the guards. "And what am I paying you for?" she continued. "How'd he get the jump on you? My Troy wouldn't let that happen."

Arin squeezed the rock shard deeper into Robin's neck. Reminding her she was there and that she had indeed gotten the jump on Troy herself a couple of days before. Robin howled and thrashed, but she held her fast.

Arin's mind flashed. *Troy.* The soldier decorated for actions throughout urban combat zones. The young man whose dying words to Arin declared he'd made a mistake. Questioning who she was. The stench of her bile filled the room. She shook her head to clear her thoughts and looked up.

Dane pinned the guard with the nasty burn on his face. The pistol lay to the side, out of reach. He was panting—grimacing from the continued buzz of the ankle cuff or the torn foot or the headache—she couldn't be sure. But he looked stable and he held his ground. The other guard swiveled his weapon between him and her, stepping back to close the angle between the two.

"Keep everyone in their place," Robin yelled to the standing guard. "The medical team will be here soon, and it won't matter. They're bringing reinforcements for the worthless pair of you, too." She swiveled her head towards Arin, minding the bite of the sharp stone at her throat. "Appropriate, don't you think? I had plans to bring you to a clean facility to continue the last phase of Project Cardinal. The company had it all set up. But you tore those fucking plans asunder and forced me to improvise. So here were are. A few moments from now, the surgeons and the backup guards will be here, and we'll begin." Robin looked to the side, toward the front door, listening.

Arin watched her turn back to the others, then do a double-take back toward the door. A loose memory flickered during that movement of Robin's head, and she tried to pin it down.

Arin looked and noticed something, too. Around the edge of the entrance door, but not yet in view. She made eye contact with Dane, who had a better angle through the door. He tilted his head—seeing something, too, but not directly.

Robin squinted her eyes again and began to speak, but held back.

Arin gasped. That was it—the memory. A video recorded years before. She almost let her hold on the older woman go, but recovered it and held her fast.

She saw Melanie stir, moaning but awake.

Ross held his wounded arm but remained seated, unmoving, save for his jagged breath.

The source that grabbed their attention near the entranceway appeared. A bobcat slinked around the corner. It froze, then snarled and emitted a hideous cry, like a human child in pain. It was the cry she and Melanie had heard by the ravine. Everyone recoiled. Arin caught a flash of movement from her other side, and the cat turned and bolted from sight.

The movement that scared the cat away was Ross hurling a stone block at the distracted but still armed guard. Dane, who had the other guard pinned, dove toward the loose gun.

The guard dodged the flying brick, and turned to fire at Ross, but swiveled to Dane when he saw him reach the pistol. Dane fired a wild round and dove behind the low partitian wall. The cuff on his ankle went with him. He howled as he squeezed off a few rounds into the other guard's chest.

Arin tried to shout a warning about the tranquilizer in the cuff, but Robin threw a vomit-encased elbow into her face and writhed out of her grip.

Dane's cries from behind the low wall told her he hadn't reached the tranquilizer distance yet.

"Here!" Ross panted and pulled a black box from behind the stone he'd pulled loose. "Dane knew it was near here. His sight—he saw the varied heat of the cuffs and triangulated. Quadrandgulated. Whatever." He pulled an adjacent brick loose and pulled up to smash the device against the floor.

"NO!" Arin yelled. "That'll put us all out. We need that signal active. Give it here. Stay with me." She looked at Melanie, moaning on the floor. "Shit."

Arin leaned down and whispered in her ear, then stood up. "She'll forgive me. You can walk?" she asked Ross. "Stay close."

Dane and the other guard traded shots from behind the far sides of the low walls surrounding the open floor.

Robin was gone.

Arin and Ross ran low along the wall towards Dane, the transponder in her pocket. She heard a yelp behind her as they moved farther from the wall.

Sleep well, Mel. She didn't dare ask Ross if being tranqued during active trauma would help, or hurt.

Dane bolted up the stairs at the far end of the room. The transponder in her pocket was too far away.

Arin yelled for him to stop but watched Dane stumble and reach for the ankle cuff before falling on the stairs. He writhed for a heartbeat or two and then lay still.

"Don't shoot!" Arin yelled at the guard. "He's down. Remember what she said about killing us? She said no."

The guard swiveled his gun toward them, and they dropped behind the wall. No shots came, nor did any words from the guard.

"Go!" Arin yelled at the guard. She'd read his reactions well when Robin was speaking. He had maintained composure, but this was just a job. He wasn't an animal. "You're not part of this. That woman fled already. She's a terror—you heard it. We're no threat. Go."

The guard hesitated, looked at his companion crumpled at the end of the room, and eased toward the grand stairway. He climbed toward Dane's unconscious body and snatched the other gun. Facing Arin, he backed away toward the entrance and disappeared across the yard.

Arin turned to Ross, who slunk to the floor, writhing in pain.

"My endorphins are dropping." His voice began slurring. "I have a bullet in my arm. Or through it. Can't tell."

"You're the doctor, but I'm saying you'll survive. You know that, too." She pulled the transponder out of her pocket. "Want me to put you out?"

"I don't think that's...need to heal...pulse will drop."

"You're in pain. This will help." She put the transponder in her back pocket and ran out the door. A yelp from Ross followed. She was building a list of people who would need to forgive her.

She ran across the yard in pursuit of the one person who deserved no forgiveness.

39

DANE COUNTED TO ten but knew that trauma threw his sense of time off kilter. If he ever saw Ross again, he might ask how perception of time works. If he saw Melanie again, he'd ask her, knowing the effects of trauma, how witnesses could ever give accurate accounts. If he ever saw Arin again, he'd ask her where the word *kilter* comes from.

The cavernous room was quiet after the guard fled toward the front, Arin ran toward the back, and Melanie and Ross were sprawled on the floor, tranquilized and wounded.

Dane opened his eyes and found himself effectively alone. His ankle screamed. He'd borne the low-level shock for a long minute, risking everything hoping that the cuffs were designed for quick but effective inputs, not prolonged activation. His swollen ankle blunted the effect of the electric jolt, and he'd sustained it long enough for the battery to run dry.

A risk without thought. Without emotion. With pain, but it worked. The agonizing buzz faded, and he faked the rest until everyone assumed he was out cold.

Even if he'd had a chance to let Arin know, he didn't want to. With the team of immoral doctors and well-paid guards on the way, she was safer away from this place. He would keep her as far away from them as possible.

He limped down the grand staircase where he'd fallen a moment before, then hobbled outside. He pulled a folded paper from his shirt pocket. The map showing the bike race course had stayed with him, intact, through the last couple of days. He recognized the area, and through another desperate gamble, he pinned not just his hope but all of theirs on the chance that he read the map correctly. That the course passed through the nearby woods.

He spent invaluable seconds studying the map, and then he ran. Limped, but it was a hasty limp. He followed a game trail down a steep bank, his ankle protesting at every step. Up the other side of the bank and a pain-filled hundred yards further into the forest, he broke onto the recognizable hardpack of a singletrack bike trail. Still miles from the nearest road, but his hope—his perilous need—was for a savior on winged wheels to sail his way.

Dane trudged up the path, against the direction of the course and shortening the time to meet a possible oncoming biker. By the sun's angle, the hour was still early, but Dane hadn't spent enough time in the woods to know for sure.

If the race hadn't started, he'd meet nobody. Robin's crew would arrive. They'd find Arin. They'd find him. Project Cardinal would continue.

Dane shuttered. Robin wasn't clear whether her intentions were for a single collection event or something prolonged. Over cycles.

He forced himself to run.

The violation for him—which would never fucking happen, he told himself—would be traumatic enough. But for Arin?

He ran faster, up the trail, through the searing pain. He heard the familiar clicks of a well-tuned mountain bike through the trees. He shouted and waved his arms as Trish—coworker of the almost date—skidded in front of him. She'd be running a prerace loop to check for downed trees and missing signs.

"Dane? Where—"

"Trish! I missed you. Hard. But I have no time now. If I'm not fired already, I will be, but it doesn't matter." His urgency effected genuine concern from her, and he didn't wait to roll any dice on his response. "I'm taking your phone, your bike, and a kiss."

He took all three, leaving the biker bewildered and stranded on the remote loop of the course. She hadn't resisted and didn't shout after him in fury. Didn't throw a stick his way, either. At least not one that came close enough for him to notice. If he made it through the morning there was hope, he told himself.

He churned back down the game trail, thumbing in numbers with one hand while steering the confiscated bike with the other.

THE LONG AND TWISTING ROAD leading up to the hospital was empty, as it had been most days in the years following Gina's death. Dane's mother had traveled up this road. She hadn't come back down. Dane flew down it, hoping never to return.

If Robin's crew of rogue doctors and backup mercenaries had passed while Dane was scouting for a bike in the forest, then all was for naught. They'd have Arin already. Melanie and Ross would be dead.

278

And they'd be hunting him. He would lose any reason to start a life again or to continue with any version of what he had now.

He sailed down the road, the cold morning wind snapping his shirt and hair, his eyes watering, his injured ankle screaming.

The wind blocked any chance of him hearing a vehicle from a distance, but he didn't need to hear it. He'd see them coming before they saw him. Through the trees, the heat of their vehicle broadcasting their approach. He'd turn to the side and find something to block their path. The further down the road, the better. Safer for Arin and the others. He'd throw the high-end bike in front of the wheels to stop them if he couldn't find a downed limb. He'd throw himself if he needed to.

With his vision blurred from the wind-induced tears, he didn't see the truck until it was in his actual, normal human line of sight. And they saw him.

His plan to ambush their vehicle wouldn't work now. He knew it wouldn't work before. He'd let his worthless concerns—his emotions—talk him out of what he needed to do.

He knew what that was. He made sure they saw his grimacing face.

Robin would have sent them photos, so he needed to be unmistakable. He held his head high as he popped the brakes wide open and let the finely-tuned machine and gravity itself deliver him to the approaching box truck full of people who would use him and Arin and anyone else they could profit from.

Dane would give Arin the best chance to escape that he could. He knew these people needed to keep him alive. He'd make them work really fucking hard at it.

The truck started to slow when the driver realized the biker was speeding up. It began to swerve, but no vehicle is as nimble as a bike.

A second from the front of the truck, Dane did what any biker knows never to do. He clamped down on the front brake lever. The front tire locked and the bike snapped into an upward pivot. The rider, along with all of his pain and memories and hopes, hurtled through the air.

He pummeled into the windshield as thousands of dollars of bike crumpled beneath the skidding van. Forces beyond calculation careened him off the roof, *shitter over spitter,* and strew him onto the road behind.

Dane's world exploded and then constricted into a tunnel. His last thought before blackness overtook him was that he'd managed to lose yet another bike.

40

EACH FOOTFALL PULSED pain through Arin's swirling head as she bounded out of the ruined shell of the god-forsaken hospital. She coursed into the bright sunlight and cutting wind of the high hills after her quarry.

Quarry. The word bubbled through the fog as she sought out the remnants of heat indicating where Robin went. The term referred to prey, but its origins meant the entrails of prey given to hounds as a prize. That thought drove her forward. She would not be a prize given to anyone. She would retain her own fucking entrails.

Sharp wind dissipated the vile odor of her drying vomit. Low morning sun cast long, sharp shadows across the yard. She used the biting cold to sharpen her clarity. A person fleeing through the woods brushes against plants. Braces themselves with a hand on a tree. Crushes leaves and moss, leaving a recognizable heat signature against the undisturbed surrounding areas. She understood those concepts now, and she used them.

She charged through the woods, guided by her augmented perception. She knew how to filter out the noise to discern what she needed. This immoral hell on a hill had given her that, and she would wrest all she could from it to end it here.

She tracked and caught up to the older woman within a frantic moment. Despite Arin's poor condition and bound hands, Robin was no match for the former track star driven to free herself and reclaim her life.

They stood at the edge of the same ravine where a hapless mental patient had died years ago during a storm. Before the place was shuttered and abandoned, where it should have stayed. Robin stopped and turned at the unmistakable sound of Arin's approach. Her face twisted as she began to speak.

"You don't get it—"

"Yes!" Arin interrupted as she stopped to square herself a few paces away. "I do get it. I understand what you are. Not why you made your choices in life, but that's your problem."

Arin paused and worked through her pounding head to lace the last pieces of information into something coherent.

"The campaign video," she continued. "Your speech at the power plant. When you were a candidate for Congress. Senate, whatever it was you failed at. My head is a fucking jackhammer and I'm days behind on sleep so it took me a moment to realize where I'd seen that look when the bobcat walked in. You turned your head, then did a double-take before it was around the corner and in line of normal human sight. I saw that same look in the news footage of that ill-fated campaign stop. You looked at the failing transformer before anyone else did. You did that same double-take a few times before anyone else looked that way."

Robin stared, giving away nothing.

"Your son, Troy," Arin continued, her frantic breath calming and coalescing into something cold. "He built a reputation for his prowess in close combat. Urban warfare. Where doorways hide death if you don't know what to look for. But he did. Do you know what his last words were?"

That got Robin's attention. Her face softened for a flash before she closed up again. "He looked at me," Arin stated, her glare piercing. "Looked into my eyes and realized he'd made a mistake. He apologized."

"You lie!"

"Believe what you want. I don't care. Back to the campaign stop. That's how the company found you, isn't it? The video with national coverage. They'd been tracking you, waiting for a sign that their pernicious program wasn't fully dead. Then you fell in with a K-Street group and got tangled in a foreign mess that brought FBI and DOJ heat. The company set it all up, didn't they? They ensnared you, then gave you no choice but to work with them to further their despicable ends on a promise to bail you out. Set you and your son up with a new life somewhere overseas. Am I anywhere near the mark here?"

Robin wrestled to unclench her jaw. She spoke before succeeding. "I called the medical team and told them to bring more guards. The patients will need extra precautions, I said. They'll be here in a moment. We'll finish this."

"You made a call? There's no signal out here."

"My phones are better than yours, but believe what you want. It won't make a difference. You have something that's not yours, and you're going to share it."

Arin used both pointer fingers from her bound hands. "You know who I am to you. And your son did, too, in the end. You never told him. Just used him." Arin held the staredown until Robin broke and cut her eyes across the forested ravine.

"Marshall—my grandfather that your thugs killed last night—he left the program before Carmen died. He brought my father and Dane's mother to an orphanage. Your company didn't know that, did they? If so, they would have known us already, but they lost track. When our good friend in there, the med student you ordered shot for fun, posted my test results, that's the first time they found me.

"But the company had you already, right? And Troy? What Marshall didn't know was that Carmen was pregnant for a third time when he fled. She kept his pattern of giving kids names based on her own, but that last time, when he wasn't around anymore, she chose it. Carmen Redwood gave birth to Robin Carmine, didn't she? And the company that sponsored Project Cardinal kept tabs on that little girl. She grew and became politically successful. Until she wasn't. They coerced her into dealings that locked her out of legitimate options. Surely paid her a lot. Getting any closer now?"

Robin turned back to Arin. "Must be a good school you kids go to. So fucking clever."

"Now this woman," Arin continued, "former politician turned enemy of the state, was too old for the company's needs. Past that critical age." She saw Robin wince. She was honing in. "You didn't want to send your son into their filthy claws, either. So you set on this path that ended with ordering your own father killed and orchestrating plans to destroy your niece and nephew to feed some foreign war machine and then fly off to hide on an island until you die, old and withered and drowning moral remnants in fruity cocktails. How fucking close am I now?"

"Get over yourself. Cut the sentiment. All humans are related and it doesn't mean a damned thing in the end. We still kill each other."

Arin tilted her head skyward. A low thumping echoed over the hills. "Do you know what *Cardinal* means?" she continued. "Yeah, I go to goddamned good schools. It means a *hinge*. The cardinal direction of the wind *hinges* on a weathervane with a big red rooster on top.

284

The actions of a church *hinge* on the guy in the big red robe. The Cardinal controls them and guides them against Cardinal Sins. Or often towards them—they're no different than anyone else. The paths our lives take *hinge* on our decisions. Or ones of those who control us."

Arin squared herself, flexing her arms in the cuffs.

"And I'm deciding that you don't get away from this. Not today. You and your company will answer for your heinous crimes."

The thumping behind them grew louder. A dark helicopter popped over a distant hill, pitched forward and racing toward the hospital grounds. Arin turned back to find Robin with a black device in her hand. The same type as she had in her pocket.

"That would be the team I requested. They heard my call, it seems. Didn't know they had a chopper nearby, but that makes things easier. We'll find another hole to keep you in. And this," Robin held up a secondary transponder, a grim smile cutting through her shaking visage, "will end your fruitless observations."

She clicked a button. Arin's leg twitched from the sharp sting on her right ankle.

Bitch. The tranq shot. She had seconds.

Her right leg went numb and she stumbled forward. With bound wrists, she struggled to hold her balance. She drove her left leg into her best hurdle leap and closed the distance—airborne—between herself and Robin. They collided and locked and sailed over the bank.

Clutching Robin's shirt with her bound hands, Arin tumbled down the steep ravine in a twist of disorienting color, pulling the older woman with her. Each slam into the ground was another second passing and more of the drug pulsing through her heart. Her adrenaline sped that process to a shocking efficiency.

Bright and dark flashes alternated as she flipped. A cacophony of sound and a constellation of pain blended with the pulsing light into one unified blur of madness.

Arin jolted from a hollow-sounding impact, and her world slowed.

A fresh pain grabbed her skull, then drifted outward, like she was somewhere else. She closed her eyes. A cold caress enveloped her ear, then her cheek, and then her mouth.

She heard a distorted ringing rise and then ease and flow away with the tranquil brook water.

Stillness overcame her.

ECHOES. SHOUTING.

Wet and cold and a foul stench.

Pain. More hurt in more places than she could count. She tried to open her eyes but drifted away.

"ARIN, THERE YOU ARE." THE metallic voice sounded, distant. She peeled her eyes open, her vision blurred and her world loud. Shaking. Tilting.

Straps held her down, but she rubbed her face with unshackled hands and turned her heavy head to look around.

She was secured to the floor of a swift helicopter. A thick headset covered her ears and piped her into comms.

Linda, her contact at the DOJ, hovered over her.

"Sorry for the straps, but we didn't want you waking up and rolling out of bed up here. You and your friends are quite the sight. And the smell, if I'm being honest here. Don't fret. We'll get you all patched up. The nearest ER is a few hills away."

Linda reached down and loosened the straps around Arin's chest and legs. She tried to speak into the mouthpiece, but only a coarse utterance escaped her swollen tongue. A water tube appeared from somewhere, and she drank deeply.

"How did we find you? I'm guessing that's your question. A town cop a few hours east of here investigated the sounds of gunfire at an RV camp last night. He showed up, and hey, those are dead bodies! So, he called in State and they gathered heaps of evidence. Including a half-burned notebook at the edge of a campfire. Someone tried to burn it with a lot of other things, but it must have slipped out. Not much was left, but that local cop was given the task of looking through it for clues. He came across a number for a guy in New Jersey."

Arin pushed through her fatigue enough to lift her head and scan the cabin's interior. Ross rested against the seat behind her, fast asleep, a thick bandage around his arm.

"Mel... Melanie?" Arin forced the words through her uncooperative mouth.

"On the road, in an ambulance. She has internal damage from the GSW, but they say she'll recover. So that number in Jersey—"

"Can you call her?"

Linda paused, then hit a button on the side of her headset. She shook her head, then switched her channel back.

"She's asleep. But stable."

Arin sipped more water as Linda continued.

"So Jersey guy was Dane's father, I'm sure you know. He had a note Dane had left with my number and the license of an RV. When the troopers called him, he called me. The RV plate scanned at an exit in the Berkshires. We headed this way but had no idea where to look until I got a call from Dane."

Arin looked around the interior of the helicopter again.

"He's also in the ambulance. Serious head trauma and a lot of broken bones. But he's a tough kid."

"He has some minor legal issues pending in Manhattan," Arin noted. "Another favor, if you will."

"Done." Linda reached out and squeezed Arin's hand. "Arin, we have a group of private security guys and a few doctors, at least they claim to be, held on the driveway up to the site. We arrived before they did, but only because Dane slowed them down. Honey, when you're back to something approaching functional, we need to talk. I have a lot of questions."

Arin nodded and started to close her eyes until Linda tilted her chin back up.

"Including," she said, "explaining how the woman who was recently exonerated from our arrest charges ended up drowned in a brook. Next to you, the person upon whose testimony hinged her warrant."

Arin looked out the helicopter door at the rolling hills below. Filled with families hiking and cooking and playing games. Robin wasn't wrong about all humans being related. She was wrong about that fact making it all meaningless. That's where the meaning came from.

People had suffered and died on the path to create what she and Dane had. No one group or one country can own that. She watched a hawk circle in the distance. She pictured a songbird, maybe a brilliant red one with a crested head, at the other end of that hawk's keen vision. The bird of prey dove from the sky into the trees, locked onto its target.

When Ross woke, she'd talk to him about his thesis. He needed to publish it all. Study the shit out of her and Dane and share it with the world.

She'd help Dane recover his new life. Heal and settle wherever he wanted. It might be that same little town in the hills, but that would be his choice.

And Melanie. Notebook half-burned or not, that girl would write a story to rattle the world. Arin envisioned her smile as she curled on the shaking floor and welcomed sleep.

EPILOGUE

Two years later.

ROSE CAME TO WORK EARLY. There wasn't much extra to do. She had the routine down and the paperwork finalized, but she always gave herself extra time to double-check everything.

And to spend a little more time with the fortunate child. Pick-up days were bittersweet. She had to say painful goodbyes, but sending her wayward children to a good home was her purpose in life.

The cookies the children helped to cook the day before were still sitting out. She nibbled on a corner and turned her face. Someone hadn't stirred in the baking soda well enough, and she caught a big clump. She freshened up her coffee cup and washed the bitter taste away.

At 8:40, twenty minutes before the appointed time, the couple showed up. She greeted them and welcomed them to some cookies.

If they caught any more baking soda lumps, they were polite enough not to show it.

"So, these are my favorite days, I'll have you know. I'm beyond happy that one of my children will be going home with you. Now, I know you've been through all the checks, and the state says you're good people, but I have one more question. I'm sure you saw the apple trees driving in. Tell me, what's your favorite apple?"

She got a pair of easy laughs in response, then the taller blonde woman said, "Macintosh."

"Wonderful. I can't trust a person who doesn't have a favorite apple. Learned that from a wonderful old soul who used to work here. Now, let's see. What kind of home are we looking at for little Owen? We have a reporter, that's fantastic. And a history teacher. A high school classics teacher, it says here. Just lovely. I know he'll be in the best of arms with you two."

Rose witnessed the new family meet, cry, and leave together, as she'd done many times before. She stood at the entrance to the orphanage until the dust from the departing car settled. She bit into another cookie and was treated to another lump of baking soda. She let the bitterness linger and then ate the remainder.

ACKNOWLEDGEMENTS

I **AM GRATEFUL** to you, the reader, for letting me share this story with you. Your time and your thoughts are invaluable.

I am grateful to my fellow scribes who shared advice and drinks along the way. I am grateful to my parents, who signed the note for the school library allowing me to check out Stephen King's It at nine years old.

Above all, I am grateful to my wife and children for the support and inspiration along this journey. The hours I've spent in these pages are numerous, but I appreciate that you see the joy this project has brought me.

—JORDAN

ABOUT THE AUTHOR

THE CARDINAL LINE is Jordan's debut novel. As an avid reader from early youth and occasianal writer of short stories and blogs, he answered the call of the muse to scribe and share this story.

Jordan grew up in rural New Hampshire, traveled the world as a US Marine, and lived in New York's Hudson Valley for nearly two decades. He holds a B.S. Electrical Engineering degree from SUNY New Paltz. He currently calls Washington home, where he and his wife and two children explore by foot, bike, boat and car.

Contact:

www.jordanwrites.net

jordanfitchauthor@gmail.com

Made in the USA
Middletown, DE
27 November 2023